A Death at the
Yoga Café

Also by Michelle Kelly

Downward Facing Death

A Death at the Yoga Café

MICHELLE KELLY

MINOTAUR BOOKS

A THOMAS DUNNE BOOK

NEW YORK

A THOMAS DUNNE BOOK FOR MINOTAUR BOOKS.
An imprint of St. Martin's Press.

A DEATH AT THE YOGA CAFÉ. Copyright © 2017 by Michelle Kelly. All rights reserved. Printed in the United States of America. For information, address St. Martin's Press, 175 Fifth Avenue, New York, N.Y. 10010.

www.thomasdunnebooks.com
www.minotaurbooks.com

Designed by Omar Chapa

Library of Congress Cataloging-in-Publication Data
Names: Kelly, Michelle (Romantic fiction writer) author.
Title: A death at the yoga café / Michelle Kelly.
Description: First Edition. | New York: Minotaur Books, 2017. | "A Thomas Dunne Book."
Identifiers: LCCN 2016037562 | ISBN 9781250067388 (hardback) | ISBN 9781466875654 (e-book)
Subjects: | BISAC: FICTION / Mystery & Detective / Women Sleuths. | GSAFD: Mystery fiction.
Classification: LCC PR6111. E5226 D43 2017 | DDC 823/ .92—dc23
LC record available at https://lccn.loc.gov/2016037562

Our books may be purchased in bulk for promotional, educational, or business use. Please contact your local bookseller or the Macmillan Corporate and Premium Sales Department at 1-800-221-7945, extension 5442, or by e-mail at MacmillanSpecialMarkets@macmillan.com.

First Edition: January 2017

10 9 8 7 6 5 4 3 2 1

For Alfie, my little miracle

Acknowledgments

To all who helped take Keeley's story from an idea to a reality: Isabel Atherton at Creative Authors, Anne Brewer and Jennifer Letwack from Thomas Dunne, and all those who helped me through the writing process with cups of coffee and words of encouragement, a very sincere thank you.

A Death at the
Yoga Café

Chapter One

Strawberries and sympathy. In Keeley's experience, they went well together.

Keeley passed a bowl of said strawberries and dairy-free cream over the counter and smiled with the prerequisite sympathy at her customer. Duane had become a regular visitor to the Yoga Café in the last few weeks, his recent heartbreak leaving him at a loose end.

"I just can't believe she would leave me for him," Duane said for about the twentieth time that morning. Keeley gave him a polite, less sympathetic smile. Duane seemed to be the only person in the entire town of Belfrey who wasn't aware of the gold-digging tendencies of his now ex-girlfriend Raquel Philips. Glamorous, spoiled, and Keeley's high school nemesis, Raquel had always had an eye for older men with money, so when she recently dumped Duane after a few months of dating in order to take up with the town mayor, Keeley thought it a characteristic act.

The handsome gym instructor, however, was clearly struggling to understand Raquel's decision. Keeley could see why. Duane was more than aware of his good looks and buff physique and had a natural tendency to assume all women in the near vicinity were his for the taking. Given that Keeley herself had also turned him down prior to his taking up with Raquel, she could well imagine that Duane's notorious ego had taken a mighty blow.

Nevertheless, weeks of hearing about it had left Keeley feeling more than a little bored with the subject. She tried to look interested as Duane sat down at a table with his strawberries, only to launch into another monologue about his lost love. Keeley looked over at the door, praying for a sudden influx of customers to give her an excuse to not listen. Then her conscience pricked at her. It was all right for her, after all. Her fledgling relationship with Detective Constable Ben Taylor was going well. More than well. In fact, there were times when Keeley felt she should pinch herself, that it was a dream come true that a man like Ben would not just want her, but treat her as though she were the only woman on earth. Not to mention the fact that Ben had been her high school crush, and had seemed just as unattainable to her then. They had finally gotten together a few months ago after Keeley moved back to Belfrey, following a ten-year absence, to pursue her dream of turning her father's old butcher's shop into a vegetarian café. A move that had coincided with a nasty murder that Keeley had inadvertently found herself slap-bang in the middle of.

Not to mention a suspect in. Her reunion with the object of

her high school affection had been more a case of answering questions on her whereabouts at the time of the victim's death rather than any rekindling of old desires. Still, at some point she had found herself once again head over heels for Ben Taylor, the best-looking boy at school, and now, at least in her humble opinion, the best-looking man in town.

Not that it was just his looks that had attracted her. If she had only wanted pretty, perhaps she would have ended up with Duane, thereby saving him from his recent heartbreak with the beautiful but malicious Raquel. If anything, Ben's chiseled cheekbones, full mouth, and effortlessly strong body had been a deterrent to Keeley, who had had her heart broken too badly by her ill-fated first love to trust a man with such obvious charms. No, it was Ben's courage, loyalty, and all-around sense of decency that had won her over. For that, she thought she could ignore the odd bout of grumpiness and a tendency to wear mismatched socks.

And she could afford to have a little more patience with poor Duane. Taking a slow, deep breath, Keeley tried to conjure up feelings of empathy, poured herself a cup of mint tea, and sat down in the chair opposite him.

"I thought we were perfect together," he said, pushing his strawberries around with his spoon. "I had real plans for the diner, you know? We were thinking of launching a new menu, with a range of healthier foods, even vegetarian ones . . ." Duane trailed off as Keeley raised an eyebrow at him, her empathy fast disappearing. Raquel owned the diner around the corner near the bus station, and had made her initial feelings about Keeley opening up a new café so close to her own loud and clear. In spite of Keeley's protestations that they would be catering to very different tastes, the diner serving more traditional English countryside dishes, the other woman had continued to see her as a rival. The fact that she too had a crush on Ben probably didn't help; in her less charitable moments Keeley had often thought that Raquel had only begun dating Duane in a misguided attempt to annoy her. Now, Keeley couldn't help feeling hurt that Duane had been intending to help Raquel set up a menu surely intended to rival her own. Failed date or not, she had thought Duane was her friend, especially when he had been so instrumental in helping her set up yoga classes at the Belfrey Leisure Center, and she had also grown very close to his cousin Megan, who owned the local New Age shop.

"I see," Keeley said in a curt tone. Duane had the grace to look shamefaced.

"She was quite jealous of your success, you know. She always said a vegetarian café was a stupid idea around these parts; then when she saw you doing so well, she just wanted to expand a bit."

"I see," Keeley said again, and Duane fell silent, no doubt realizing his attempts to appease her were only making things worse. Still, she supposed she should be flattered. Many of the locals had voiced their reservations concerning the wisdom of opening a vegetarian café in a traditional farming town, and on the site of her father's old butcher's shop no less, but these first few months had proven the café to be, if not a roaring success, certainly not a flop either. She was already turning a small profit, and in today's small-business climate that was more than Keeley had hoped for. More important to her than the finances was that the café was fast becoming the go-to place in Belfrey for fresh food and friendly faces. Her plans to hold yoga classes in the upstairs apartment had been hampered by her having to move up there after the macabre incidents at Rose Cottage in the spring, but all in all her dreams for the Yoga Café were turning into reality. Even her mother would surely find no cause to complain.

Keeley thought about her mother and grimaced, revising the thought. Darla Carpenter could always find something to complain about, especially when it involved her only daughter. In fact, the only blot on Keeley's horizon was her mother's impending visit. Remembering that, any annoyance at Raquel or Duane faded into the background. Darla made Raquel look almost pleasant, and that was on a good day.

The truth was, Keeley had never felt good enough for her ultracritical and impeccably groomed mother. Keeley had been an overweight, shy child and had grown up seeing the disappointment in Darla's eyes every time she had looked at her daughter. Although her father's adoration had made up for the lack of maternal warmth, his death ten years ago had only pushed mother and daughter farther apart. After a painful heartbreak, Keeley had left for India and then America. She had returned a successful yoga instructor, tanned and lithe, but her mother could make her feel like that chubby teenager again in a heartbeat. Even though she knew that expecting any approval from her mother was an unrealistic dream, she couldn't help but hope that Darla would be impressed by what she had done with her father's shop. She looked around the room, allowing herself a stab of pride. Gone were the linoleum floor and large meat counter, and the awful smell of fresh pork, now replaced by blond wood floorboards, matching tables and chairs, and the small counter with its colorful drapes that matched the canvases on the wall, mostly pictures of fruits in bright, fresh colors that looked almost edible. A salad bar and smoothie machine stood in the far corner, and there were fresh flowers in the windows and on the tables. She had wanted the Yoga Café to be appealing to the eye as well as the taste buds, and felt she had achieved her aim. It had been no mean feat, given that she had arrived back in Belfrey to find the café smoke-damaged and cordoned off with police tape after it had been the site of an attempted arson and grisly murder.

If she had been expecting life in the country to be quiet, her first few months had been anything but. Now, though, her days had settled into a pleasant rhythm, busy certainly, but nourishingly so. Her days were taken up by the café, yoga classes, Ben, and her friends.

The door tinkled and she looked up to see one of them come in, her blond dreadlocks swinging. Megan grinned at her and came over to envelop her in a patchouli-scented hug. Keeley hugged her friend back with warmth, looking over her shoulder at the two people who accompanied her. A young woman with spiky pink hair and stars tattooed across one cheekbone hung off the arm of a man who rivaled Duane for healthy good looks. He smiled at Keeley, and the woman stepped closer into him as if warning her off. Keeley raised an eyebrow at Megan.

"Keeley, this is Suzy and Christian. They're staying with me for the Art Festival. In fact, I have a favor to ask." Megan looked at her with wide, hopeful eyes, and Keeley suppressed a smile. As much as she loved Megan, some of her views on life and some of her friends were, to put it nicely, a bit wacky. She had never forgotten the time she had found her in the yard with a few of her New Age friends, attempting to cleanse the café of "negative energy." Megan's idea of a favor was likely to include anything from using the café to hold a séance to roping Keeley into a spot of water divining.

"You know the art festival usually consists of an art trail, with a lot of the residents opening their houses to showcase various artists' work? We thought it would be a good idea to get some of the local businesses involved, and I was wondering if you would be happy to exhibit some of Suzy's work?"

Keeley looked at Suzy, who looked back at her with an expression that could be interpreted as nothing short of hostile. She was tempted to say no; there was something about the pink-haired woman that put Keeley on edge, but then she immediately felt guilty for being so uncharitable. There was also the fact that the Belfrey Art Festival had been going for years, held every year over the August bank holiday, and it often brought a lot of visitors from out of town. Opening up the café to display some of Suzy's work could bring in a lot of customers, and it wasn't as though she had plans over the bank holiday; Ben was, as usual, working. As the only nonuniformed officer in Belfrey and the three surrounding villages, he was a lot busier than one might expect for a village policeman, plus he was chasing a promotion to Detective Sergeant.

Keeley opened her mouth to say she would consider it when Megan's next words made her mind up for her.

"Christian's already got his work into the diner, so Raquel will be opening up."

Keeley pursed her lips at Megan, who had a mischievous glint in her eye. Keeley normally tried her best not to encourage Raquel's rivalry with her, believing that there was plenty of room on the High Street for both of them, but Duane's admission of

Raquel's plans to start serving a vegetarian menu ignited a spark of competitiveness in her.

"Okay, sure, I'd love to." Megan and Christian beamed at her, while Suzy only offered her a surly smile better suited, Keeley thought, to a thirteen-year-old than a grown woman. Still, she tried to be kind. Perhaps Suzy was just awkward around new people.

"What type of art do you do?" she asked politely, belatedly realizing she had agreed to display the woman's work before even asking what it was.

"I work with acrylics," Suzy said, her chin jutting forward. Her dark eyes had an intense look to them that highlighted the brightness of her hair and the candy-colored stars tattooed on one side of her face. Behind her quirky looks she was, Keeley realized, stunningly beautiful, with perfect bone structure and a pouting mouth. Much like Christian himself, though with his tanned skin and tousled light brown hair he was rather more wholesome looking. They both had the same full mouth and high cheekbones, and Keeley wondered if they were in fact brother and sister rather than a couple.

"Charcoal's Christian's medium. We met at art college," Suzy informed her before sliding her other arm around Christian's torso, which made him look slightly uncomfortable. *Definitely a couple then.*

"You know Raquel?" Duane piped up, then blushed as four confused faces turned toward him. "You said you were displaying your work at the diner," he explained.

"No, I just popped in and told her about my work and she offered to display it. She seems a lovely woman," Christian said, causing both Suzy and Duane to glower. Keeley raised her eyebrows at Megan, who shrugged. She could imagine Raquel would have been all over the handsome young artist; perhaps that was why Suzy was now clinging on to him for dear life. Keeley couldn't help thinking that they seemed an odd couple; Suzy's pink hair, tattoos, and ripped jeans were a stark contrast to Christian's natural good looks, with his lithe physique clothed in blue jeans and a simple white tee that accentuated his tan. It looked like a natural tan too, rather than the orange glow that Duane often sported. In contrast Suzy was porcelain pale. In fact, from first impressions, even their personalities seemed at odds with one another. Christian gave off a warm, easygoing air, whereas Suzy seemed, to put it in the nicest possible terms, rather intense.

Chiding herself for being judgmental, Keeley gave the pink-haired artist a friendly smile, only to be rewarded with a deeper glare.

"Friend of yours, is she?" Suzy snapped. "This woman at the diner?"

Keeley hesitated. "More of an acquaintance," she said, ignoring Megan's suppressed snort of laughter. There was no love lost between her friend and Raquel; Megan had made her disapproval of Raquel and Duane's relationship loud and clear, although Keeley had thought they were well suited to each other.

"She was my girlfriend," Duane said in a doleful tone. Megan looked at Keeley and rolled her eyes. Suzy looked at him, however, her head cocked to one side and eyes narrowed. She looked like a bird of prey about to strike, Keeley thought.

"Was?"

"Suzy," Christian admonished, but Duane was only too happy to answer.

"Yeah, she left me. I gave her everything. I really thought we were going somewhere, you know? We had plans for the future, plans for the business—" He caught Keeley's eye and looked away, guilt crossing his face. "—and, you know, *goals*. Then she threw it all away for some old man." His face twisted at his last words, a bitter tone to his voice that Keeley had never heard from him before. Perhaps she and Megan shouldn't be so quick to dismiss Duane's heartbreak, Keeley thought with a pang of compassion. He was hurting more than she had understood.

"That's rough, man," Christian said, disentangling himself from Suzy and sliding into the chair opposite Duane. Glad he had someone to talk to, Keeley turned back to Suzy and Megan.

"So, how many paintings would you like to display, Suzy?"

Suzy pursed her lips and looked around at the café in a critical manner that reminded Keeley of her mother.

"There's not much space, is there," the artist said, "but I could hang a few of the smaller canvases on the walls, I suppose. And I'd like to create a bigger piece for the window, which I wouldn't unveil until the day of the festival itself."

"That sounds interesting. What would be the subject?" Keeley hoped that was the right term; she didn't really know much about art. Suzy looked at her and blinked slowly.

"Why, I don't know yet," she said in a singsong sort of voice, "it depends where the Muse takes me."

"Right," said Keeley. She looked at Megan, baffled, but her friend was nodding with enthusiasm.

"You should let me make you a crystal charm," Megan said, "there are lots of crystals that are good for creativity and inspiration."

Keeley excused herself to go behind the counter and started wiping it down, although it was already sparkling. As much as she loved Megan, she was often bemused by some of her friend's views on life. Still, she supposed that many of the residents of Belfrey, particularly the older generation, had felt the same about yoga and vegetarian food.

"Shall we get something to eat while we're here?" Christian asked Suzy, who shrugged, looking bored.

"Oh, you should!" Megan said, handing a menu to Suzy. "Keeley's ice cream smoothies are delicious, and she's got a lovely summer stew on the menu if you want something more substantial."

Keeley smiled at her friend's impromptu sales pitch, although Suzy managed to turn her button nose up even more.

"I'll just have an herbal tea, please. We're not hungry."

"Actually," Christian admonished, giving Keeley a warm smile, and ignoring the answering glare from Suzy, "I'd love to try your summer stew. What's in it?"

"Oh, a mix of vegetables, mostly squash and zucchini, with basil, oregano, and garlic for flavor," Keeley said with more than a touch of pride. She had added the recipe to her menu a month ago, and it was selling well.

"Sounds lovely, I'll try it," Christian said, giving Keeley another of those warm smiles. If she wasn't with Ben, she would definitely have been attracted to the man. She could see why Suzy was possessive; he must unwittingly charm women everywhere he went.

Keeley made Suzy her tea and then retreated into the kitchen and busied herself with Christian's stew. She could hear Duane launching into his familiar monologue about Raquel,

and Christian making sympathetic murmuring noises. Megan
sounded as though she was trying to make small talk with
Suzy, from whom there seemed to be little response. She wondered how Megan knew the couple, and if the girl was really
that moody, if it was some kind of "artistic temperament," or
if it was an affectation deliberately put on. Or perhaps she was
just having a bad day.

The sound of shouting from outside startled Keeley out of
her musings. She came out of the kitchen to see her friends staring out of the window at a couple involved in a heated argument.
There was no mistaking the shrill tones of the woman. It was
Raquel, looking as glamorous as ever but equally as furious,
shouting at a flustered-looking Gerald Buxby, the local mayor
and the man who had stolen Raquel away from a heartbroken
Duane. Duane had gotten to his feet and was making his way
to the door when Megan laid a hand on his arm.

"Keep out of it," she told her cousin firmly. Keeley moved
forward to the window, intending to pull the blinds but becoming interested despite herself. The café door was ajar, and when
Gerald began to shout back at Raquel in his gruff voice he could
be easily heard.

"You're just want, want, want, all the bloody time. Don't
I give you enough?"

Raquel looked furious, her face flushed and her dark eyes
glowing like hot coals. Gerald must be angry to speak to her like
that, Keeley thought, knowing all too well from her own experience just how formidable Raquel could be when her blood was
up. Gerald's words, however, didn't bring forth the torrent of
abuse Keeley was expecting; rather the other woman stiffened,
then gave Gerald a haughty look. Keeley couldn't quite hear her

next words, but the sneering look on her face left no doubt that they were poisonous. Whatever she said, Gerald's usually mottled complexion went pale. He opened and shut his mouth like a goldfish, as Raquel turned on her very expensive heels and walked off down the road. As she did so she looked toward the café and spotted its inhabitants in the window, shooting them such a look of malice that Keeley found herself shrinking back. Raquel stopped, and Keeley thought she might come over and give them a piece of her mind, when Gerald shouted something at her that took her attention well away from the café.

"You're nothing but a spoiled little gold digger!" The mayor shouted. Raquel seemed to falter at that, and then walked off quickly without looking back. Even from across the road Keeley could see that the woman's face was burning. She felt someone push past her, and saw Duane rush out of the door and across the road after Raquel, who turned and fell dramatically into his arms, sobbing into his shoulder.

"Crocodile tears," Megan snorted. Keeley turned away, feeling bad for snooping, just as Gerald threw up his arms in seeming exasperation and walked off in the opposite direction from Duane and a now distraught Raquel. Something made Keeley look back, and as she did so she caught sight of Raquel's face over Duane's shoulder. In that instant, she didn't look as though she was crying or even upset at all, but was watching the retreating back of Gerald Buxby with an icy glare that made Keeley shudder.

"Well," Christian said, looking bemused, "that was unexpected. Is it usually so dramatic around here?"

"Hardly," Keeley said, at the same time as Megan gave an enthusiastic nod. "Oh, it all goes on in Belfrey," Megan told

Christian, causing Keeley to squirm in embarrassment. "Keeley solved a murder back in April, you know. In fact, it happened upstairs, where she's now living." Megan ignored the look Keeley gave her. Suzy gazed at Keeley with rather more interest.

"Really? That is fascinating. I wouldn't have thought you were so interesting."

"I didn't really solve it," Keeley said, ignoring the woman's jibe, "it was more a case of being in the wrong place at the wrong time."

"She's far too modest," said Megan. "Keeley faced the murderer down herself; she was in terrible danger. Thank God DC Taylor turned up. He's Keeley's boyfriend now, it's so romantic."

Suzy and Christian were now staring at her with rapt attention. Keeley excused herself and escaped into the kitchen, having no wish to talk about the gruesome events of last April, even if they had made Keeley something of a local heroine, not to mention boosting sales on the opening day of the Yoga Café.

The truth was, memories of that day, when Keeley had narrowly escaped becoming a victim herself if it hadn't been for Ben's timely appearance, still left her feeling shaky. It didn't help that circumstances had dictated that Keeley move into the apartment above the café, a space she had been planning on using as a yoga studio to hold private classes, and the site of the murder of Terry Smith, a local businessman who had known her parents. Sometimes, late at night when she woke in the dark to the sound of foxes calling or the chiming of the church bells, Keeley fancied she could sense him. It was silly, of course, she didn't believe in ghosts, but it was harder to hold on to rational thought when alone in the small hours. Only Ben knew of her discomfort, and as a result they had been spending the night together more often, whether at his house down by the Water Gardens or upstairs in her cramped apartment. She didn't dare tell Megan; her friend meant well, but would probably suggest some type of exorcism ritual or something equally offbeat.

"Keeley, are you okay?" It was Megan, entering the kitchen behind her. Keeley smiled at her friend, giving herself a mental shake to clear her head of morbid thoughts. It was a beautiful day, and she had tonight with Ben to look forward to.

"Of course. I wonder what was up with Raquel and Gerald?"

Megan shrugged. "Who knows? By the sound of things Raquel is just being her usual self and Gerald has finally seen through her. I would say it served her right, but no doubt she'll leech back onto poor Duane."

"He does seem to be very fond of her," Keeley said in a neutral tone. Megan rolled her eyes.

"They're both as narcissistic as each other, that's why. Probably spend all of their time gazing into each other's eyes at their own reflections."

Keeley bit her lip to stop from laughing. Instead she jerked her head in the direction of the other room, where Suzy sat waiting for Christian to finish his stew.

"What's the deal with those two? Do you know them from college?"

Megan shook her head. "Christian's from Bakewell, same as me. Our mothers are friends; well, they were, his moved to Nottingham a few years ago now. Christian went off to study art and came back a couple of years ago with Suzy. She's brilliant, her work's amazing."

"She's very intense," Keeley said diplomatically. Megan grinned and said, "Artistic temperament, isn't it? They say geniuses are all a little mad. She does leave a very heavy aura behind; I'm going to have to do a sage cleansing at my cottage when they've gone."

"Right," said Keeley, wondering what on earth a sage cleansing was and deciding she didn't need to know. "Christian doesn't seem to be like that, though."

"Christian's lovely, but don't let those puppy dog eyes fool you. He's very passionate about his work."

They fell silent as Christian came into the kitchen, carrying his empty bowl.

"That was great, Keeley, I really enjoyed that. You have to serve it for the art festival."

Keeley smiled at the praise, feeling the warm glow of satisfaction a successful recipe always gave her.

"I've just thought, your mum will be here in time for the festival, won't she?" Megan looked anxious. She had never met Darla Carpenter, but Keeley knew she had told her friend enough that Megan had cause for concern.

"Yes, I think she's coming at the end of this week."

"It won't be too much for you, will it?"

Keeley shook her head. If anything, preparing menus for the festival would be a welcome distraction from Darla. Hopefully her mother, who never cooked if she could get someone else to do it for her, wouldn't attempt to get involved in the running of the café during her stay.

"Well, I suppose we had better be going. I said I'd show Suzy and Christian around Belfrey." Megan gave Keeley a tight squeeze on her way out. Keeley followed them out of the kitchen, waving at Megan as they left. Christian gave her another smile, but the only good-bye from Suzy was a surly mutter with no eye

contact. Keeley swallowed down her annoyance at the girl's rudeness. Considering she wanted to use the Yoga Café to display
her work, though, she would have expected at least a pretense of
friendliness. Perhaps she was just shy, and covered it up with that
teenager-like demeanor.

Keeley set about tidying up and switched the sign on the
door to CLOSED. She had no classes that evening, so she would
have time for her own practice and a relaxing bath before she
got ready to go and see Ben.

Thinking about Ben made her forget about the festival, Suzy,
and even her mother. It had been a few days since they had spent
time together and she had missed him. She was also looking forward to a night in his king-size bed, rather than the cramped
divan upstairs.

She was leaning over clearing the utensils away when she
heard the door open and the clack of stilettos behind her. It was
a noise she always associated with Raquel, and Keeley straightened, expecting to see her would-be rival.

Instead a very different woman stood in front of her, groomed
to perfection, her expertly made-up eyes looking around the café
with a haughty contempt that even Raquel would find difficult
to muster. Those eyes then looked Keeley up and down with
equal disdain.

"Hello, dear," said her mother.

Chapter Two

It had been one of her mother's disappointed looks that had sent Keeley off to India to study yoga in the first place. Not that she had gone with the intention of becoming a yoga instructor at all, but rather to get well away from Darla, and from the pain of her first heartbreak.

She had been unable to believe her luck when she had started going out with Brett. He had been so handsome, so charming, and, as her mother lost no time in telling her, ridiculously out of her league. They had met at the gym, when Keeley had finally decided to do something about the "puppy fat" Darla constantly nagged her about and then discovered a genuine passion for yoga and nutrition. She had stopped eating meat after the death of her beloved father, after finding him dead of a heart attack amid the animal carcasses he worked with as a butcher.

Brett had swept a shy, awkward Keeley off her feet and proposed within a year, much to Darla's delight. Her mother had been full of warnings and advice on how to "keep him." *Sit up straight, that slouching is so unattractive. Don't show so much of your teeth when you smile. For God's sake, hang on to him, Keeley, you won't get another chance like this.* Her mother's warnings had rung in her ears every time she had been with Brett, and she found she had become desperate to prove herself, to be the perfect girlfriend and, perhaps more importantly, the perfect daughter.

Looking back, Keeley knew that Darla had become more critical than ever after her husband's death; no doubt her way of coping. Her mother wasn't one to cry; in fact, Keeley had never seen her publicly grieve her father. Only after a revealing telephone call earlier in the year during the run-up to the opening of the Yoga Café had Darla opened up about the death of Keeley's father and how deeply it had wounded her. Back then, Darla had withdrawn behind her icy demeanor, leaving Keeley to grieve by herself. Brett had, she supposed, been something of a rock. She had been so pathetically grateful for his declared love, so intent on becoming the girl that he and her mother seemed to want, that she had turned a blind eye to things she should have been fully aware of. The answering machine messages from other girls that he never fully explained, the smell of unfamiliar perfume, the evenings when he suddenly canceled their plans without a plausible explanation. She hadn't dared confide in her mother, because she hadn't wanted to admit that she was losing him just as Darla had always told her she would.

In the end, when she finally caught him cheating in spite of her own attempts to ignore what was going on in front of her own eyes, it had been her mother's reaction that had wounded her more than Brett's, who had at first tried to minimize his behavior and then shrugged it off with a "it was never going to work anyway." He had gotten engaged to the other girl within a week of Keeley returning her own ring.

When she had told Darla, her mother had turned that look of utter disdain on her, coupled with a kind of disappointed resignation.

"I suppose," she had said, her voice dripping with all the ways in which Keeley had let her down, "it was to be expected. It was too much to hope for that he was going to stay with *you*." The emphasis on the word "you" had cut Keeley to the bone. Once again, she had felt like a failure in her mother's eyes.

She had gone to India within a month, and after finishing her studies in yoga and nutrition had moved to New York with a friend and started to grow a successful business, teaching yoga to the hip and the happening. Her contact with her mother dwindled to stilted long-distance phone calls and even more stilted Christmas visits. Then Darla had announced her intention to sell George's old shop, and Keeley had found herself back in Belfrey at the age of twenty-seven, ten years after she had left it in the wake of her father's death. Her homecoming had certainly been eventful, what with the murder of Terry Smith and the ensuing drama that Keeley unwittingly got caught up in the center of. There had been a brief time when certain revelations had left Keeley thinking she and Darla might be able to rebuild their relationship, but now, once again on the receiving end of Darla's icy disapproval, she realized both that she was still as eager as ever for her mother's approval, and still just as unlikely to ever get it.

"Well, this is . . . quaint," Darla said, taking in the interior of the café in one panoramic glance. Keeley straightened her shoulders and attempted to smile at her mother.

"I didn't think you were coming until next week."

"I thought I'd surprise you," her mother said, walking into the kitchen with the air of a hygiene inspector. Keeley half expected her to run her finger across the surfaces and inspect them for dust.

"How was your journey?" she said, aiming for politeness and wincing at the sullenness in her tone.

"Absolutely dire," Darla said, emerging back out from the kitchen and raising one immaculate eyebrow at her daughter. "You know how much I dislike traveling by train." As if Keeley was personally responsible for all the ills of the British public transport system.

"Is it always so quiet?" Darla said, her words a blatant accusation. "I thought you said business was doing well?"

"It's doing very well," Keeley said, trying not to bristle at her mother's words. "I was just closing up for the day. That's why the sign on the door says CLOSED."

"Don't be sarcastic, dear, it really doesn't suit you. Where am I sleeping? Get my bags will you, I'm quite exhausted. A lie down and a cup of tea will do nicely."

Keeley tried not to seethe as she dragged her mother's luggage up the stairs and into the small apartment. It really was small, consisting only of a main room with a bed, a meager living space, and a kitchenette. There was a separate bathroom at the top of the stairs, with a shower over a bathtub so small she couldn't stretch her legs out in it.

"This is tiny!" Her mother said in horror. Keeley sighed. "I did warn you it was cramped. There's a lovely bed and breakfast across the road with very reasonable rates if you'd prefer." She held her breath, wondering why she hadn't thought of that before.

"Absolutely not," Darla snapped, dashing her fledgling hopes. "I'll be staying here. You'll have to take the sofa, I presume. You can't possibly expect me to, with my back."

It was the first Keeley had heard of her mother, who was only forty-seven and as fit as a fiddle, having a bad back, but she knew better than to push it and instead gave a resigned sigh. After all, it would only be for a few days or so. She could cope. She closed her eyes and took a few deep breaths, inhaling through her nose and out through her mouth, a beat between each breath, feeling her chest and stomach rise and fall. It was a basic breathing practice that usually calmed her instantly, but today it just wasn't having the desired effect. She opened her eyes to see Darla staring at her curiously.

"What on earth are you doing?"

"*Pranayama.* Breathing practice. It's great for stress levels and the immune system." Keeley responded automatically, surprised to see genuine interest in her mother's face.

"I might just try one of your yoga classes, you know. My friend in London swears by it for keeping her trim and her blood pressure down."

"That would be great," Keeley said, caution in her voice.

"You are properly qualified and insured, I hope? After all, you did it all abroad."

"Yes, mother," Keeley said, knowing that to Darla, "abroad" encompassed anywhere that wasn't England, and was to be treated with inherent distrust.

"Well, get the kettle on then, dear. Or do I have to make it myself? Honestly, I've traveled all this way, and you don't even think to offer me a drink. Still selfish, I see." She said the last with a tinkly little laugh, as though doing so would take the sting out of her words. Or rather, give Keeley no cause to complain without her mother informing her that she was still oversensitive as well as selfish, or whatever the criticism of the day might happen to be. As Keeley retreated into the kitchenette she could feel the irritation bubbling inside her and below it, dull and throbbing, the hurt. Having Darla here was going to be a test of all the hard-won serenity that ten years of yoga practice had given her and that could still, on a bad day, be elusive.

She made her mother a cup of English Breakfast, being sure to add two and a half sugars and to stir counterclockwise. Even so, Darla pulled a face as she tasted it.

"How can you hope to run a café, Keeley, when you still can't make tea properly?" She gave another of those tinkly little laughs. Keeley gritted her teeth.

"Would you like me to make you another?" she asked, trying to imagine her mother as a difficult customer, rather than the bane of her life.

"No, it will do," Darla said, with pointed distaste, before sitting back on the sofa and kicking off her pumps, crossing her slender legs.

"So, what shall we do tonight? There must be somewhere nice to go for dinner. I heard Belfrey had improved since we left; God knows it needed to."

Keeley felt her heart sink, remembering she had plans. *Ben.*

"I'm already going out tonight."

"Oh? On my first night here?"

"Mum, I didn't know you were coming today," Keeley said, praying that for once, her mother would be reasonable.

"Well, surely I can accompany you." A demand, rather than a request.

"I'm going round Ben's. For dinner. A romantic dinner, for two," she clarified, before Darla could possibly suggest coming along. The thought of introducing Ben and Darla made her apprehensive; although she couldn't think of anything about Ben for her mother to complain about, she knew well that Darla could always find something.

"How nice. Ben Taylor, isn't it?"

"Yes," Keeley nodded, feeling a spark of hope. When Keeley had been young, everyone in Belfrey had known everyone else, and Ben's father, a retired army colonel, had been the sort of person whom Darla might actually approve.

"Well, do try and hold on to this one, won't you, dear?" Darla said, before taking a decor magazine from her designer handbag and settling down to read it, dismissing Keeley. Keeley swallowed down her resentment and went over to the small bedroom space, unrolling the yoga mat next to her bed. As she went through a few Sun Salutations, a flowing series of movements designed to warm the body and energize all the muscles, it didn't escape her notice that her movements were more vigorous than usual, driven by the uncomfortable feelings provoked by her mother. She tried to align herself with the rhythm of her breath and her movements, but the usual peace that accompanied even a short practice eluded her. No matter how she tried to lose herself in the moment, she was acutely aware of her mother's presence in the room just a few feet away, fancying she could almost feel Darla's ongoing disapproval of her daughter emanating from her, a tangible presence in itself.

Keeley's yoga practice was a constant in her day. She aimed

for at least twenty minutes every morning, again after work, and a short meditation and breathing practice before bed. If she had time, she would do an hour in the morning, and of course she taught classes too, currently doing three hours a week at the center and a few one-to-one sessions in her apartment. It had become part of her daily life, a complete mind, body, and spirit system that kept her healthy and balanced, and even, at times, at complete peace with herself and her surroundings. For Keeley, who had been a shy, awkward teenager constantly questioning her place in the world, it was nothing short of a transformation.

Yet, just a few choice words from her mother and she felt like that chubby teenager all over again.

She finished her practice with a short *Savasana,* a lying-down pose that looked rather like one was dead, and usually brought deep relaxation, but a pointed cough from Darla had Keeley cutting her time on the mat short.

"It all looks rather odd; I don't think I'll try it after all," Darla said, shaking her head at her daughter before turning her attention back to her magazine, something glossy about homes and gardens. Keeley didn't reply; instead she went for a quick shower, trying to imagine as she did so that the water was washing away her resentments. Feeling somewhat calmer she got dressed, choosing a knee-length flowered dress she knew Ben loved and leaving her hair to dry naturally into loose waves. She tried to avoid looking at her mother, who put her magazine down every so often to watch her, sometimes letting out a soft sigh, no doubt of disappointment.

"There's some stew left in the fridge you can heat up," she told her mother as she shrugged on a denim summer jacket. Darla smiled thinly.

"I do think it's rather self-absorbed of you to insist on going out tonight, but if you must, you must. Do say hello to Ben for me, dear."

"I will," said Keeley, then, feeling guilty despite herself, "I'll come back earlier, okay? I'll just stay for dinner." She cringed at the petulant tone in her own voice. She had been so looking forward to some time with Ben tonight, and of course he would be expecting her to stay over, but Darla's surprise visit had scuppered those plans. Still, that wasn't her mother's fault. Feeling a pang of guilt, though she wasn't sure why, she leaned over and kissed her mother's cheek before turning to leave.

"You look nice," Darla said. Keeley looked back over her shoulder, about to utter a surprised but touched "thank you," when her mother continued, "Although I'm not sure you should be wearing a skirt that short. You've still got a touch of cellulite, I see."

The smile froze on Keeley's face and, murmuring a good-bye, she hurried down the stairs, feeling her cheeks flame. Why, she asked herself, her eyes stinging with sudden tears, could her mother not just be *nice,* for once?

The walk to Ben's just a few streets away calmed her. Belfrey really was beautiful in the dusk, with its cobbled High Street and picturesque stone cottages, some with gables that made her think of gingerbread houses, and the rolling hills all around, in whichever direction one cared to look. A summer mist came down from those hills, adding a pleasant coolness to the air, brushing her fevered cheeks like a caress. She slowed her steps and breathed in the evening air, feeling the calm that had been so elusive to her in the apartment settle over her. As she neared Ben's she felt the usual fizz of excitement low in her tummy.

It had been a few months now since they had become a couple, but even so the thought of him made her feel a little giddy. There was something strong, yet inherently tender, about Ben Taylor that had swept her off her feet years ago at school and had never really let her get back up again. When she had bumped into him in less than favorable circumstances, on her first day back in Belfrey last April, she had tried hard to dismiss him as another arrogant jerk. Another Brett. Especially when he had treated her with the suspicion befitting a prime suspect in a murder case.

Now, though, she couldn't imagine being without him.

Ben answered the door within a few seconds of her knocking, and she drank in the sight of him for a few delicious moments before he pulled her into his arms for a kiss. His dark hair was due a cut, and looked becomingly tousled on top, and he was dressed, as he usually was when he was off duty, in a simple white tee and blue jeans. She felt a wide smile break over her face.

"You, Keeley Carpenter, look good enough to eat," he said as he nuzzled her hair, pushing the door shut behind her.

"Ditto," she murmured, brushing his lips with hers. He kissed her back, harder, and for a few moments she forgot all about her mother, in fact about anything except the feel and taste and smell of him. By the time he let her go, they were both grinning at each other.

"I've bought some of those Egyptian cotton sheets you keep going on about," he said, frowning as Keeley looked crestfallen. "What's the matter?"

"I can't stay tonight," she said with a sigh, "my mother arrived this evening."

"Already," Ben frowned, ushering her into the dining room. "Wasn't it supposed to be next week?"

"She decided to surprise me," Keeley said drily. Ben raised an eyebrow at her, looking half amused, half concerned.

"And are you okay?"

"I am now that I'm here," she said, kissing him again before taking off her jacket and sitting at the table, which Ben had already set. "What are we eating?"

"Takeaway pizza," Ben said, making her laugh. "I didn't get back from the station till late and, well, you know cooking isn't my favorite thing."

Keeley shook her head at him, giggling, as he pushed a takeaway leaflet toward her.

"Veggie pizza it is then."

As Ben poured her a glass of wine he asked her about her day, carefully avoiding the subject of her mother. "It has to be more interesting than mine; I spent most of it doing paperwork."

With a start Keeley realized that in the aftermath of her mother's appearance she had all but forgotten the events of the day. She told Ben about Suzy and Christian and agreeing to take part in the art festival, and then about Raquel and Gerald's rather public argument, feeling a little guilty for gossiping, but knowing that it would be all around Belfrey by morning in any case.

Ben passed her wine to her and sat down, stroking her forearm almost unconsciously. She smiled at him and lifted her feet into his lap, feeling any final cares of the day draining away from her at his touch.

"I'm sure they'll sort it out by morning," Ben said, diplomatically, then frowned. "So Duane was hanging around the café again?"

"Only to moan about Raquel." She wondered if Ben was still a little jealous of the fact that she had been out on an ill-fated date with the gym instructor, but his face was now carefully blank. She gave a wry smile as she took a sip of her wine. She wasn't immune to the odd twinge of jealousy either, particularly around the fact that Ben and Raquel had dated, albeit back in their college years. "Maybe they'll get back together after he rushed out to comfort her."

"Doubtful; he hasn't got nearly enough money to keep Raquel in the style she's accustomed to. Although she might use him for a bit of comfort if Gerald doesn't take her back. I wonder what they were arguing about? It must have been serious for him to call her a gold digger; it's not like Gerald to be that nasty."

Keeley thought about that. She wasn't so convinced that the mayor's jovial, blustering demeanor didn't hide a meaner side. Earlier in the year she had suspected him in the murder of Terry Smith, and he had become quite nasty when she had confronted him about it. Not as nasty as his ancient housekeeper Edna, however, who was a force to be reckoned with. Keeley thought even Darla was scared of her.

"Enough about them anyway." Ben leaned in for another kiss, which Keeley gave him gladly. Later, in the lazy afterglow of intimacy, they lay upstairs on the bed, eating a vegetarian pizza that Keeley privately thought wasn't a patch on her own recipe, and talking, finally, about Darla.

"She won't stay long," Ben predicted, "and if she gets to be too much you can stay here, Keeley. She's a grown woman, she doesn't need babysitting."

"I know, but I can't just leave her to fend for herself."

"It's not as though she doesn't know her way around Belfrey," Ben pointed out. "She lived here for years with your father. It hasn't changed that much. I'm just saying, if you need a break, you can come here; I like having you here. In fact, I'll get you a key." He said the last matter-of-factly, as though it were nothing more than a perfectly practical suggestion, but as Keeley nestled into the crook of his arm she wondered if it heralded a new phase in their relationship. They hadn't yet discussed the possibility of moving in together, although she had found herself staying at Ben's more and more, if only because it was a deal more comfortable than her cramped apartment.

"I'd like that," she said, almost formally. Ben kissed her lightly on the head.

"That's settled then, I'll get you one cut tomorrow."

They lay in comfortable silence for a while, until Keeley looked at the clock and realized it was ten o'clock and dark outside. She sat up, sighing.

"I had better go, I told Mum I wouldn't be back too late," she said, feeling like an errant schoolgirl who had stayed out past her curfew. Ben looked disappointed, but nodded.

"I'll pop in the café and see you tomorrow. Perhaps I could take you and your mum out for dinner tomorrow night? Let her get to know me."

"Sounds like a plan," Keeley said, kissing him on the end of his nose, then wincing as she thought about how the night was likely to go. "I'm sure she'll love you, which no doubt means she'll spend most of the evening wondering loudly how I managed to snare you."

Ben laughed and tumbled her back onto the bed.

"You snared me, Keeley Carpenter," he said, nuzzling into the ticklish spot between her neck and collarbone and making her giggle, "because you are funny, sexy, caring, and the best maker of fruit sorbet I've ever met."

"Oh, you just love me for my sorbet," Keeley teased. Ben pulled away then, looking down at her with a serious expression in his green eyes.

"I love you because you're you," he said, and leaned down to kiss her again, slowly this time. Keeley wrapped her arms around him, entwining her hands in his hair, and was just about to lose herself in him again when the shrill sound of his phone ringing startled them both. Swearing, Ben sat up and reached for his phone, answering it with a curt "DC Taylor."

Then his face changed and his body went very, very still and Keeley sat up, watching him, knowing at once that it was something bad.

"I'll be there as soon as I'm dressed," Ben said, closing his phone and looking at Keeley with a grim expression, one that Keeley recognized.

"Someone's dead, aren't they?" she asked, feeling a chill go through her.

"Yes. In fact, it looks as though Gerald and Raquel won't be getting back together after all; the mayor has just been found murdered in his sitting room."

SAVASANA

Otherwise known as Corpse Pose. A relaxing, restoring pose usually used at the end of yoga practice or any time one needs a break from a hectic day.

Method

- Lie down on your back in a warm, well-ventilated room. Close your eyes and lie with your legs a little apart and your arms resting away from your body, palms facing up.

- Allow your fingers to curl naturally.
- Begin to tense all the muscles in your body, from your feet all the way up to your head, including your jaw, buttocks, and fists. Hold your whole body tensed in this way for a few seconds, clenching everything as tight as you can.
- Release all of your muscles at once on an exhale. Stay lying on your back, breathing deeply through your nose, for at least five minutes. Try not to get distracted by your thoughts, but just listen to the rhythm of your breath and allow your body to relax. Imagine your body is sinking into the floor beneath you and that you are safe and protected.
- When you are ready, open your eyes and bring your knees into your chest, clasping them as if giving yourself a hug. Roll onto your side and get up slowly.

Benefits

A great stress reliever. Relaxes the central nervous system. Promotes whole body relaxation. May help with insomnia and headaches.

Contraindications

If you have lower back problems, consult your doctor before attempting this pose. A cushion or bolster under the lower back region may help. If more than three months pregnant, lie on your side in the fetal position instead. If you are worried about falling asleep, set a timer to wake you with a gentle sound.

Chapter Three

Keeley woke up wondering why her neck was so stiff and her bed suddenly so uncomfortable before a soft snore from her mother reminded her that she was, in fact, sleeping on the sofa. She sat up, rubbing her neck and stretching, and then jumped to her feet as she remembered the events of last night. Walking quietly into the kitchenette so as not to disturb her mother, she started to brew a pot of lemon tea, staring out of the window at her backyard without taking in the view.

Gerald Buxby, mayor of Belfrey, Matlock, and Ripley, was dead. Murdered. Ben hadn't been able to tell her an awful lot; he had dropped her back at the café then hurried off, phoning briefly an hour later only to tell her that Gerald had been stabbed—information he warned her to keep to herself—and that he might need a statement from her concerning the mayor's street argument with Raquel. Keeley wondered if Raquel would be the prime suspect; after all, partners were usually the first ones to warrant suspicion. There had been a time when Keeley had thought Raquel most definitely capable of murder, but now she wasn't so sure.

She continued to muse over the fate of poor Gerald as she finished her tea, had her morning shower, and rolled out her yoga mat, again careful not to wake Darla, who was flat on her back, a silk eye mask covering most of her face.

Taking a few deep breaths, Keeley tried to clear her mind as she launched into a few Sun Salutations and standing postures, but images of Gerald and his angry face the day before found their way into her mind unbidden. When her unruly thoughts had her wobbling in one-legged Tree Pose, she gave up on the more strenuous postures and got down on the mat for a few forward bends and seated twists, leaning into the stretch and imagining her concerns flowing out of her, leaving her clear-headed for the coming day and whatever it might bring.

"You look like a pretzel." Darla's voice was strident in the small apartment.

"It's good for the digestion," Keeley murmured, closing her eyes.

"Breakfast would be even better," Darla snapped, getting to her feet and going to the kitchen where she began to noisily open doors and bang utensils. "Don't you have any coffee?"

"There's lemon tea in the pot," Keeley said, arching her back into Cobra Pose and trying to breathe in patience and tolerance.

"I'm not drinking that. It smells like washing-up liquid. Honestly, Keeley, you know I drink coffee in the morning."

"Mum, I haven't lived with you for eight years," Keeley pointed out. She gave up on her practice, finishing by folding into Child's Pose for a few moments and then standing up, feeling self-conscious with her mother's eyes on her. Only when she was rolling her yoga mat and Darla was tentatively sipping a cup of lemon tea did she remember that her mother would have known Gerald. In fact, the mayor had always spoken highly of her parents.

"Gerald Buxby was found dead last night, Mum. They think he was murdered."

Darla went very still, like a statue, then gave a little shudder as though she had mentally shaken herself. Her penciled eyebrows shot up her forehead. "Goodness! Are you sure?"

Keeley nodded. "I was with Ben when he got the call."

"Well," Darla said, for once seeming lost for words, "how terrible."

Keeley nodded again, looking out of the front window at Belfrey High Street, with its cobbled stones and range of shops, from the vintage hairdressers to the key cutters, and the local pub, the Tavern, something of an eyesore in the picturesque street with its unkempt, dingy appearance. Belfrey looked so serene this early in the morning, the kind of place where bad things just didn't happen. And yet this was the second murder of a local resident in just a few months, the first one coinciding with Keeley's arrival. Morbidly, she couldn't help feeling that she was somehow jinxed.

She finished getting ready in silence, watching Darla as she flitted around the small apartment, tutting at the lack of space and Keeley's apparent lack of organization, obviously already recovered from her shock at the grisly news.

"What are you planning on doing with yourself today, Mum? I'll be in the café until three."

"Well, I thought I'd come and give you a hand. You were saying last week you could do with taking someone on."

"Thank you," Keeley said, surprised and more than a little pleased. Darla was right; Keeley did need an extra pair of hands around as the Yoga Café continued to get busier and busier. Megan, who opened and closed Crystals and Candles whenever she seemed to feel like it, often came in and helped out in return for a free meal and endless cups of chamomile tea, but Keeley didn't like to take advantage and besides, she knew that, sooner rather than later, she really would need to employ someone.

"Well, I need something to do with myself," Darla said briskly.

Keeley soon found herself regretting her gratitude for her mother's offer of help when Darla proceeded to criticize the decor of the café, refused to tie her bobbed hair away from her face—"Darling, I spent a fortune having this styled yesterday"— and turned her nose up at Keeley's breakfast menu. Keeley could feel any glimmer of tolerance slipping away fast, to be replaced with her usual feelings of utter inadequacy around her mother. She gritted her teeth and tried to ignore her sniping, but the last straw came when Darla tutted loudly about the dust— alleged dust, as Keeley couldn't see any—on the table near the window.

"You're going to have to keep things better than this, dear. We don't want the hygiene people round."

Keeley exploded before she could stop herself.

"Why do you always have to be like this, Mum? Why are you always trying to make me feel like I'm not good enough?"

Darla, leaning over the offending table, went very, very still, before she straightened up and turned to look at Keeley with a funny look on her face. It was a most un-Darla-like look, Keeley thought. In fact, it was almost like guilt. She noticed her mother was wringing the polishing cloth between her hands. She had actually upset her, she realized.

"Mum, I'm sorry . . ." Keeley went to apologize, and was shocked into silence when Darla cut in.

"No, dear, you're probably right. I can be too hard on you. I just want the best for you, that's all; I want you to have all the things I didn't."

Before a stunned Keeley could respond, Darla had bent back over the table and resumed her polishing.

"Mum," she began, but Darla was already tutting over the bedraggled-looking vase of daisies on the windowsill. With a sigh, Keeley gave up and let her mother get on with refolding napkins and arranging the flowers in the center of the tables, feeling strangely emotional. That was the nearest thing to a genuine apology she had ever gotten from her mother, and she wondered if she, in turn, was being too hard on Darla in her opinions of her. Darla had never been someone who showed her affections easily; she had nagged and sniped at her husband too, but the jovial George had taken it in stride. Taking a deep breath, Keeley got on with preparing breakfasts.

At eight o'clock, she opened the café and waited. Her weekday regulars appeared first: Ethel, who owned the arts and crafts shop around the corner came in for her usual scone and homemade jam, and Lucy, who owned the local nursery, popped in for her usual before-work omelet. Keeley loved that she had regulars now, that her café felt like not just a business but a community.

She glanced at the clock. Tuesdays weren't her busiest mornings, but news of Gerald's demise would be winging its way around Belfrey by now and the gossips would soon be out in full force.

She didn't have to wait long. At 8:34 Norma and Maggie came in. Both middle-aged women, they were nearly always seen together, and were notorious as village gossips. Although Keeley didn't like to think the worst of anyone, the fact that the pair rarely frequented the Yoga Café but were staunch fans of Raquel's Diner told her they were there for more than a breakfast smoothie.

"Have you heard? Isn't it awful?" Norma said as she entered. Her eyes were wide in an expression of shock, but there was an eagerness to her voice that belied her words.

"Awful," Maggie echoed. "Poor Gerald. It will be that woman he took up with, you mark my words."

"Raquel?" Keeley asked, marveling at how fast they were to find a villain, at how Raquel, a resident of Belfrey and very well known to the women, had now become "that woman."

"Well, who else? The diner isn't open either; I wonder if she will have been arrested already." The way Norma peered at Keeley, she knew it was a question rather than a statement of wonder. As the girlfriend of the local police detective, Keeley was used to being questioned about the particulars of any crimes that happened in Belfrey. As if Ben ever told her anything, really. She had been surprised at his disclosure of Gerald's mode of death, putting it down to tiredness. Ever since Keeley's involvement in the Terry Smith case, Ben made very sure to keep his work and their private life separate.

"I would imagine she's grieving," Keeley said.

Maggie snorted. "Grieving? Her? She'll be on to the next one by the end of the week."

Keeley went to defend Raquel again, then fell quiet as she remembered the way the other woman had thrown herself into Duane's arms the day before. Still, Gerald had been alive then. Quite why she felt the need to defend Raquel at all she didn't know; there was certainly little love lost between them, mainly because Raquel insisted on viewing Keeley as a rival. Nevertheless, they had been friends at school. If "friends" was the right word—Raquel had been happy to get Keeley to do her homework for her and be the obligatory plain, chubby friend to Raquel's effortless beauty, but had dropped her like a hot potato when there was a better prospect on the horizon. Shy and awkward, Keeley had been grateful for the crumbs of Raquel's friendship, not seeing it for what it was until her father had died tragically and Raquel had barely even asked how she was, never mind offered any support. They hadn't kept in touch during Keeley's ten-year absence, and when she had returned slimmer, more confident, and opening a café of her own, Raquel had gone out of her way to make Keeley feel unwelcome.

Although, Keeley thought with a twinge of guilt, the situation had hardly been helped by Keeley suspecting her of having been the one to kill Terry Smith. Perhaps that guilt was part of the reason why she felt the need to defend her now—that, and the secret Keeley had discovered about Raquel's parentage.

There had been an awful moment when Keeley, having discovered that Darla had once been unfaithful to her beloved father, had thought it was her own parentage that was in question, and the relief when she had discovered the mix-up had been palpable. Ever since, she had felt a softening toward Raquel, and tried not to engage in the other woman's antagonism. She wasn't the nicest woman, but Keeley was almost sure she wasn't a murderer either. Almost.

"I'm sure that's not the case; I would imagine Raquel is very upset," Darla said, straightening up in the corner where she had been organizing the morning papers. Norma and Maggie's eyes went wide in genuine shock as they recognized her.

"Darla Carpenter? Well I never!" Norma gave her mother a large, insincere grin. Darla merely looked at her, then gave a tight little smile that looked more like a grimace.

"Norma. Maggie."

"You look amazing," Norma said with obvious envy, her small eyes sweeping over Darla's immaculate appearance like lasers. The look Darla gave her in return made it all too clear that unfortunately, she wouldn't return the compliment.

"Thank you. Are you ordering anything? Keeley's very busy, I'm sure she doesn't have the time to stand around gossiping."

Keeley hid a surprised smile. Both Norma and Maggie looked taken aback, before Maggie said in a slightly haughty voice, regaining some composure, "No, no, we had better be off." They mumbled good-byes in Keeley's direction before bustling their way out of the door. Darla watched them go with pursed lips.

"Never could stand that pair. They were always in here when it was your father's shop, spreading their poison and trying to barter with him on prices as if he were a market trader."

"Thanks, Mum," Keeley said, feeling strangely touched at her mother's intervention.

Darla gave a graceful, one-shouldered shrug.

"You should be more selective about your customers," she said, and turned back to the newspapers. Shaking her head in amusement, Keeley went back to preparing the fresh produce for the day's salad bar. It had been an extraordinarily warm summer, and her salads, smoothies, and homemade ice cream had been selling like hotcakes. There were two pastimes that made Keeley happy: yoga and cooking. Sometimes, when she was in the middle of chopping or whisking or even dreaming up a new recipe, she found herself in that ultrafocused yet relaxed state that a good yoga practice gave her. To many people, her friends often among them, they seemed like mutually exclusive activities, but to Keeley one complemented the other perfectly. In yogic philosophy, food was more than fuel; it was a form of connection, both to oneself and others and the world around you. As far as Keeley was concerned, there was no better way to feel a part of the community around her than by sharing her love of tasty foods. Although her first few months as proprietor at the Yoga Café had been hard work, it had also been fulfilling, and given her the sense of purpose and grounding she had so desperately needed.

If it hadn't been for a tendency to get herself involved in grisly murders, in fact, these first few months would have been perfect.

As she watched her mother bustling around, somehow managing to convey the impression of being busy without actually doing anything useful at all, she thought about how important it was to her that Darla understand, even be proud of, what her daughter had achieved, of the success she was making of George Carpenter's old butcher's shop. Her mother's out-of-character comments this morning had given Keeley a glimmer of hope that it may not be such a hopeless wish.

"It's rather cramped in here, isn't it?" Darla said with a long-suffering sigh, making much of squeezing herself between tables to get to the bathroom even though, in Keeley's opinion, there was ample room for her mother's lithe frame.

Customers began to trickle in and Keeley was soon busy with breakfasts. Her vegetarian breakfast and summer fruit por-ridge had proved to be popular dishes over the last few weeks, and she was soon knee-deep in cooking and serving, and began to find herself grateful for Darla's presence as her mother took over the till and serving drinks. Although her mother served people with an air of offended disdain, as if she couldn't quite believe she was having to do so, she was efficient and organized. It certainly took off the pressure of the morning rush, and she thought again that it really was high time she hired someone to help her out on a regular basis.

As she had expected, the locals were full of talk about Ger-ald's death. Jack Tibbons came in with his old wolfhound, Bambi, clutching the midmorning papers. A large picture of Gerald in full mayor regalia dominated the front page under the headline "MAYOR MURDERED," which was certainly to the point if a little lacking in imagination.

"Seen this? Right bad business," Jack said in his rough voice, putting the paper down on his usual table, in the corner near the counter. Then his eyes went wide as he spotted Darla, and his face softened into a wry grin.

"Darla Carpenter? It's been a long time," he said. Darla gave him a brusque nod.

"Jack. What can I get you?" Her voice was as briskly efficient as it had been all morning, but Keeley thought she detected just a hint of warmth in it, a slight softening of her mother's stance. She watched the pair with interest. Jack had worked with her father and had carried on managing the butcher's after George's death and Darla's departure, until his late wife's ill health had turned him into a full caregiver and, later, a widower. Jack was the sort of taciturn older man that Keeley often thought of as typical of Belfrey: down-to-earth and with a keen eye for bullshit. Not really the sort of person one would expect Darla to warm to, but Jack had been loyal to their family, and Keeley suspected her mother was a deal more fond of him than she liked to make out.

"It is a bad business," Keeley said softly, returning to the subject of Gerald's death. Jack had known Gerald well, as had most of the long-term residents of Belfrey, and the mayor had been a popular character. His murder would be a shock to the whole village.

"Has anyone seen owt of Raquel?" Jack asked. Keeley shook her head just as Megan entered, smelling of lavender and looking the part too; her blond dreadlocks had been dyed lilac. A man was with her, with long hair and a beard and what looked to be a white dress over white trousers. Keeley blinked, before arranging her face into one of polite friendliness. Megan's companions were often a little "out there," and the impending art festival was bound to attract a few unusual types.

"She's with my cousin," Megan said, coming over and kissing Keeley on the cheek while Darla looked at the newcomer with barely disguised horror, taking in her unusual hair, hippie style of clothing, and the prominent nose ring. Then her eyes went to her companion, and she closed them, looking pained.

"This is David," Megan said, "he's here for the art festival." Keeley smiled at the man, who didn't speak but gave Keeley a serious look and then inclined his head in a regal motion that made Keeley almost want to curtsy.

"Mum, this is David, and my friend Megan." Keeley introduced them before turning back to Megan and asking, "She's with Duane? Is she all right? It must have been a shock."

"I haven't seen her; Duane phoned me earlier. He sounded in shock himself. Apparently Raquel was being questioned by Ben this morning." There was a question in her voice, and Keeley shook her head in answer. "I haven't spoken to him since the early hours," she said. Megan looked around the café, where more than a couple of customers had paused mid-mouthful to look very interested in their conversation, and lowered her voice. "I've got a bad feeling about this, Keeley. I looked at the cards this morning, but they wouldn't tell me anything."

Jack, next to them, gave a disbelieving cough.

"I don't think them funny cards of yours will tell you anything, lass; best to leave that sort of thing to the police," he said. Megan looked offended and Keeley, ever the peacemaker, cut in with an offer for Megan to try out her new smoothie recipe on the house. Megan followed her over to the salad bar as she began to whisk up a mango and cucumber smoothie, leaving Darla and Jack chatting in low voices. David sat by the window looking out onto the street, his face in a serene expression, seemingly oblivious to anything going on around him.

"Apparently Raquel turned up at Duane's crying early this

morning after the police had finished talking to her. He said she was in a right mess."

"Did she have any idea what had happened?"

"You mean, who did it? No. She kept saying Gerald was a nice man and didn't have any enemies. She said she hadn't seen him since their argument outside here yesterday. That's all Duane told me."

He wasn't so nice yesterday, Keeley couldn't help thinking, remembering that very argument and the way Gerald had shouted insults at Raquel. Megan seemed to be thinking the same thing.

"So if he didn't have any enemies, and Raquel was the last person to argue with him . . ." Megan said, letting her words hang in the air. Keeley looked around the café, sure that there were ears straining to hear their conversation even though nobody was looking their way.

"Let's not jump to conclusions," Keeley said. "The police have spoken to her and clearly found no reason to keep her in."

"I've always said she was a nasty piece of work, though. It's her aura; it's very draining. She's like a psychic vampire."

"I don't know what that means. But whatever it is, it doesn't make her a murderer," Keeley said firmly. It wasn't like Megan to be so hostile, but she had an aversion to Raquel, who had always been at best condescending and at worst downright rude to her, particularly since Keeley had become a close friend.

Megan shrugged. "Maybe not. Ben will sort it out, I'm sure."

Keeley nodded, thinking about her friend's statement. Ben was the only local detective, his superiors being based at the main station in Ripley, and there was every chance this case would fall primarily into his hands. If it did, and he solved it successfully, it might mean the promotion to Detective Sergeant he was looking for. A double-edged sword, then, made all the sharper by the fact that the victim was someone he had known well. Keeley felt a shudder go through her, as well as a wave of sympathy for Ben. Although he preferred not to talk about work, she knew a case like this would be hard for him. Ben loved Belfrey, and had preferred to stay and work his way up in the village even when the chance of a transfer to Derby would have upped his prospects, but the downside of working in such a close-knit community meant that cases inevitably hit a little too close to home.

"How are your guests?" Keeley changed the subject. It worked to lighten the mood, as Megan gave a chuckle at the mention of Suzy and Christian.

"Interesting, to say the least. I found Suzy making stone rubbings on the cottage wall at six this morning. Said she was getting a feel for the place, inviting her muse in."

"I thought you liked all that sort of thing?"

"Well, I do, but she said it in such a patronizing way, basically implying that I would never understand because I'm not an artist. I tried to talk to her about spirits of the place and how Belfrey is a very spiritually rich place, and she said she didn't care about any of that, all that mattered to her was her art."

"I wonder how poor Christian feels about that?"

"Well, considering they kept me awake half the night in their throes of passion, I don't suppose he cares," Megan said, wincing.

"Oh, dear. That's a bit rude, when you've been good enough to let them stay. Perhaps you should say something?"

"I know, but how do I bring that up? 'Excuse me, can you keep your love-making down?' It's hardly over-the-breakfast-table conversation, is it?"

Keeley burst into laughter at her friend's words. Megan could always cheer her up. She finished making the smoothie, to Megan's appreciation, and was just clearing tables when the door chimed again. She looked up, feeling the flush in her cheeks as she recognized that familiar footstep. A few months in, and Ben still had that effect on her.

He kissed her cheek, his lips lingering just for a moment over her skin. Up close, she could see how tired he looked.

"How are you? I've still got plenty of breakfast left, if you want some?"

He shook his head.

"I've got to get back to the station and write these witness statements up properly, but I'll have a quick coffee. Real coffee, not decaf."

"Come into the kitchen. Oh, and this is my mum, Darla. Mum, you remember Ben?"

Darla looked up, and her stern features became a charming smile as she took in the grown Ben Taylor. Her mother was still very beautiful, Keeley thought.

"Well, look at you! You look wonderful. How are your parents?"

Ben exchanged a few pleasantries with Darla, his voice friendly but his eyes wary, before following Keeley into the kitchen.

"How has it been this morning?" he asked as he pushed the kitchen door closed behind him, and Keeley knew he wasn't referring to business at the café or even the mood of her customers following the tragic news, but rather the presence of her mother.

"She's actually been quite helpful in her own way," Keeley acknowledged. "When she goes back to London, I'm going to have to get some help in. But enough about me, how has your morning been? You look exhausted." She wound her arms around his neck, and Ben pulled her into him for a brief embrace.

"Busy," he said, "and likely to get busier still. And it's a strange one, Keeley; so far, no one seems to have seen or heard anything, not even that housekeeper of his. But there are no signs of forced entry."

"So it was someone he knew," Keeley said, feeling queasy. "I heard you had questioned Raquel?"

"Of course; she was the first person I spoke to. I'm going to have to take statements from everyone who witnessed their argument as well. I've already spoken to Duane. Raquel claims to have been with him at the time of the murder."

Keeley raised an eyebrow. If Gerald had been killed early last night, that implied that Raquel and Duane had at least spent part of the night together.

"Megan's here, she heard them. And the two art students."

"I'll get to it later," Ben said, moving his mouth to hers and kissing her briefly before pulling away with a sigh.

"I've got to go."

"I thought you wanted coffee?"

He gave her a tired grin, and she saw the dimples at the side of his mouth, making his face suddenly boyish. She felt a tug in her chest, felt the instinctive pull this man had on her.

"No, I just wanted to get you on your own for five minutes. I'll call you as soon as I can." He kissed her again before leaving, saying his good-byes to those in the café. He gave Darla an extra-charming smile, and Keeley was amazed to see her mother actually pat her hair in an almost simpering gesture. Ben winked at her as he left, and Keeley stifled a smile.

"He's absolutely adorable, Keeley," her mother said. She braced herself for the next comment about how lucky she was to get him and how it would be a miracle if she could keep him, or similar, but it didn't come. Instead her mother busied herself collecting plates. Keeley raised her eyebrows at her mother's back, wondering at this softening of attitude.

She had little time to wonder, as just as they had cleared away from breakfast, it was time for lunch. The next few hours blurred into a rush of cooking and serving, and thankfully left her busy enough to avoid questions from those locals who had heard about Gerald's murder, which after the midmorning papers was more or less everyone, and who also knew she was the girlfriend of Belfry's only detective constable—hopefully soon to be detective sergeant. As she had predicted, the café was a lot busier than it would normally be early in the week, and Gerald seemed to be the sole topic of conversation. Murder, it seemed, was good for business. Of course, there was the fact the diner was also closed, causing many of Raquel's regulars to drift into the Yoga Café, swapping their pork burgers for tofu ones. Keeley marveled at the disloyalty being shown as they cheerfully echoed Norma and Maggie's earlier sentiments. The general consensus of the village seemed to be that Raquel was the villain of the hour. Although instinct told Keeley that wasn't true, nevertheless there was something nagging at her, something Ben had said, or maybe Megan, that she just couldn't quite put her finger on.

It was midafternoon before the café slowed and Keeley and Darla were able to sit and enjoy a cup of tea and a meal. Or at least, Keeley enjoyed it. Darla's unexpected and more open mood seemed to have evaporated over the course of lunchtime, and she soon proceeded to turn her nose up at every item on the menu.

"Don't you serve any actual real food, dear? I'm surprised the café is doing as well as it is. I do hope this isn't just a novelty and you don't start struggling to keep customers."

Keeley gritted her teeth at that to stop herself retorting. The café had a good base of regular customers, many of them also visitors to Keeley's yoga classes, but the fact remained that it had always been a risky venture opening a vegetarian café in a traditional farming community like Belfrey, and her mother's words only echoed Keeley's own early fears. She had worked hard to make the café part of Belfry, making sure all of her dairy and eggs were sourced from local organic farms, as well as using local fruit and vegetables where possible, and getting involved with community events, such as the upcoming art festival. Her work had paid off, but she also knew she had been given a head start by the fact that she had been born and raised in Belfrey and her father, George, had been a popular local figure. Keeley shuddered as she remembered how she had even been accused of "betraying his legacy" by transforming his shop.

There was another reason Keeley bit her tongue at her mother's comment; Darla still owned half the premises, making her in effect a sleeping partner. Her mother's decision to visit had made her more than a little nervous; although Darla had no reason to complain about the way her daughter was running the business, given that it was already turning over a small and increasing profit, it would be out of character if her mother didn't attempt to have some kind of influence.

Indeed, Darla was looking around the café, her eyes narrowed.

"Perhaps we should change things just a little? Give it more of a vintage feel, serve more cream teas and cakes? Those types of places are very popular, you know, and are less likely to be just a fad."

"I don't think people regard the Yoga Café as a 'fad,' Mum," Keeley said softly, though her mother's words had stung her, "and there are three of those teashop-type places in Belfrey already. This place is unique."

"Well, it's certainly different," Darla said with what sounded like a long-suffering sigh, as if this was a quirk of Keeley's she must endure. Keeley resisted the urge to roll her eyes, glancing at the clock.

"I think I might close up and pop into the Tavern for a glass of wine, if you'd like to join me?" Keeley asked, feeling mean as she knew she hoped her mother would refuse.

"Oh goodness me, no, I wouldn't set foot in that dump, I never understood why your father liked the place. No, I'm going upstairs for a lie down, today has been absolutely exhausting, and my manicure is ruined."

Darla left Keeley to tidy up, and Keeley found herself, after such a busy morning, glad of the solitude. Except it was hard not to think of the demise of Gerald Buxby without anything else to distract her. She tried to push the thoughts out of her mind, her natural curiosity warring with revulsion at the news of another murder in Belfrey.

After locking up, she walked over to the Tavern, blinking as she walked from the sunny High Street into the pub's smoky gloom. The interior hadn't changed from as far back as Keeley could remember, and it had been shabby then. Still, she had an enduring fondness for the place, remembering many an afternoon sitting with her dad and his friends after school had finished and the butcher's had closed. She smiled to see Jack and

Bambi at their usual spot, and pulled out a chair to sit next to them. Bambi laid his great head in her lap, looking at her with doleful eyes. Keeley scratched him behind the ears.

"Aye; the dog's got a fondness for you. How was the rest of your afternoon, lass?"

"Busy," Keeley said. Jack peered at her, taking a long drag on his pipe.

"And with your mother? She's not the easiest woman to please."

Keeley grinned at him, grateful for his astuteness. She never could get anything past Jack, and of all the older residents in Belfrey he had known and remembered her family well, having not just worked for her father but been one of his close friends also. He would have known Darla, and all of her idiosyncrasies, all too well. Even so, although he had always seemed to have the measure of her mother, he nevertheless always spoke of her with a kind of grudging respect. He had told Keeley, once, that he had never been in any doubt as to Darla's love for her husband, and that seemed to be enough for Jack to hold her in higher esteem than he perhaps otherwise would have. He had been one of the few people Keeley had found herself able to confide in when she had discovered her mother's infidelity before Keeley had been conceived.

"It's not been quite as bad as I expected, to be honest," she admitted, burying her hands in the fur around Bambi's neck and being rewarded with a happy shudder from the dog. "I suppose having her around just puts me on edge. I always feel like everything I do isn't good enough for her, and I so want her to be proud of what I've done with the café. Then earlier, she actually admitted she could be too hard on me sometimes, which isn't like her. So now on top of everything else I feel guilty for feeling cross at her." She stopped abruptly, embarrassed at her own openness. She had always found Jack easy to talk to, but even so she had barely admitted those feelings to herself all day, never mind anyone else.

"I'm sure she is proud," Jack said with a wry smile, "just as I'm sure she'll find it near impossible to tell you. She was as proud as punch of you as a kid, you know, always talking about how clever you were to people."

"Really?" That was news to Keeley, who wasn't sure how she felt about Jack's revelations. She was beginning to wonder if she had her mother all wrong. "She was in a better mood than I expected. She seemed to like Ben. But then she started being all critical about the café again."

"Maybe she's a bit shook up as well. She knew Gerald quite well when you were young; it's not good news to come back to."

Keeley nodded thoughtfully. In all honesty she hadn't stopped to consider how Darla might be feeling about her return to Belfrey, ten years after the death of her husband. It could be quite painful for her. Keeley felt a stab of guilt, realizing she had been so caught up in her own feelings she hadn't acknowledged that her mother may be struggling with her own. That was Darla's way: to be so guarded about her emotions it was easy to assume that she just didn't have any. Other than contempt, of course, and irritation. She did those well enough. Defense mechanisms, Keeley thought with a rare wave of sympathy for her mother.

"Maybe I should do something nice for her; take her out to dinner. Ben suggested it too."

Jack took another drag on his pipe. "Maybe you should. You

can come to me one night as well if the pair of you would like to, and bring young Ben. My housekeeper does a lovely lamb casserole; I'm sure she can take the meat out of yours."

"That would be lovely!" Keeley felt a rush of warmth for the older man, leaning over and giving him a brief hug. Jack flushed and puffed again on his pipe. Gently pushing Bambi's head from her lap, Keeley got up to go to the bar and order herself that glass of wine. The barman, Tom, gave her a weak smile.

Tom was what was affectionately known—or perhaps with less affection from the older locals—as a "metal head" due to his love of heavy metal music, which he partially expressed with a tendency to wear all black, sport a long beard and hair, and have various pieces of metal adorning his lips, brows, and ears. Keeley remembered Tom from school as a shy, unassuming boy, and the transformation never failed to startle her.

"Heard the news?" he asked, reaching for a small glass and a bottle of house white.

"I was with Ben last night when he got the call," Keeley confessed. "It's a big shock."

"Dunno who would want to murder the mayor."

Keeley thought about that. Any murder of a resident would send shock waves through the local community, but even more so when that resident was such a prominent figure, the public face of Belfrey in a sense. And so close to the annual art festival too. Keeley wondered if the festival, which had been hugely popular until recently, would pull in more visitors this year as a result. Tragedy was good for tourism. As awful as it was, she knew it was only the truth, as the day's influx of visitors to the café had shown.

"Me neither," Keeley murmured, taking a grateful sip of the

wine Tom handed to her, which was cool and sharp in her mouth. She smiled at him, glad that, unlike everyone else that day, he didn't seem to automatically want to put Raquel in the frame.

Until his next words.

"Raquel will be in trouble, won't she?"

Keeley frowned. "As they were going out, of course she would be one of the first to be questioned," she said, aiming for diplomacy and wondering if Tom had heard about yesterday's argument in the street outside the café.

"Yeah, but I mean because she was the last person to see him alive. She was with him last night, wasn't she." A statement, not a question. Tom picked up a glass and started cleaning it.

"I don't think so." Keeley thought about what Ben had said, that Raquel had been with Duane all night. Again she had the niggling feeling that she had missed something.

"Yeah, I saw her on the way home from here last night," Tom said. "Coming out of the mayor's. So if he was killed last night, then she must have seen him just before."

Keeley felt as though a bucket of ice had been tipped down her back. As Tom's words and their implications sank in, she remembered what it was that had been bothering her.

Ben had said Raquel claimed to have been with Duane last night. Which was at odds with Tom seeing her coming from Gerald's house. But from what Megan had said, Raquel had turned up at Duane's early that morning.

Which meant not just that Raquel was lying, but that Duane was providing her with an alibi. And innocent people didn't need an alibi.

Chapter Four

Keeley looked up as Ben entered the café. She was sitting at the corner table by the window, looking out over the High Street and wondering if she had done the right thing in ringing Ben, after explaining to Tom how important it was that she tell him. Tom had seemed happy enough to do so, after Keeley had reassured him that no, Ben wouldn't be searching him. Although Tom never openly admitted it, the permanently stoned expression and often suspicious smell that clung to him left no one in any doubt that his rolled cigarettes contained something stronger than tobacco.

Right thing to do or not, Keeley couldn't help feeling disloyal, even though she knew that she owed Raquel no loyalty, not really. Even less so after Duane's revelations that the other woman had been planning on introducing dishes similar to Keeley's onto her menu. Perhaps the feeling came from all those times at school when Raquel had used Keeley to cover up for her by telling her parents they were doing homework together when she was in fact off to meet a boy, or to go and hang around with the older crowd in Ripley, an area often regarded as "common" by the residents of Belfrey, and certainly by Raquel's parents, who could give Darla a run for her money in the snobbishness stakes.

Ben, who knew Keeley well enough by now to guess how she was feeling, wrapped his arms around her and kissed her firmly on the lips before sitting in the chair next to her. It was evening now, a few hours after he had spoken to Tom and then pulled Raquel and Duane in for questioning. Keeley had spent most of it anxiously waiting for news. Even cooking a large pot of spicy summer casserole for tomorrow's main dish hadn't calmed her racing thoughts. She looked at Ben with a question in her eyes. Ben sighed.

"She's been released pending further inquiries. She admitted to using Duane as a false alibi; she wasn't with him last night when Gerald was killed. I say admitted it; it was more a case of tripping herself up and then realizing and becoming completely histrionic." He looked even more exhausted than he had earlier. No doubt a few hours in an interview room with an overwrought Raquel had been less than pleasant. "But it came out in the end; and then Duane confirmed it; I think lying was getting to him."

Keeley raised a hand to her mouth. "She admitted she was at Gerald's?" The rest of the question hung unspoken in the air between them. *Did she kill him?*

"No. She says she was alone until she saw Duane this morning."

Keeley frowned. "How can she explain away the fact that Tom saw her?"

"She can't. She was just adamant that she went nowhere near Gerald's last night."

"So she's lying? Or could Tom be mistaken?" For some reason, Keeley found she truly didn't want Raquel to be responsible.

"Well, I wouldn't class Tom as an immediately reliable witness, and it was dark. He didn't attempt to speak to her, and it was across the road. It's possible he just saw a dark-haired woman leaving the mayor's house and assumed it was Raquel. If it ever went to court, they would pull that apart. But realistically, given the situation? It was most likely her, Keeley. I've just got to find the evidence to prove it."

Keeley sucked in her breath sharply. The situation, which had so far seemed a little surreal, now hit her in all its enormity. Raquel—school friend, rival, nemesis—could be charged with murder. And Ben thought she was "most likely" guilty. Had she been living and working next to a potential murderess all these months?

"Did she say what she and Gerald were arguing about?"

Ben hesitated before answering, and Keeley felt a flash of annoyance that he was so reticent with her about the details. She understood, of course, about his position and that he couldn't just disclose every detail to her, but quite often lately Ben would discuss aspects of his cases with her, welcoming Keeley's insight. He often commented that she would make a good detective herself. Still, she supposed that he had to be careful with this case because it was, well, personal. Even so, she couldn't help taking it personally, as though he didn't trust her. After all, she told Ben everything.

"He was accusing her of flirting. With that friend of Megan's you were talking about."

"Christian?" Keeley thought about that and decided it was more than likely to be true. Raquel was a notorious flirt and there was no denying that Christian was an attractive guy. She remembered the look on Suzy's face the day before at the mention of Raquel and Christian exhibiting his work at the diner. She had looked angry, as well she might if Raquel had been all over him.

Even so, Keeley somehow just couldn't picture Gerald being the possessive type; he had surely known what he was taking on when he had got together with Raquel. She said as much to Ben.

"Who knows what goes on behind closed doors? And he seemed smitten with her; perhaps if he saw her getting close to a younger man, he realized he might be in danger of losing her."

"He called her a gold digger," Keeley said, thinking back to the previous afternoon, "so maybe he saw her cozying up to Christian and got nasty, realizing his money and status were the only things he could offer her. Still, it's not a motive for murder is it? Just because he embarrassed her in the street? I know Raquel can be spiteful, but that can't be all there is to it."

"I doubt it is all there is; at the moment I've only got her word for it. And there's every likelihood that she's lying."

Keeley studied Ben's face. Although he was sitting close to her, leaning toward her with an easy intimacy, his face when he spoke about Raquel and Gerald was guarded.

"You really think she did it, don't you?"

Ben looked at her for a long moment. "It's bothering you, isn't it? Why, because you know her?"

Keeley shook her head, staring out of the window. In the

hazy glow of summer evening, Belfrey High Street looked post-card perfect.

"It just doesn't feel right. I don't think it was her; I can't explain why."

Ben reached for her hand, turning it palm up and rubbing that palm with the pad of his thumb in a gesture that felt oddly intimate. He carried on stroking, looking out of the window in the direction of Keeley's own gaze as he continued.

"Often, with these cases, there is no big reason, or compli-cated motive, or surprise killer. The simplest explanation is usually the most accurate one. Raquel and Gerald had an argu-ment earlier in the day, then a woman matching her description is seen leaving his house and then her alibi turns out to have been fabricated. There's not enough evidence to charge her yet, but it's my guess that sooner or later, there will be. I'm sorry, I know that's not what you want to hear."

"But you will explore other angles?" Keeley heard the note of pleading in her tone and had to wonder why she was so in-tent on being in Raquel's corner. The other woman certainly wouldn't have done so for her.

"I'm a detective, Keeley; I'll explore every angle there is." His words were light, but Keeley couldn't help but feel she might have offended him. She closed her hand around his and leaned toward him, brushing her lips against his own.

"I'm sorry; I'm not trying to tell you how to do your job. It's all just so awful."

He kissed her gently, before sitting back and squeezing her hand.

"What are you doing tonight?" he asked, changing the

subject. "I was hoping to see you, but I think this is going to keep me busy most of the evening."

"I'm going to see if Mum wants to go out for that meal. Try and build some bridges. She really did try to be helpful today. She even said sorry for being mean—well, sort of."

Ben gave a nod and squeezed her hand again before standing up. "Okay. Well, I'll ring you later, maybe if I get finished in time I could come and join you, if that's not gate-crashing?" He looked suddenly apprehensive.

Keeley stood up with him and leaned up on her tiptoes to kiss him. God, but she loved this man. "Of course not, I'd love you to come."

They kissed again, deeper this time, and Keeley felt herself as usual overwhelmed by the nearness of him and his strong body pushing against hers. Just for a moment, all thoughts of murder were forgotten and everything was all right with the world.

"I love you," Ben whispered to her before turning to leave.

"I love you too," Keeley said. Ben paused, his back to her, then turned to look at her over his shoulder.

"Keeley? You won't get involved, will you?"

He left before she could answer, leaving her staring after him. He had sounded concerned, worried even, and she didn't know whether to be touched by his obvious care for her or angry at his assumption. She had become involved in the Terry Smith murder through no fault of her own; it wasn't as though she had set out to find the killer.

Well, not at first anyway.

Keeley went into the kitchen to make sure everything was

turned off and locked up, thinking back over the day and feeling a wave of exhaustion wash over her. What she really needed was some time alone with her yoga mat, and a good night's sleep. She wasn't likely to get either with Darla staying.

Thinking of her mother, she heard her stilettos outside in the café and came out of the kitchen, summoning a weak smile and hoping Darla's earlier good mood had been restored. But it wasn't Darla who stood before her with red-rimmed eyes, quivering in anger.

"Raquel!"

Keeley made to go forward as if to embrace the woman, then stopped herself, knowing Raquel wouldn't welcome such a gesture. Especially as Raquel was looking at Keeley with an expression that could only be described as rage.

"I hope you're happy," the other woman snapped, tossing her mane of glossy dark hair. Even after the night and day she must have had, and with her expensive makeup streaked from crying, Raquel looked amazing.

"Oh Raquel, of course I'm not. Would you like a cup of tea?" Keeley felt a pang of compassion for the clearly traumatized woman, but at the furious look Raquel gave her she remembered she was in fact alone in the room with a suspected murderer and felt a twinge of fear. Then the anger drained out of Raquel's face and she sank into the nearest chair, slumping forward and putting her head in her hands. Keeley went behind the counter and began to make a pot of tea, waiting for Raquel to speak.

"I didn't do it," Raquel said at last, looking up as Keeley sat down opposite her with a tray containing a pot of tea and two mugs. Keeley didn't answer, just nodded and started to pour. Raquel's next words, however, caused her to look up in surprise.

"You have to help me, Keeley."

"Me? How can I help you?" When Raquel didn't answer, Keeley thought she understood what she meant. "Just because I'm with Ben, that doesn't mean I have any influence over him or his cases, Raquel. He has to investigate." *And you're the prime suspect,* she finished the sentence in her head.

"I didn't do it," Raquel repeated as if Keeley hadn't spoken, her beautiful face set now in stubborn lines.

"Then I'm sure Ben will find that out," Keeley said, trying to sound soothing but wincing as her tone came out more patronizing. Raquel glared at her.

"I bet you're loving this, Keeley Carpenter. You've always wanted to push me out of the limelight."

"That's ridiculous," she said, although her voice wasn't unkind. "And being questioned for murder is hardly being kept out of the limelight."

Raquel seemed to deflate a little at that, sinking back into herself. She reached for her cup of tea, wrapping her hands around it and pulling it toward her. They sat in silence for a while, both drinking tea, until Raquel gave a little sniffle.

"I did care about him, you know. Everyone seems to be forgetting I'm actually the one bereaved."

"I know," Keeley said softly, wishing there was something she could say in sympathy but knowing there were no words that could soften the blow of a sudden loss.

"I know you saw us arguing yesterday," Raquel said abruptly. Keeley hesitated before she answered, choosing her words carefully.

"It looked like you were having a bit of a disagreement. There were a few people here who saw."

"Duane was the only one who bothered to come out and see if I was okay," Raquel said, and Keeley felt a twist of guilt before she remembered that Duane had also tried to provide Raquel with a false alibi. She wanted to ask Raquel why she had lied, but Ben's voice came back to her, pleading with her not to get involved, and so she looked down at her hands and said nothing.

Raquel repeated her earlier words, this time as more of a demand than a request.

"You have to help me, Keeley."

"How can I possibly help you?" Keeley hoped she wasn't going to ask her to lie for her too. But her request was even more startling.

"You could find out who really did it. You solved that other murder."

Keeley felt her mouth fall open in shock. She lifted her cup to her mouth to cover her reaction, taking a long swig, then set it down and took a deep breath before answering.

"I don't know if 'solved' is really accurate. In any case, I can't see how I could possibly help find Gerald's killer. I'm sure if you leave it to the police, they will find out the truth. If you're innocent, then you've got nothing to worry about."

"Of course I'm innocent," Raquel snapped, "but innocent people get charged and convicted for things all the time, don't they, and now that idiot Tom has claimed to see me coming out of Gerald's; as if anyone can believe anything that freak says."

Keeley winced at that; Tom was a nice guy, in spite of his unconventional fashion sense and penchant for marijuana. Even so, she had to admit Raquel was only echoing her earlier thoughts that Tom's account may not be entirely accurate. She was beginning to wish she had never convinced him to tell Ben what he had seen. At the time the evidence against Raquel had seemed weighted heavily against her, but Keeley found that, after talking to her, she believed her first instincts had been correct. Raquel hadn't killed Gerald.

But if it hadn't been Raquel, then who? Who had been the woman Tom saw? Keeley leaned forward, finding that she had so many questions the other woman might be able to answer about Gerald and who may have had reason to harm him, but then she again remembered Ben's admonishment and she sat back, swallowing them down.

"The police will get to the bottom of it, Raquel, I'm sure," she said instead. Raquel glared at her.

"You don't want to help me; of course you don't. I don't know why I even asked." Raquel stood up, wiping at her eyes impatiently, and Keeley saw that she had been on the verge of angry tears.

"I'm sorry," she began, but Raquel was already leaving, shutting the door none too gently behind her. Keeley watched her go, a mix of emotions warring with each other.

Did Raquel really think that she, Keeley, could help her? It would have been an oddly flattering thought had the circumstances not been so terrible.

She locked up, a whirl of thoughts, images, and feelings fighting for supremacy in her mind. As she walked the stairs up toward the flat, she braced herself for all the likely outcomes of Darla's moods, and was relieved to see her in the kitchen, humming to herself as she made a sandwich.

"I was wondering if you wanted to go out, Mum? My treat, somewhere nice?"

Darla looked up at her and blinked in surprise, then shook her head firmly.

"Actually, I'm going out already with an old friend in Matlock."

"I didn't know you stayed in touch with anyone from Amber Valley." Keeley was surprised, given that her mother had moved back to London as soon as possible after George's death and had never spoken about Belfrey in favorable terms since.

"There's a lot you don't know about me, young lady," Darla said, and then hesitated for just the briefest second. Keeley flushed, remembering the revelations of her mother's infidelity. Mumbling a response, Keeley took herself for a shower.

As she let the warm water fall over her, she felt some of the tension drain away, leaving her with a raw, almost scrubbed-out feeling. The combination of her mother's impromptu visit with Gerald's murder and Raquel's subsequent questioning had been a lot to take in. A night in on her own might be just what she needed. Nevertheless, as she sat on the sofa and watched Darla get ready to go out, she felt suddenly lonely. Maybe she could call Megan and invite her around while she had the apartment to herself for a while; but when she tried to ring her friend's phone it went straight to voicemail.

Instead, after Darla left she unrolled her yoga mat and lit some incense. But even a few restorative poses only cleared her head for so long. She gave up after a while and instead made herself an omelet and settled down with a romance novel, only to find the usually delicious meal tasted like sawdust in her mouth and the words swam on the page in front of her. Sighing, she tried Megan again, this time leaving a brief message when her friend failed to pick up.

Keeley had just switched off the lamp and was trying unsuccessfully to get comfortable on the sofa, realizing that an early night wasn't going to be easily accomplished given her current sleeping arrangements, when her phone rang loudly. Ben. Keeley answered it, trying to sound more cheerful than she felt.

"Hello, sweetheart, how are things?"

"I'm exhausted," said Ben, giving a loud yawn. "I'm just heading home now. Do you want to do dinner tomorrow?"

"I'd love to; if you can get away from work," Keeley said, trying not to sound petulant. She had accepted the reality of Ben's often long working hours when they had got together.

"I'll make sure of it," Ben said. "I've spent all evening questioning Gerald's sisters and elderly aunt. Absolutely dotty, the lot of them."

Keeley stifled a reprimand, knowing that if Ben was being uncharitable about people, then he was even more stressed than he was letting on.

"Did you find out anything?"

Ben hesitated. "Not really," he said, suddenly distant. "I had better go; I'll call you tomorrow. Love you." He was gone before she could finish her own good-bye. Keeley frowned at the phone. His reluctance to tell her the outcome of his talk with Gerald's family, coupled with his urging earlier for her to keep out of it, left Keeley feeling as though he didn't trust her. As much as she tried to tell herself that was rubbish—that Ben was just being overprotective because he loved her—the feeling niggled at her as she tried to sleep.

Chapter Five

Keeley woke with the sun in her eyes and a crick in her neck. She heard humming and sat up quickly, confused. Darla was up and awake and making toast.

"Would you like some? I noticed you had some homemade jam in the fridge that needed eating."

"Please," said Keeley, trying to hide her shock. She was beginning to wonder if her mother was experiencing some kind of midlife crisis.

"Mind you, you shouldn't have too much sugar; not with your thighs," Darla said, and although she winced Keeley felt oddly relieved to hear her mother acting in something more like her usual fashion. Even so, she stole a suspicious glance at her thighs. Darla could always be relied on to subdue her hard-won body image.

"I heard that Raquel was taken in for questioning for Gerald's murder," Darla said as she handed Keeley her toast and a glass of fresh orange juice.

"Thanks, Mum. And I don't think she's actually been charged."

"Do you think she did it?" Darla asked, sitting across from her and peering at her eagerly.

"I hope not. Did you know the mayor well?"

Darla looked thoughtful. "Quite well. Of course he wasn't the mayor then. Your father played bowls with him sometimes. Has anyone questioned that housekeeper of his? I'd be surprised if she didn't know anything."

Keeley had all but forgotten about Edna, a sour woman of indeterminate age who had been Gerald's housekeeper for several years and by all accounts was infatuated with her employer. She had no liking for Keeley, ever since she had asked Gerald questions about the unfortunate Terry Smith. Her mother was right; as far as she knew Edna had still worked for Gerald at the time of his murder, so surely she would have seen or heard something. She made a mental note to ask Ben, and then remembered he had been less than forthcoming about the case.

"I'm sure Ben would have questioned her," Keeley said, taking a large bite of her toast. The jam was delicious, the strawberries having been picked locally from the Glovers' farm. She had Diana Glover coming for a private yoga session that morning before she opened up; she would have to take it downstairs, rather than subject Diana to the appraisal of her mother.

"I had better get ready," she said, looking at the clock and seeing she had overslept. No doubt a night of tossing and turning on her couch hadn't helped. Her mother, on the other hand, looked as fresh as a daisy.

Downstairs she saw Diana already waiting outside, her hands clasped together in their usual nervous gesture, long fingers fidgeting with each other.

"Morning, Diana, how are you?"

Diana gave her a weak nod as she came in, yoga mat under her arm, not quite meeting Keeley's eyes. Diana was a regular at Keeley's class at the leisure center, and had recently started having one-to-one sessions with her. She was a timid woman who worked hard on the family farm under the watchful eye of her bullying husband, Ted, and Keeley often thought that the yoga classes were the only time Diana had to herself, and wondered if the mysterious backache Diana claimed as the reason for her interest in yoga was simply a convenient reason. Keeley pulled out her bolsters and her own mat from where they were stored under the counter.

"If you don't mind, we'll have to practice down here today. I'll push the tables over and keep the blinds down."

Diana just nodded and began to help move the tables. She was even quieter than usual, and as the sunlight came through the slats in the blinds and alighted on the older woman's face, Keeley saw the mark of a yellowing bruise, barely covered by cheap powder. Her stomach rolled and she turned her face away before Diana caught her staring, telling herself sharply not to jump to conclusions.

"So how are you feeling?" she said instead, rolling out the mats. "How is everything at the farm?"

"Just busy. I've been very tired. My back's been aching something fiendish this week."

"In that case we'll concentrate mostly on some restorative

poses," Keeley said. Not only were restorative poses good for aches and exhaustion; they were an antidote to emotional trauma also. Although Keeley had no way of truly knowing what went on behind closed doors at the Glovers' farm, she had the innate sense that Diana was a deeply unhappy woman.

She sat down cross-legged on the mat, indicating for Diana to copy her, and then took her through a few rounds of Skull Shining Breath, a breathing exercise designed to clear the mind and increase feelings of happiness. After just a few minutes Keeley saw some of the tension drop from Diana's face, the lines on her forehead seeming to smooth out and a soft smile relaxing her mouth. She really was quite pretty, Keeley thought; most likely a stunner in her youth, before life and marriage had taken its toll on her.

Keeley then led Diana through some forward bends and other sitting postures that she knew would be good for the other woman's back, and after a while Keeley felt a sense of peace settle over herself as she led Diana through a kneeling spinal flow, feeling her own tensions, which she hadn't even been aware of carrying, ebbing away from her.

To finish the practice Keeley spent the last twenty minutes taking Diana through some lying-down poses, propped up where needed by the bolsters. Although Keeley's own practice tended to be a lot more energetic, as she watched Diana lie on her mat, radiating serenity, she realized it might be a good idea to allow herself more time for some deep relaxation. Things had been so manic the past few months that she often felt as though she didn't have chance to pause for breath.

As she waved Diana off, Keeley thought it was strange that

Diana hadn't mentioned Gerald's murder; perhaps, stuck up on the farm, she hadn't heard about it yet, or perhaps she had forgotten in the wake of her own obvious problems.

She watched Diana walk away, her steps lighter and her shoulders less hunched, and allowed herself a warm glow. This was what it was all about for her, really: serving others. Although often forgotten in the modern craze for new exercise routines, the cornerstone of yoga practice wasn't postures or flexibility but living by spiritual principles, of which helping others was one of the most important. Back in New York Keeley had taught a number of nonprofit classes for inner-city teens or at rehab centers and had always got more satisfaction from them than the higher-paid sessions she taught at expensive studios. Sometimes she missed all that, but Belfrey was her home again now and the Yoga Café her dream; and perhaps she was still able to help, if Diana's face was anything to go by.

But you wouldn't help Raquel, piped up an inner voice that Keeley pushed away with a mixture of guilt and frustration. Ben was probably right; the case was something she should keep out of. It was in Ben's hands and if Raquel truly was innocent, then she was sure the truth would come out. Pushing away thoughts of news stories of innocent people being convicted for crimes they didn't commit, Keeley started pulling the tables into place and getting ready to open up for the day. She would be glad when the murder was solved and the whole thing done and dusted. Quite what Raquel thought she could even achieve for her, Keeley had no idea. Perhaps she thought Keeley could pull some strings with Ben, not understanding, as Keeley did, that Ben was straight as an arrow when it came to his role as a police detective. It was one of the things about him that she loved most, even if there were times when his black-and-white view of the world infuriated her. She pushed away the small voice in her mind that told her that maybe she could help Raquel, and if she could, then she should.

As the morning wore on, with Darla staying upstairs, having apparently decided not to risk her hair and nails that day, Keeley couldn't push Raquel's request from her mind. Later, when Megan came in with Christian for a flapjack and a smoothie, she shook her head at Keeley, the colored beads in her dreadlocks dangling.

"I don't know why you're assuming it isn't her. All the evidence points to it, and I've always thought she had a viciousness about her."

"I don't think she's capable of this. I mean, where's the motive? An argument about her flirting hardly warrants murder." Keeley fell quiet as she remembered it was Christian himself who she had apparently been accused of flirting with. Christian, his hair flopping becomingly over one eye, gave a graceful shrug.

"I didn't even think she was being flirtatious with me, although Suzy wouldn't agree. But then"—he grimaced—"Suzy can be very possessive."

"Where is she today?" Keeley asked, although she was quite relieved that the intense young artist wasn't there; Suzy set her on edge.

"She's working on a new piece that she wants to unveil here the first day of the festival."

"Oh? What is it?" Although Keeley was quite looking forward to turning the café into an art gallery for a few days, it occurred to her that she hadn't even seen Suzy's work. She hoped it wasn't going to be nudes, or something equally shocking to the older residents of Belfrey.

"I don't know, she's being very secretive about it, she always is when working on a big piece. It will be wonderful, I'm sure," Christian assured her. "She's incredibly talented."

"She's using my attic as her studio at the minute," said Megan in carefully neutral tones that Keeley understood meant that she was less than thrilled about this new arrangement.

"Here." Christian showed Keeley his phone. "Here's some pictures of Suzy's last exhibition."

Keeley took the phone and scrolled through the pictures of Suzy's work. Keeley knew next to nothing about art, but there was no denying the girl was good. She used a mixture of acrylics, pencils, charcoal, and even unusual mediums such as pieces of glass and what looked like dirt to create undeniably beautiful pictures, mainly of young women in fantastical surroundings wearing tortured expressions. Beautiful, but dark. Still, she hadn't expected pretty pastoral scenes.

"They're very good," Keeley said, handing the phone back. "Have you got any of yours?"

He handed it back, to reveal mostly charcoal sketches of local landmarks, including a detailed one of the local windmill, a popular tourist attraction, as it was the country's only existing windmill that still produced grain. Although his work lacked the undeniable brilliance of Suzy's, he was obviously very good, and it was much more in keeping with the kind of thing Keeley expected the average citizen of Belfrey to enjoy. She sighed, wishing Christian had come to her before Raquel. Then she frowned as she had a thought.

"Will you still be exhibiting at the diner with everything that's happened?" She couldn't see Raquel rushing in to open up at the moment. It wasn't as if she needed the money—Raquel's parents were quite well-off and had purchased the diner for their daughter more to give her something to do with her time until she snared a rich husband than anything else. Raquel did little of the work there herself, employing a cook, two waitresses, and a cleaner.

"I believe so. I'm going round to see Raquel this evening; I expect to discuss that very thing."

Megan raised an eyebrow. "Is Suzy happy about that?"

Christian looked uncomfortable.

"Well, I haven't had the chance to tell her yet; she's been painting all last night and this morning, and it's always best not to disturb her when she's involved with her work. I'll tell her later. I expect she'll end up coming with me." He said the last with no indication that that was in any way a bad thing, but there was a slightly pained expression in his eyes that made Keeley feel instantly sorry for him, wondering how hard it must be to cope with Suzy's possessiveness. She thought again of Diana Glover and the haunted expression she so often wore. *I'm so lucky to have Ben,* she thought with a rush of love.

"I'd be surprised if she doesn't keep the diner shut for a while," Megan said. "It was closed when I walked past on my way here. Perhaps she's going to tell you she can't exhibit your work after all."

Christian looked crestfallen.

"If that's the case, perhaps you and Suzy can both display here? Or you could use Crystals and Candles?"

"I've already got my friend displaying her range of hand-painted tarot cards, and David is coming in on the first day to create a sculpture. He's a druid, you know, so I'll be displaying some of his work too. Otherwise I would have loved to," Megan explained.

Wondering exactly what a druid was in its present-day form, Keeley shrugged at Christian.

"Well, you and Suzy are more than welcome to share the space here if necessary."

"Thank you," he said, looking relieved and giving her a sweet smile. Keeley thought again that she really wouldn't have put him with the intense Suzy. Still, opposites attract, she supposed. In many ways she and Ben were chalk and cheese also, yet she felt they fit perfectly. Suzy no doubt had her softer side; people were rarely just one thing.

"That's settled then," Keeley said, and then moved further down the counter to serve two teenage girls who had just come in, while Megan and Christian took their pot of herbal tea and sat down at one of the tables. The lunchtime rush soon started, and Keeley wondered as she rushed around doing three jobs at once just what her mother was doing upstairs, and how amenable she was likely to be to giving Keeley some help.

As it turned out, not at all. Darla appeared in a haze of perfume and powder, announced she was off to Matlock to do some shopping, and disappeared before Keeley could make any request. It really was high time she took some help on; she would start advertising this week, she decided.

The afternoon was getting on before the line of customers slowed down, and Keeley retreated into the kitchen to phone Ben, hoping he wasn't too busy to answer.

He answered on the third ring, his deep voice evoking a fluttering feeling in Keeley's belly that hadn't subdued after four months of dating.

"Dinner tonight?" he said after she had given him a brief rundown of the morning. "Perhaps we could go to the Wheatsheaf and take your mother."

Keeley tried to sound enthusiastic. As much as she appreciated Ben's efforts to get on with Darla, in all honesty she would prefer to keep her mother as far away from her boyfriend as possible, perhaps worried that Darla's often critical analysis of her only daughter would rub off on Ben. She should really give him more credit; Ben showed her how much he loved her so often, and in so many ways, that Keeley knew it was only her own often-fragile self esteem that kept her from sometimes fully accepting it.

"Sounds great. How has your day been? Any headway on the Gerald case?"

There was a noticeable pause before Ben answered, sounding suddenly distant. "Not as yet. I'd better go, I've got a ton of stuff to do; I'll ring you later to sort out tonight. Love you." He rung off before Keeley had even had the chance to form her own words of good-bye. She glared at the phone, feeling annoyed. She was really starting to get the feeling that he was shutting her out over this case, ever since his comment the day before about staying out of this one. They had never really spoken about her involvement in the Terry Smith case since they had gotten together as a couple, and Keeley wondered if he still for some reason resented it. It had certainly caused friction between them when they had first met, but Keeley, knowing herself to be in danger, had found herself unable to just sit back and let events unfold.

If it hadn't been for her, the murderer might well have never been caught. Not that that was any great reason for pride, she told herself sharply, given the fact that right up until the end she had been certain that Raquel was the villain.

Perhaps, she mused to herself, drumming her fingers on the work surface in front of her, that was why she felt the need to defend Raquel's innocence now: because of a misplaced sense of guilt. Just because the woman hadn't been responsible for Terry Smith's death didn't mean she wasn't responsible for Gerald's. Besides which, it was nothing to do with her. She had been unwittingly involved last spring; this time there was no reason for her to be concerned. Except that Raquel had directly asked her for help.

"I need you to help me, Keeley Carpenter," came the voice of Raquel herself, causing Keeley to nearly jump out of her skin. She spun around, seeing Raquel in the doorway of the kitchen. She had been so lost in thought she hadn't even heard the jangling of the café door that indicated a customer.

Although Raquel's tone was as imperious as ever, she looked awful, Keeley thought, her usually glowing skin gray and dry, her hair greasy at the roots and lines of fatigue around her mouth and eyes. Her face was puffy too, as though she had been crying, and Keeley had the urge to throw her arms around the girl, although it was an urge she resisted. Instead, she ushered Raquel back into the café, turned the sign on the door to CLOSED and put the kettle on.

"English Breakfast, two sugars?" she asked. Raquel nodded, giving Keeley a weak smile.

"You always remember everyone's drinks. And names. I wish I could be like that at the diner."

Keeley tried to hide her surprise at the other woman's compliment and admission of anything less than absolute perfection. She carried two mugs and a pot of tea over to the table and sat down.

"I'm sorry if I was short with you yesterday," she began, pouring Raquel a mug, noticing as she did so that the other woman's hands were shaking. "But I just don't really see how I can help."

"Find out who did it," Raquel said abruptly. Keeley nearly dropped the sugar. She looked at Raquel with wide eyes.

"I can't do that, Raquel. It's a matter for the police." She could hear Ben's voice again, warning her away, and again felt a flash of annoyance. If Ben wasn't her boyfriend, would she be more open to helping Raquel? Keeley thought that she would, and that made her feel instantly guilty.

"The police think it's me," Raquel pointed out, oblivious to Keeley's mental wranglings. "It wasn't, you know, it really wasn't. I haven't seen Gerald since we had that row. It was just a silly argument." She shook her head, blinking rapidly as if fighting back tears, and Keeley felt her heart go out to her. All of her instincts screamed at her that Raquel was telling the truth. But then, the voice of reason countered, if she had been wrong about Raquel's guilt before, how could she be certain she wasn't wrong about her innocence now?

"I believe you," she said. "I don't know why," she went on more honestly, "but for some reason I do."

Raquel nodded. "Thank you."

There was an uncomfortable silence, Keeley thinking of all the times Raquel had been hostile toward her or mocked her since her return to Belfrey, and now here she was asking for her help. Reflecting on how proud, if not downright arrogant,

Raquel usually was, she thought that the girl must really be desperate.

But desperate because she was innocent, or desperate because she was guilty? In spite of her gut feelings that Raquel was genuine, Keeley was under no illusions that the other woman was quite capable of putting on a contrite façade in order to manipulate her.

And yet . . . Keeley looked at Raquel, so uncharacteristically forlorn, and made her decision. She could worry about the implications with Ben later.

"Okay," she said, trying to sound forthright, though her stomach was fizzing as she understood what she was about to take on. "So if you didn't kill Gerald, why did you get Duane to provide you with a false alibi?"

"I was scared," Raquel said simply. "I knew they would look to me as his girlfriend and because everyone had heard us arguing, and I was just covering my back."

"So where were you really?"

"At home by myself. Duane came back with me for a bit after I argued with Gerald, then from about eight o'clock I was on my own. I was waiting for Gerald to call me and apologize, but he never did. Now I know why." She looked down, her expression bereft, and Keeley got the feeling that she was indeed now playing on it.

"So you're saying it definitely wasn't you that Tom claims to have seen leaving Gerald's?"

"No. I didn't leave the house."

Keeley sighed, rubbing her hand across her forehead. It didn't make sense. What other dark-haired woman would be leaving the mayor's house late at night?

"What happened to Edna?" She remembered the house-keeper. Raquel pulled a face.

"That horrible old bat. Gerald persuaded her to take retirement. She wasn't doing her job properly, she was too old to cope with the cleaning. And I found her snooping around in my drawers. Not that Gerald believed me, he said she was probably just getting confused. But I managed to convince him that keeping her on given her failing health was a cruelty. She didn't take it very well," Raquel said with an obvious relish that made Keeley shudder. As much as she herself disliked Gerald's sourpuss of a housekeeper, she took no joy in the old woman's dismissal, knowing that she had been devoted to the mayor.

"Why, do you think it's her?" Raquel said with a gleam in her eye. "I wouldn't put it past her, you know."

"She's quite old," Keeley pointed out, "and I would imagine Gerald was a lot stronger than her." Still—Keeley continued her musings silently—it didn't take a huge amount of strength to stab someone, only the skill—or luck—to get the blade into the right place. "Besides, she was devoted to Gerald, I'm sure she wouldn't kill him."

"She might, if she felt rejected."

Keeley nodded, taking a long drink of her tea, the taste pleasantly strong in her throat. She didn't drink what the villagers termed "proper tea" very often, preferring herbal, so when she did it was always a treat. The occasional jolt of caffeine couldn't hurt either.

"I wonder if she would have been vindictive enough to set you up?" Keeley said. In the few dealings she had had with Edna, the woman had shown herself to be both spiteful and incredibly protective of Gerald. That sort of possessiveness could easily turn into hate. "I mean, if she thought it had been you who had influenced Gerald's decision to let her go, maybe she was trying to get revenge on both of you?"

Raquel nodded, a smile on her lips.

"That makes perfect sense, Keeley. See, I knew I was right to come to you!"

Keeley shook her head. She was getting ahead of herself.

"Raquel, we don't have a lot to go on. I don't even know all the details—the murder weapon, the exact way he died—so anything we think of is just pure speculation."

"But you're not going to let me go to prison for a crime I didn't commit. You're going to help me, aren't you?" Raquel's eyes widened and her mouth formed a small "o." Genuinely upset she might be, but Keeley knew a melodramatic expression when she saw one.

"I'll ask a few questions, see what I can find out," Keeley said, trying not to feel gratified by the way Raquel's eyes lit up with gratitude. After a childhood of Raquel's particular brand of toxic friendship, she couldn't deny there was a certain satisfaction to having the woman so genuinely ask for her help. "I very much doubt it's going to come to that, Raquel," she said in a sensible tone, as much for herself as Raquel. "If you're telling the truth and you were nowhere near Gerald's that night, then you've got nothing to worry about. There's barely enough to charge you, never mind take you to court." Keeley was tempted to tell her that Ben had said as much himself, but knew he would be furious if she divulged his forecasts to the suspect in question. Instead, she tried to reassure her. "I'm pretty certain of that; I've listened to Ben talk about his work enough. If you're innocent, Raquel, then it will all come out."

"But people will still think it's me," Raquel pointed out. "Even if there's not enough evidence to charge me, if the real killer isn't caught, people will still always think it was me. I'll be a pariah. Mummy and Daddy are barely speaking to me as it is; they've threatened to cut my allowance."

Keeley bit her lip to prevent making a comment on her surprise that a grown woman in her late twenties still got an allowance. This, she thought, was the real crux of the matter. It would be too out of character for Raquel to not be motivated by a good dollop of material self-interest.

"I'll do what I can, but you're going to have to be completely honest with me," she said. Raquel had a tendency to bend the truth to suit herself, and also wasn't likely to want to reveal anything that might put her in a bad light. In the Terry Smith murder it had turned out Raquel was keeping secrets, all because she didn't want the fact of her cosmetic surgery to be made public. Although Keeley didn't think anyone could fail to realize that Raquel's gravity-defying assets were less than natural.

She didn't trust Raquel, if she was going to be brutally honest, but she still couldn't shake the conviction that the other woman hadn't done this, and that was enough for her to want to help.

Ben isn't going to be happy, came the rational voice inside her head. Keeley sighed to herself. She would see Ben that night, and ask him about the possibility of investigating Edna. Maybe, she tried to convince herself, he would even be glad of some informal help. He had welcomed her input before. Surely, she rationalized, he couldn't expect her to just ignore Raquel's pleas?

She turned her attention back to Raquel herself, who was looking decidedly shifty after Keeley's comments about honesty.

"Is there anything else you want to tell me?" she asked. "I can't help you if I don't know everything."

Raquel shrugged.

"It's probably nothing . . . but Edna isn't the only person Gerald got rid of lately. Because of me," she admitted, looking down at her hands.

"Okay," Keeley took another sip of her drink. "Tell me about that?"

"You know he had his gardens done recently? The man he employed, John, used to come in here on his lunch break." Raquel sniffed, obviously offended that the man in question had chosen to frequent the café rather than her own diner.

Keeley thought back and nodded. She remembered the man, a swarthy, rugged-looking guy in his early forties who hadn't spoken much, and had surprised Keeley by ordering herbal tea and tofu burgers every day. He had seemed pleasant enough, if somewhat reticent.

"I remember him. Why did you get him sacked?"

Raquel shifted in her seat, looking uncomfortable. She didn't meet Keeley's eyes when she spoke.

"He was rather inappropriate with me. Tried it on, you know?"

Keeley looked at her. The almost informal way Raquel had said that, coupled with the other woman's inability to meet her gaze, told Keeley a different story. She thought back to what she remembered of the gardener. John hadn't spoken much, but when he had he had mentioned a wife and young baby, and his face had lit up as he had done so. Had he really made advances on Raquel? Or would it be more likely that it had been Raquel, and he had turned her down? Keeley had no doubts that the woman was vindictive enough to then lie to Gerald to get him sacked—a woman scorned and all that—but was that a motive for murder? It might be, if the man had a new baby to support and Raquel's lies had left him in dire straits.

"But wouldn't he be more likely to be angry with you than Gerald?" Keeley asked, thinking aloud. Raquel looked shocked.

"I could be next!" she exclaimed. Keeley fought the urge to roll her eyes. After all, if someone was crazy enough to commit one murder, who could say it would indeed stop there?

"I'll talk to him. He left me a card, I'm sure I've still got it somewhere. Did you tell Ben about this?"

Raquel shook her head, flushing slightly, and Keeley thought that if her suspicions about the real story of John the gardener were correct, then of course Raquel wouldn't mention it to Ben, possibly the only other man in Belfrey to ever turn her down. Raquel was attractive, and her ego knew few bounds. A man with the sense to not succumb to her obvious charms would be anathema to her.

Keeley sighed. She knew she should really tell Raquel to tell Ben this information, just as she knew that Raquel would probably do anything but. She was going to help her; she could question John and Edna at least, and if she found out anything useful she would pass it on to the police. Ben could hardly complain about that. It wasn't her fault if people chose to confide in her, she thought mutinously.

Raquel left after giving Keeley a Chanel-scented hug, promising to call her if she thought of anything else. Keeley watched her go, feeling strangely excited about the possibility of investigating again. Only as she was clearing up did the reality of the situation hit her. If Raquel was, as Keeley believed, truly innocent, then there was another murderer still running free around Belfrey. Someone capable of stabbing the mayor to death in apparent cold blood. The gardener seemed to have a motive, but it had been a few months since he had done Gerald's gardens. Although Edna struck her as more than capable, it seemed too surreal that it could be the elderly housekeeper. But if not them, then who? As Keeley looked out of the window at the picturesque Belfrey High Street she wondered, and not for the first time since her return, just what secrets were lurking behind its closed doors.

MARICHYASANA—SEATED TWIST

A pose named after the sage Marichi, more commonly known as Seated Twist. A gentle spinal twist that is good for digestion, flexibility of the spine, and gentle toning of the abdomen and torso. A good pose to practice if you have been sitting at a desk all day.

Method

- Sit on your mat with your legs straight out in front of you and your spine tall, looking ahead. Your arms should be straight, with your hands palm down on the mat behind you, fingers facing away.
- Bend your right knee, pulling your foot in as close to your buttock as you can, keeping your foot flat on the floor.
- Exhale and turn your torso to the right, toward your bended knee. Inhale and bring up your left arm, bent at the elbow, and place your left elbow on the outside of your right knee, your forearm vertical.

- With each inhale, focus on lengthening and stretching your spine and twisting your torso around to the right. Do not strain; this should be a very gentle pose. After at least one minute, exhale and release, and repeat on the other side.

Benefits

Relieves digestive problems such as constipation. May be useful for lower backaches and menstrual cramps. Stretches the shoulders and boosts energy.

Contraindications

This pose isn't advisable for those suffering from migraines, insomnia, or diarrhea, or those with high or low blood pressure.

Chapter Six

Dinner began, to say the least, a little strained. Darla had returned from Matlock in a sour mood, having got caught in a sudden downpour and then been reacquainted with the haphazardness of the public transport system in Amber Valley—namely, if you got a bus within an hour of its scheduled time, you were lucky. Nevertheless Darla had seemed keen to go for dinner with Ben and Keeley, but then proceeded to moan about everything from the decor of the Wheatsheaf to the limitations of its menu.

"Mum, this isn't London," Keeley reminded her.

"I can see that, dear. Honestly, I had forgotten how backwards this place could be," her mother said, shooting a nasty look at the waitress who was belatedly clearing their table. The poor girl flushed, mumbled an apology, and hurried away. Keeley shot a glance at Ben, who was carefully expressionless, though she saw the flash of amusement in his eyes as he met her gaze. Keeley felt herself relax. Ben could handle her mother's sniping, she was sure. She felt him reach for her hand and squeeze it under the table and gave him a grateful smile.

Then she remembered Raquel.

After they had placed their orders, Darla finally settling for a salmon salad, Keeley saw her chance when her mother went outside for a cigarette, grumbling about the smoking ban.

"Raquel came into the café today. She really is very upset."

Ben's expression was instantly wary.

"I hope you're not discussing the case with her, Keeley. She's the prime suspect at the minute."

Keeley decided not to mention that Raquel had all but begged her for help.

"I know she is, but I still find it hard to believe she did it. I'm sure she's really grieving for him." *And her allowance,* she couldn't help but add to herself. Ben snorted with skepticism, reading her mind.

"She's more likely to be worried about embarrassing Mummy and Daddy and having her generous allowance cut off. I'm surprised you're so interested, Keeley; she's hardly been the friend- liest of folks towards you."

Keeley thought about that. She really didn't owe Raquel any- thing. Yet her innate sense of justice wouldn't let her sit by and watch an innocent woman be wrongly accused.

"I just feel, in my gut, that it wasn't her. I can't really explain why; intuition perhaps."

Ben grinned.

"You sound like bloody Megan, with all her batty goings-on about energies and aurals."

"Auras," Keeley corrected, smiling back. Although she wanted to reprimand him for calling Megan batty, she was glad the atmosphere between them had lightened again.

Perhaps now would be a good time to mention her decision to help Raquel. Maybe she could start with asking him about Edna.

"Speaking of auras, that housekeeper of Gerald's came across as quite a nasty woman. I suppose you've questioned her already?"

Ben's smile vanished.

"You're doing it again."

"Doing what?" Keeley was genuinely baffled.

"Trying to get information out of me. Do you not trust me to do my job properly, Keeley? It's bad enough having the senior officers at Ripley breathing down my neck without you questioning me as well." He sounded both hurt and annoyed.

"Of course I do. I think you're wonderful at your job," Keeley said with sincerity. "I was just curious. I really don't think Raquel did it, so I just wondered about Edna, that's all. From what I know of her she's a pretty nasty piece of work." Keeley bit her lip, aware she wasn't being entirely honest, but realizing that Ben was going to be far from happy about her involvement.

"She's got to be nearly seventy, Keeley; she's hardly in the frame for this. Now can we please stop talking about work?"

Keeley nodded, swallowing down the retort that Ben was perfectly happy to talk about work when it suited him. The atmosphere felt awkward between them again and she reached for his hand, but then saw Darla returning and thought better of it. She hoped her mother wouldn't notice that there was anything wrong. The last thing she needed was Darla waxing forth on their relationship.

Fortunately Darla had other things on her mind. She sat down with an impatient sigh, patting her hair frantically.

"This rain just keeps ruining my blow-dry. Honestly, I had forgotten how awful the weather can be up here. It changes every minute."

"Your hair looks wonderful, Darla," Ben said smoothly. Darla gave him a small smile.

"Thank you, dear. But really, I will be glad indeed to get back to London. There weren't even smoker's shelters outside here; I had to stand in the rain."

"We should have gone to the Tavern," Ben said with a quick wink at Keeley, "they don't care so much about the smoking ban in there; they've still got ash trays on the table."

Darla wrinkled her elegant nose.

"I wouldn't be seen dead in that place."

"It's true," Keeley said, "I always see Jack Tibbons in there puffing away on his pipe."

"Speak of the devil," Ben murmured. Keeley looked up, surprised to see Jack, for once minus Bambi, entering the doors of the Wheatsheaf. She was even more surprised when her mother raised her arm and waved for his attention.

"Jack! Over here," Darla called. Jack's creased face broke into a smile when he saw them, and he made his way over to the table.

"Mind if I join you? I was just on my way back from the Pooch Parlor, thought it was high time Bambi had a trim. The old fellow's looking a bit scraggy."

"I don't know how you can take that mutt everywhere,"

Darla said, though there was a lack of the usual disdain in her tone as she moved over to let Jack sit down.

Dinner progressed quite pleasantly with Jack regaling them with stories of Belfrey when Keeley had been a child and her father the local butcher. Keeley loved hearing about her father, and even Darla's eyes lit up when she talked about her late husband. Keeley felt a rare flush of affection for her mother then. Ben seemed to relax, and by the end of the evening she was nestled into him as they sipped on their after-dinner coffees.

She was disappointed when he insisted on dropping them both off afterward. She had assumed she would be going back to Ben's, if not for the night then at least for a few hours of alone time, but Ben said he was tired and had an early start the next morning.

"It must be very draining, this awful business with Gerald," Darla said as she went into the café, Ben having walked them to the door. She air-kissed Ben's cheek then disappeared up the stairs, leaving Ben and Keeley alone. Keeley turned to Ben and wound her arms around his neck, breathing in the familiar yet exciting smell of him.

Then she stepped away as Ben remained rigid in her arms, feeling a flicker of insecurity.

"What's wrong? And don't say 'nothing,'" she said hurriedly, seeing a stoic expression come over him. Ben sighed at that and rubbed his hand over his chin, a sure gesture that he was both overwhelmed and frustrated.

"Keeley, please promise me you'll stop talking to Raquel about the murder. Or anyone else."

Keeley winced. This wasn't going to be the right time to tell him about her decision to find out what she could for Raquel.

"That's daft," she said bluntly. "The murder is all that anyone is talking about, Ben. It's difficult to avoid, especially when I run a local business."

"Don't be obtuse," Ben snapped, the sudden irritability in his tone causing Keeley to take a step back. "You know what I mean."

Keeley wasn't so sure that she did. Was he really so annoyed about the idea of her talking to Raquel about the murder? Perhaps it was just as well she hadn't told him about Raquel's pleas for her to help, or her own acquiescence.

"I don't want to fight," she said in a soft voice, and the anger drained out of Ben's eyes. "I'm sorry, Keeley," he whispered into her hair after pulling her back into his arms. "It's just been a long day."

They kissed then, slow and lingering, and by the time Keeley had said her good-byes and gone upstairs to the apartment, a tension she hadn't even known she was carrying had eased. It would all be fine, she was sure. If she found out anything useful, she would tell Ben, and surely he would see that her intention was only to help.

She treated herself to a long bath with candles and scented oils, a few relaxing yoga poses, and then curled up on the sofa and, for once, fell asleep as soon as her head hit the cushion.

The next morning, she woke to birdsong and the sound of her mother singing under her breath as she made tea in the kitchenette. Keeley sat up, shocked, and stared across the room at her.

"Morning, dear."

"Morning," Keeley said, feeling bemused. Since her arrival in Belfrey, Darla's moods had been so mercurial that Keeley wondered if her mother was going through the Change. She was in her late forties, after all. As much as she quite liked this mellow version of her mother, it also made her feel strangely un-anchored. If there was one certainty in life, it was Darla's displeasure at anything to do with her daughter.

"Would you like some help in the café today, dear?" her mother asked as she handed Keeley a cup of herbal tea. Keeley stared at her.

"Er, that would be nice. Although I don't open until ten today; I've got a class up at the leisure center. Why don't you try it out?"

Darla shook her head, her lips pursing in something like her usual expression.

"I don't think so, dear. I tell you what, why don't I open up and watch the café for you? I can at least serve tea and toast and things."

"Really? I mean, thank you, that would be great." Keeley watched her mother's retreating back with something bordering on suspicion. She couldn't shake the feeling that her mother was up to something; why else this sudden interest in the Yoga Café? She pushed back the thought that as her mother still owned the premises, she could take as much interest as she liked; Keeley felt a surge of possessiveness sweep over her at the thought of Darla taking over the business she had worked so hard to get off the ground. She was being ungrateful, she chided herself. Worrying about Raquel and Ben was making her close-minded.

She showed Darla everything she needed to know to open up, prepared the salad bar, and left for her class at the center.

Belfrey Leisure Center was the only one of its kind for miles, and so it attracted a lot of clientele not just from Belfrey but the neighboring towns and villages. It had an excellent fitness suite and a spacious, mirrored studio in which Keeley taught her classes. It reminded her a little of being in New York, especially with the fitness instructors with their suspiciously white teeth and perma-tans.

The class was larger than normal, with a few of the older residents from Belfrey attending with Norma and Maggie, the local gossips. Maggie was a regular, although she spent most of the sessions peering at her fellow yogis as if she could discover any juicy secrets simply by osmosis. Keeley's heart sank as she saw the two of them together, along with their friends. As she expected, within seconds the studio was full of chatter about Gerald and his tragic murder. Keeley unrolled her mat and turned on her stereo. Sounds of chanting set to the haunting sounds of pan pipes filled the room, only to be drowned out by the braying tones of Norma and company.

"Namaste," Keeley said, then repeated herself more firmly when the ladies continued to chatter. "Namaste!" she all but shouted. Finally Norma fell silent and looked around in surprise.

"Let's begin," Keeley said. She led the class through a few Sun Salutations. They were great for the butt too. She found herself going at a slightly more vigorous pace than usual, perhaps in a bid to keep Norma and Maggie slightly out of breath and therefore less likely to start chattering. She then took the class through a series of standing poses, Seated Twists, and back bends before finishing with some core work. By the end of the class the women were glowing, and Keeley felt invigorated herself. Teaching always gave her a buzz. She was smiling to herself after the class as she packed away when she heard footsteps at the door to the studio. She looked up to see Duane.

"Hey," Keeley said, thinking he looked a little nervous under his glowing tan. "How are you?" She hadn't spoken to him, she realized, since the day Raquel had argued in the streets with the mayor. The day of his murder.

"I'm not too bad, Keeley, a bit shaken up with things if I'm honest."

"I'm not surprised," she said, giving him a hug. He squeezed her back more forcefully than usual, and when he stepped away she could see he was struggling to keep his composure. "I'm just really worried about Raquel," he explained, blinking rapidly as though he was fighting back tears. *He really does love her*, Keeley thought. She wondered if Raquel truly understood that, and if she still would have gone off with Gerald if she had.

"She came to see me yesterday."

"I know," Duane said, looking a little sheepish, and Keeley sighed, thinking that Duane coming in to the studio wasn't just a social visit.

"If you're coming to plead with me on her behalf, you don't need to, Duane," Keeley said. "I already agreed to help." Duane was the picture of wide-eyed innocence.

"I don't know what you're talking about," he protested, then at Keeley's cynical smile he held his hands out beseechingly, giving her his best puppy-dog look. "Okay, she might have asked me to have a word yesterday morning. I haven't seen her since, so I didn't know you'd agreed. I'm so glad; there's no one else to help her, Keeley. Everyone's convinced she did it. Some of the village kids even threw stones at her yesterday."

Keeley bit her lip. "That is awful," she said with genuine horror, feeling certain then that she had made the right decision. "I just hope there's something I can do," she mused aloud.

"You found out who killed Terry Smith," Duane pointed out.

Keeley shook her head. "That was different. It was more a case of the killer coming to me." And that certainly wasn't an experience she was willing to repeat any time soon. "I'll ask around a bit, hopefully I can find out something." She had no intention of putting herself in danger again.

Duane beamed. "I know you will. People like you, Keeley, they talk to you."

Keeley smiled, a little embarrassed at the praise. She hoisted her gym bag onto her shoulder, looking at the clock.

"I've really got to get back to the café, Duane, I've left my mother there on her own."

Although it would probably be quiet as she was usually closed and there were no breakfasts being served, it was a good excuse to get away. She needed to think about her plan of action, and who to question first.

She pushed away the memory of Ben imploring her to stop talking about the case. After all, she never had actually promised him.

"When are you going to start?" Duane asked, looking eager and, Keeley thought, a little desperate. He must be really worried for Raquel.

"I'm going to get this afternoon done at the café and then go and talk to a few people, including Edna." She didn't mention John the gardener, wondering if Raquel would have told him.

Duane looked encouraged at that.

"Thank you, Keeley." He gave her another hug, squeezing her so tight Keeley wriggled away from him laughing.

"All right, don't crush me," she laughed, eyeing Duane's massive biceps.

"Sorry, I forget how strong I am. But she will be pleased. Do you think Edna will tell you anything?"

Keeley shrugged. "Who knows? Depends what there is to tell, I suppose."

"According to Raquel, there's plenty. The mayor was hardly white as snow."

"Oh?" Keeley couldn't help but feel curious at that. She had always thought there was more to Gerald's jovial blustering than met the eye.

"Apparently—" Duane lowered his voice and leaned in to her, looking out of the door to ensure no one was listening. "— he had a secret love child years ago, and had been keeping it quiet for years."

"Really? He told Raquel that?" Why on earth hadn't Raquel told her this yesterday?

Duane nodded. "Yeah, but she doesn't really know the details. I bet Edna would, though; I bet she knew about everything that went on."

Keeley thought he was probably right about that, considering the run-in she had had with Edna earlier in the year. The woman struck her as someone who had a lot of knowledge of other people's dirty laundry, and by all accounts she had been very close to her employer.

"Raquel didn't tell me about this." She wondered why the woman hadn't mentioned it.

"Maybe she thought it wasn't relevant?" Duane suggested. "It was years ago."

"Maybe," Keeley said. Or maybe as it didn't directly concern her, Raquel didn't think it was of any importance.

"I have to go, Duane. If you see Raquel, tell her I'll be in to talk to her tomorrow." She slipped past him and out of the door before he could crush her into another hug, hurrying out of the leisure center.

All the way back to the café, she couldn't stop herself pondering Duane's revelations. It didn't surprise her, somehow, that Gerald would have such a secret in his past; she supposed lots of affluent or powerful men did. It must have been a closely guarded secret too, otherwise it would have been brought up in the village speculation about his murder by now; she certainly would have heard about it from Norma or Maggie. Still, it didn't sound as though it was a secret that could have any relevance to his death; perhaps Raquel had been right to not give it any importance.

But if he had one secret, who was to say he didn't have many others? One of which he could have been killed for? Keeley's head was whirring with scenarios when she returned to the Yoga Café to find Darla happily in attendance, with two elderly customers sharing a pot of tea.

"Did you have a nice class, dear? That didn't take long."

"I've been nearly two hours. Have you been okay?"

Darla tutted. "I'm not an imbecile, Keeley, of course I have. It's been quiet, as you said. To be honest, I've quite enjoyed myself. I'll happily hold the fort a little longer if you have anything you need to do."

Keeley went to decline, then glanced at the clock. She had time before the lunchtime rush to pop in and see Megan and share with her the information Duane had passed on. As she made her way to Crystals and Candles, it didn't escape her knowledge that she couldn't wait to tell Megan. But Megan was her friend; she trusted her. When Ben had asked her to stop discussing the case with people, she was sure he wouldn't have included Megan in that. Although she had only been friends with Megan a few months, she had grown very close to her, and, apart from Ben, Megan was the one person in Belfrey she had really taken to her heart since her return. Megan was the person she shared her fears and insecurities with, and the one who knew she still woke up in the night sometimes, remembering the aftermath of Terry Smith's murder. She was the person she sat and ate chocolate—albeit dairy-free—and watched rom-coms with, which Ben hated. Megan was her best friend, which, if she was honest with herself, she had never really had before. She had been a shy, quiet girl at school, with a handful of equally quiet and shy friends, and of course Raquel, who had wanted Keeley's friendship when her latest plot hadn't worked out according to plan or whenever she needed help with her homework. It made Keeley cringe at herself a little now to remember how accepting she had been of Raquel's "pick-her-up put-her-down when it suited her" model of friendship. She wondered if the reason she wanted to help Raquel now was partly the old, people-pleasing Keeley rearing her head, but she didn't think so.

She had friends in London and New York of course, but they were more acquaintances than close friends, people whose company Keeley enjoyed but she never quite let her guard down with. In fact, Ben and Megan were perhaps the only two people in the world that Keeley felt really knew her, ever since her father had died. The thought of losing either of them caused a flutter of panic across her tummy; she remembered Ben's annoyed expression the night before. She really hoped he was going to understand that she couldn't just ignore Raquel's pleas for help.

As soon as she stepped into the smoky, otherworldly atmosphere of Crystals and Candles, she felt soothed. A variety of different-colored crystal charms hung from the ceiling, catching the light and sending prisms of color across the room, cutting through the smoke from the incense sticks that burned steadily in each corner of the room; vanilla and musk, she could smell today. A large oak table took up most of the room, covered in a variety of colored candles and a large selection of crystals and gemstones. In glass cabinets around the outside of the room stood the more esoteric items: dowsing rods, crystal balls, and tarot cards. A display stand near the till showcased Megan's homemade creams and potions. There was nothing esoteric about these; even the most staid of Belfrey residents flocked to Megan for her foot soaks, body lotions, and dry-skin creams.

Megan looked up from her seat behind the counter and gave Keeley a wide grin that turned into a look of concern as she eyed her friend astutely.

"Is everything okay? You seem a bit on edge."

Keeley nodded, pulling up a stool next to Megan and sitting down.

"I had a great yoga class. Then I saw Duane." She recounted her conversation with her friend's cousin. Megan sighed and rolled her eyes.

"I don't understand how he can even be trying to help her after the way she treated him. And this certainly isn't your responsibility to get her off the hook. Still," Megan cocked her head to one side, "they are right. You are good at that sort of thing."

"I am going to do what I can. Including talking to Edna," Keeley confessed, "though I'm not sure she would tell me anything anyway. I'm a bit worried about what Ben's going to say when he finds out, though." She told Megan about the strained atmosphere between herself and Ben the night before, which had only really diffused with the arrival of Jack Tibbons.

Megan looked thoughtful.

"He's just being protective, probably. He really loves you, Keeley, I don't need to be a spiritualist to see that. But, you know, maybe he feels a bit put out too."

"How do you mean?"

"Well, he's the village detective, isn't he? It's all on his shoulders to solve Gerald's murder, and let's face it, it's a pretty high-profile case. There are no real leads apart from Tom's sighting of Raquel, and then people are asking you, his girlfriend, to solve it. It almost calls his ability to do his job into question."

Keeley hadn't thought about that. It made sense; she knew how proud Ben could be.

"Then maybe I should keep out of it," Keeley said. Megan raised an eyebrow at her, then gave a mischievous smile.

"But you don't want to keep out of it, do you?"

"Well, I suppose I feel bad for Raquel, and guilty that I accused her of the last one, and then it turned out she had nothing to do with it."

"Yes, yes," Megan said, waving a hand in the air with impatience, "but it's not just that. You *like* investigating, Keeley Carpenter, I know you do. And like I said, you're good at it. Maybe you should join the police force yourself."

Keeley laughed. She could just imagine Ben's face. "Maybe you're right."

"I know I am," said Megan, without a touch of arrogance, just a simple self-assurance Keeley envied. Then she changed tack. "Do you really think that Raquel didn't do it?"

"Yes. I can't explain why, it just doesn't feel right."

"Then who? Edna's too old, surely?"

"Maybe." Keeley told her about the gardener.

"Seems like Gerald fired a few people on Raquel's behalf."

"She certainly has a knack for causing trouble."

"Including my cousin. Do you know, it sounds awful and I feel guilty even saying it," Megan began, then paused, picking up a quartz crystal and rolling it between her fingers. Keeley waited for her to go on, wondering what she was about to say. Finally, Megan blurted out, "Do you think it could be him?"

Duane? Keeley felt initial shock at the suggestion, and by Megan of all people, but then when she began to think about it, it almost made sense.

"He is besotted with her, and has done nothing but go on about how Gerald took her away from him," Keeley mused. "So I suppose you could say there's motive there. But really, Duane? You know him better than I do, do you really think he's capable of that?"

Megan shook her head, looking guilty.

"No, I don't think Duane's got a bad bone in his body. He's a little shallow, but not a killer. But who knows, love can easily turn into a destructive force. If he's been wrapped up in his own jealousy for weeks, then seeing Gerald shouting at Raquel in the street, maybe he snapped."

"He didn't seem his usual self earlier," Keeley said, cocking her head to one side as she thought back to her conversation with Duane at the leisure center. "He was quite nervous and seemed on edge. But I took that to be because he's worried about Raquel; he cheered right up when I said I was going to investigate. Surely he wouldn't be like that if he had done it himself?"

"I suppose not," Megan said, looking relieved. "It's just like you said: he hasn't been himself. I sense there's things he's not telling me."

Nobody was being themselves, Keeley thought, feeling a little glum. Megan wasn't her usual self either, questioning the innocence of her own cousin. Ben was ever more distant, and her mother's changes of mood were nothing short of unsettling.

"There's an ill wind in Belfrey at the minute," Megan said, staring out of the window at the High Street, her tone ominous. "I wouldn't be surprised if Gerald's murder wasn't the last."

Keeley felt a chill settle over her, a trickle of cold fear running down her spine. Then she tutted and gave Megan a gentle shove on the arm, forcing herself to sound cheerful.

"Snap out of it, Mystic Meg. I'm sure it had nothing to do with Duane." She had a thought. "It can't be, can it?"

Megan turned back to her, curious. "Why not?"

"Well, Tom said he saw a woman—young, brunette, possibly Raquel—coming out of Gerald's house around the time of death. Duane's not a woman, is he?"

"He has got long hair," Megan offered doubtfully, a smile beginning to return to her face.

"Yeah, but still. I know Tom isn't the sharpest person at the best of times, but I'm sure even he couldn't mistake Duane for a woman. That would let the gardener off the hook too. And surely no one could mistake Edna for a young woman. Maybe I'm just wrong, and it is Raquel after all. Duane probably suspects her too, and doesn't want to admit it, that's why he's acting so funny."

"Maybe. I wonder what Gerald's secrets were? They could provide a motive."

Keeley nodded. She had been thinking as much herself. She needed to ask Raquel more about her former lover. She told Megan as much, and her friend looked thoughtful.

"Raquel will only exaggerate anyway. Or leave anything out that she considers embarrassing to her. I think you should talk to Edna first, and this gardener, get the real story. Maybe it wasn't anything to do with Raquel, maybe he stumbled across something while he was working there."

"In the garden?"

"Maybe a body?" Megan suggested, only half joking.

Keeley shook her head. "That's hardly a reason for him to then kill him in turn," she laughed.

"Visit Edna first," Megan suggested, "you could make out you were just dropping in to see how she is. If she didn't kill him, she must be grieving."

Keeley nodded, feeling a sense of compassion for the old woman. She doubted anyone would have thought to visit her in the aftermath of her previous employer's death. As far as she knew, Edna had no real family or friends. Her bitter nature had hardly won her a slew of friends. Without Gerald, she must be incredibly lonely.

"Maybe I'll drop in after work."

"It can't hurt. The worst that can happen is she doesn't tell you anything and gets a bit rude. You never know, she might be glad of the company." Megan stood up and went over to a display stand housing a variety of crystal pendants. "Tell you what, have one of these carnelians." She handed over a thin chain with a bright orange gem hanging from it. "It will give you confidence to say what you need to say, and it promotes friendship, so she will be more amenable to listening."

Keeley fastened it around her neck, dubious but not wanting to appear rude. The last time Megan had given her a crystal it had been for protection, and hadn't exactly proved to be very successful. Still, she didn't want to hurt her friend's feelings.

"Thank you," she said, standing up and giving Megan a hug. "I had better go back, I've left Mum in the café all morning."

"Don't worry about Ben," Megan advised. "If you do find out something useful, maybe he'll stop complaining about you asking questions."

That would be nice, Keeley thought.

"Maybe. I'd better go, pop in later?"

Megan murmured her assent and they hugged again before Keeley left the shop with every intention of going back to the Yoga Café. However, almost as though they had a mind of their own, her feet took her past the café and across the High Street, cutting through an alley to a row of old stone cottages behind. Keeley paused for a moment, then set her shoulders and walked with a determined air up the small cobbled path toward Edna's cottage.

Chapter Seven

The door creaked open, and Edna stood there, her eyes black gimlets that bored into Keeley as though trying to drill right through her. The animosity coming from the woman was so strong Keeley could almost smell it. She was surprised, then, when Edna stood aside without a word and waved Keeley into her front room, giving a suspicious look out into the street before shutting the door behind them with such force that it made Keeley jump. She swallowed, realizing she was now in the dark little house alone with a sour old woman who hated her at best and was a vicious murderer at worst.

Once inside it wasn't animosity she could smell, but an unpleasant mixture of cats, lavender water, and damp fabric. The small room was cluttered and everything was covered with a layer of dust that looked to be ten years old. Keeley was surprised, remembering that when she had met Edna before, in her role as the mayor's housekeeper, the old woman had been tire-lessly cleaning away and Gerald's house had been spotless. Per-haps Edna had taken more pride in her employer's house than her own; after all, she was on her own here. Keeley felt a twinge of compassion for the woman, and tried to hold on to it as Edna glared at her with mounting hostility.

"I wondered how long it would be before you came snoop-ing around, trying to dig up the dirt. Didn't take you too long, did it? Your boyfriend send you, did he? Thought you could get more out of me than he did? It will take more than a pretty face to get me to talk, lady."

So Ben had questioned Edna. The fact that he hadn't thought to mention it when they had gone out for dinner and Keeley had been asking him about the housekeeper made her feel odd; he was definitely trying to shut her out of this case. Or perhaps he had been offended, thinking she was telling him how to do his job when it was an angle he had already covered. Keeley sighed, wondering if her visit was a waste of time, but then remembered that Raquel had told her things she hadn't told Ben. Who was to say Edna had told him the full truth either?

"I just wondered how you were," Keeley said, not without sincerity. "I know you were very close to Gerald. And if I'm here on anyone's behalf," she continued honestly, "it would be Raquel's rather than DC Taylor's."

Edna scowled.

"That jumped-up little tart? I told him to steer clear of her, said she was nothing but a gold-digging little hussy, but he wouldn't listen. Turned him against me, she did, sweet-talking him and saying how I really should be taking it easy at my time of life. Just trying to get me out of the way."

"That must have been awful," Keeley said. She realized her sympathy was genuine; for all her bristling hostility, Edna was really just a lonely old woman, if a little bitter. And twisted? Keeley had to remind herself that lonely or not, there was still every chance the sinewy old lady before her had killed her once-beloved employer.

"Why would you care?" Edna looked at her through narrowed eyes, her every pore oozing suspicion. Keeley decided to be honest.

"Can I sit down?"

Edna looked surprised, then frowned, then shrugged and motioned toward the battered old sofa of an indeterminate color that might have been dark blue, or green, and was covered with a faded throw. Everything in the little house looked old and shabby. Surely Gerald should have been paying Edna enough to keep her to a decent standard of living? Keeley sat down carefully on the edge of the sofa and a black and white cat appeared as if from nowhere, jumping on her lap and meowing loudly at her. Keeley went to stroke it behind the ears and then thought better of it as the cat fixed her with a look even more hostile than that of its owner. Edna sat down on a small wooden chair opposite, wincing as she did so, and the cat curled up on Keeley's lap at the same time, looking at her as though daring her to move it.

"The thing is," Keeley began, leaning away from the animal lying on her legs and now kneading her jeans with its claws, "I just don't think Raquel did it. I know I've never exactly seen eye-to-eye with her, but for some reason, I believe her."

"I don't think it was her either," Edna said. Keeley was surprised; she had been expecting the housekeeper to blame Raquel at the earliest opportunity. "As awful as that girl is, I don't think she would have the guts to do it."

That struck Keeley as an odd expression, as though someone had to be brave to commit a cold-blooded murder, as though it were a commendable thing. She looked down at the cat on her lap and the closed front door, which Edna was sitting directly in front of, and felt trapped.

"Do you have any ideas who did?" she asked, her throat feeling tight. "How about that guy who did his gardens for him? John? Apparently there was some trouble there." Edna sniffed with contempt.

"He was no better than he should have been, jumped-up young man, tried to say I was interfering with his work, just because I didn't like all his newfangled ideas for the garden. Then Raquel was always sniffing round him. Gerald was right to let him go; I told the man as much when he came to pick up his tools."

That was interesting. "There wasn't anyone else who might hold a grudge?"

Edna shook her head. "No. Gerald was a wonderful man. Until the end, when he got his head turned by that floozy, he was the finest man you could ever meet." The old lady's face softened, and Keeley remembered Darla previously telling her Edna had been in love with her employer for years. She was going to have to tread carefully with her next question.

"Raquel mentioned that Gerald had a few secrets in his past. A child he doesn't see? Was there still any animosity with the mother perhaps?"

Edna's head jerked up, her eyes furious. The cat dug its claws harder into Keeley's leg, making her yelp.

"I knew you just wanted to snoop! Didn't you learn your lesson last time, coming round trying to dig up dirt?"

During her investigations into Terry Smith's murder, Keeley had discovered that Gerald had been blackmailed by the man. When she had confronted him, Edna had defended her employer with her usual vehemence and let Keeley in on a few home truths—it had been Edna who had revealed Darla's infidelity to her. Keeley hoped the woman didn't know any more Carpenter family secrets.

"I don't want to dig up anything," she said in what she hoped was a soothing voice. "I'm just wondering if perhaps Gerald had any enemies from the past? As you said, everyone in Belfrey was very fond of the mayor."

Edna looked a little placated, tipping her head to one side like a bird as she thought about Keeley's words.

"That was a very long time ago. He got some little floozy pregnant, and had to pay her off when she threatened to tell his wife. As far as I'm aware, no one has heard anything since. Silly little tart, she was." Clearly it hadn't occurred to Edna that her former employer—then very much married—had any part to play in that drama.

"Do you know where she was from? What happened to the child?"

"Bakewell. She had a girl, found some silly sod to marry her and gave the child his name. I only know because Gerald still sent money to her every year, then when the girl would have been about fourteen, it started being sent back. That was eight years ago. It's old news."

"Perhaps the girl found out about her real father and

decided she didn't want anything from him, as he hadn't bothered with her," Keeley mused. Edna looked furious again.

"Gerald would have been an excellent father! Unfortunately Mrs. Buxby could never have any children."

All the more reason why the mayor wouldn't have wanted his wife to know about his extramarital affair, Keeley thought. Sleepy little Belfrey certainly had a steamy past.

Still, Edna was right, it seemed like old news, not any reason why the mayor should be murdered now. The old woman's show of loyalty to her employer, and her obvious physical frailty, indicated that it wasn't her either. But then, who?

"Did you tell Ben—sorry, DC Taylor—about this child?"

Edna tutted. "No. And I wouldn't be telling you either if I didn't now know Raquel knew. You had better tell her not to be blabbing it around the village, or I'll scratch her over-made-up eyes out." Edna looked every bit spiteful enough to do just that, and Keeley revised her last thought that Edna was incapable of murder.

"I think it might be best if you tell DC Taylor," Keeley said, trying not to flinch as Edna leaned forward in her chair menacingly. "After all," she continued in what she hoped was a reasonable tone, "I'm sure you want the murderer brought to justice, and any lead could be useful."

Edna shook her head. "I wouldn't betray his confidence," she said, and averted her eyes from Keeley, though not before she caught the look of utter anguish in the old woman's eyes. She must have really loved him.

"It must have been hard for you," Keeley said with genuine sympathy, "when he let you go after working for him for so many years." *Especially if it was because of Raquel.*

Edna looked at Keeley with a forlorn expression in her eyes, that was gone as soon as it arrived to be replaced by one of utter fury. The old woman stood up, her hands balled into fists at her side, suddenly seeming to dominate the small room. The cat dug its claws into Keeley's thighs with such force that she yelped again and pushed it off before getting to her own feet, facing Edna. The cat ran to the corner of the room before turning to hiss at her.

"What are you trying to say?" Edna said through her teeth in a tone remarkably similar to the hissing of the cat. Keeley stared at her, bewildered and more than a little unnerved by the sudden change in the old woman. She looked every bit capable of murder now, every nerve in her body appearing taut and bristling with anger. Keeley noticed how sinewy her arms were, and suspected Edna was a lot stronger than she might first appear. There was certainly nothing frail about her now.

Edna took a step toward Keeley, who stepped back and realized the sofa was behind her. She twisted to the side, stepping away from the woman and looking toward the door. A fluttering feeling of panic rose in her chest; she had been in a similar situation last year, confronted with the murderer of Terry Smith. She inhaled deeply through her nose to calm herself, reminding herself that that was over, that she was safe.

She would have felt a lot safer if Edna wasn't opposite her, visibly bristling with barely contained anger.

"You think it was me?" She said through lips pursed so tightly they were almost blue. Her sharp teeth showed, giving her a feral look.

"I didn't say that," Keeley said in a soft voice, as though soothing a child.

"But you think it. You think I killed him?"

Keeley opened her mouth to deny the accusation, but her own innate honesty made her pause, and Edna read that as the confirmation she needed. Letting out a guttural sound, the old woman launched herself forward, hands and nails outstretched in front of her. Keeley caught her wrists, but not before Edna's nails, sharp as claws, had come into contact with her cheek.

"I'll kill you!" Edna shrieked, struggling against Keeley's grip. Mustering her strength, Keeley spun the old woman around by the wrists so her back was to the sofa and then shoved her back against the cushions as hard as she could before running to the door. She barely registered the loud knock on the other side before she wrenched it open, blinking against the rush of sunlight into the dark room.

In the doorway, the light framing him like a halo, stood a very shocked Ben.

Chapter Eight

"So he arrested her?" Megan handed Keeley a mug of suspicious-smelling herbal tea. Megan brewed her own, and was always a little cagey about precisely what was in them. Keeley took a tentative sip, relieved that the dominant taste seemed to be raspberry.

"Yes, hauled her off to the station. He looked furious. The only thing is, I suspect it was as much at me as at her." She touched the small bandage on her cheek where Edna had drawn blood, hoping it wouldn't leave a scar. Megan had given her a poultice of lavender and tea tree, and some German chamomile cream to help it heal. She had also offered to perform a "quick cleansing ceremony, so Edna's aura doesn't attach to yours," which Keeley had declined, trying not to sound as bemused as she often felt by Megan's beliefs. She had to remind herself that some people would describe yoga as such. Each to their own, after all.

Keeley looked around at Megan's cottage. For all that her friend's talk about auras often baffled her, there was no denying the calming energy in her house. Rather than the kaleidoscope of colors and pungent smells that was Crystals and Candles, the house had a light, airy feel with its white walls and blond wood floors, the light glinting off the large crystal dream catcher that hung from the wooden beams on the ceiling. The interior—minus the dream catcher—reminded her of Rose Cottage, her ill-fated former home, and how cramped she was now living above the Yoga Café.

In the same place as the last Belfrey murder. A violent shudder went through her, and Megan looked at her with concern.

"Are you feeling all right? You've gone as white as a ghost."

"I'm a bit shaken up," Keeley admitted. Edna launching herself at her had brought back memories of the attack earlier in the year, and now she couldn't seem to rid herself of morbid thoughts about both murders.

"Well, I'm not surprised, I'd be shaken up too if old Edna had gone for me like that. Good on Ben for taking her in. Are you going to press charges?"

"God no, she's an old woman." Ben had arrested Edna and phoned for WPC Kate Turner to come and take a statement from Keeley. Keeley had relayed the conversation, leaving out the part about Gerald's child. She wanted to tell Ben about that herself, and had felt more than a little slighted that after making sure she wasn't badly hurt, he hadn't spoken to her since. Although she knew he had been busy questioning Edna, she also knew that Ben was angry at her. He had asked her to keep away, and she had done the exact opposite. She relayed her thoughts to Megan, who sat down next to her and put a comforting arm around her shoulders.

"Don't worry about Ben. It must have scared him too, turning up at Edna's like that and finding you there. Maybe now he's got her in for questioning and you've riled her up, she'll confess all. He'll thank you then."

Keeley frowned. "You still think it might be her?" There could be no denying after that attack that Edna was vicious enough, and probably more than physically capable of it if she had caught Gerald off guard, but Keeley remembered the look of anguish on Edna's face when she had talked about her employer's demise. She had adored Gerald, that much was evident.

But love could easily turn to hate. Wasn't that what most crimes of passion were about? She could well imagine Edna turning on Gerald in a fit of rejected rage. But there was the matter of the illegitimate child as well. Although it had been years ago, Keeley couldn't help feeling it might be significant. She told Megan about it, and her friend shook her head in disbelief.

"Randy old goat, who would have thought it? Maybe it was the long-lost daughter who killed him, or the mother. Perhaps she felt spurned all these years."

"It's a bit far-fetched, after all this time."

Megan shrugged.

"No more so than the idea that Edna did it because Gerald sacked her, and after the way she attacked you I don't think that's far-fetched at all. Honestly, Keeley, I'm still not convinced it isn't Raquel, and she isn't just playing on your guilt to get her out of it."

Keeley sighed. "Who knows," she said, feeling weariness

settle over her. "I hope you're right about Edna. Maybe she will confess and this is an end to it all." She took a large drink of her tea, then looked up sharply as she heard a door bang at the back of the house. Megan got up to check.

"It was just the wind," she said.

"Where are Suzy and Christian?"

"Christian's gone to Bakewell to see his mother, and Suzy's up in the attic. Again. I must admit I'm quite excited to see what she will unveil at the café for the art festival. It should bring in quite a few extra customers, you know. Have you thought about what dishes you're going to serve?"

Keeley gave her friend a grateful smile, glad of the change of the subject. Talking about food always made her feel more grounded.

"I'm thinking of doing some kind of tart, maybe goat's cheese from the Glovers' farm, with walnut and lemon. And definitely meringues with local berries for dessert."

"Sounds amazing," said Megan with a dreamy expression. A knock came at the door, startling them both.

It was Ben, with a closed expression that sparked an ominous feeling low in Keeley's belly.

"Would you like a lift home? We need to talk," he said in clipped tones, avoiding her eyes. Keeley nodded, gave Megan a hug and thanked her for the tea, and got into the car with Ben. He roared off without saying a word, his hands tight on the steering wheel. He pulled off outside the café, turned off the engine and shifted in his seat to face Keeley, still with the same inscrutable expression. He didn't speak, just continued to regard her with that closed, even expression.

"Are you waiting for me to confess? I feel like I'm in the interrogation room," she quipped, only half joking. Ben didn't look amused.

"What were you doing round Edna's?"

"I was passing, and wanted to see how she was after Gerald's death," she said, echoing what she had told Kate. Ben tutted.

"Don't give me that, Keeley. You were fishing for information, trying to get Raquel off the hook. It was only last night you were trying to get me to go round and question Edna again."

"You must have thought there was something in what I said," Keeley pointed out, "or why else were you going round there today, if not to talk to her about Gerald?"

Ben gave a sharp nod, conceding her point.

"You're right. I thought about what you said and decided it was worth talking to her again. Though I would have done that at some point anyway. And it's just as well I did, isn't it, or that scratch in your face could have been a lot worse."

Keeley blushed, then felt her cheeks flame even more as Ben went on, his closed expression being replaced by such raw hurt that she felt tears spring to her eyes.

"Do you have any idea," he said through gritted teeth, though she could tell he was more upset now than angry, "how it felt to turn up there and find you putting yourself in danger, again?"

Keeley felt stung. "That's unfair. Last time wasn't my fault; I was already in danger before I even arrived in Belfrey. I was involved in Terry's murder whether I wanted to be or not."

"And yet that wasn't enough to convince you to keep out of things this time? For God's sake, Keeley, this isn't a game. Some-one's been killed!" He was all but shouting at her now, and when Keeley shrank away from him, reaching for the door handle, he looked immediately contrite. His shoulders slumped, the anger seeming to drain out of him.

"I'm sorry, sweetheart; I am. But I've got enough to deal with on this case without having to worry about you as well."

Keeley nodded, feeling guilty.

"Is it proving very difficult then, this case?" she asked, then hoped she didn't sound too interested lest he question her motives. If she was honest, after what had happened with Edna she could happily never hear about Gerald Buxby again. Even so, she still believed in Raquel's innocence.

But she cared about Ben too; more than cared, and looking at the dark shadows under his eyes and two-day stubble on his chin, indicating he hadn't even had time to shave, she reflected that she had been so wrapped up in her own feelings about and investigations into Gerald's murder that she had given only the barest of thoughts to how it must be affecting Ben. She laid an apologetic hand on his leg as he answered her question.

"There's just no real leads, other than Tom claiming to see Raquel. To my mind that's not enough to charge her, not without some forensic evidence. We still haven't established—or found—the murder weapon. But I'm getting pressure from the new chief at Ripley to wrap this up. Gerald was the mayor, Keeley; it reflects badly on Amber Valley law enforcement if we can't even get justice for our own."

Keeley hadn't even thought about that. Of course—Gerald being a prominent public figure meant ten times the pressure for Ben. Reading between the lines of his words, Raquel could be seen to make a convenient scapegoat.

"So they want you to charge her?"

"That was the unspoken implication. But no one wants the

Crown Prosecution Service to throw it out of court before it even gets there, so the onus is on me to gather the evidence. And as much as I hate to admit it I am coming around to your way of thinking, Keeley; I don't think Raquel did it."

"You don't?" Keeley felt both surprise and pleasure at his statement.

"No, I don't. But then the problem is, who else could it possibly be?"

Keeley touched the small bandage on her cheek, wincing.

"Didn't Edna reveal anything?"

Ben shook his head. "Hoping for a confession?" he said wryly. "Afraid not; turns out she has an alibi, apparently she was at Bridge Club." He grinned at Keeley's blank expression. "It's a card game," he explained.

"Right."

"So I'm afraid Raquel is still the only suspect I have. I understand that you want to help her, Keeley, I really do, but you could have got seriously hurt today."

"I'm sorry too," Keeley said, then she remembered what Edna had told her. "I did find out something, though; Gerald has a secret daughter." She gave him the details as she knew them from Raquel and Edna. Ben leaned forward, interested, but by the time she had finished that closed expression was back on his face.

"You didn't tell Kate any of this when you gave your statement?"

"I was still shocked from Edna flying at me like that. And," she added honestly, "I suppose I wanted to tell you myself."

"So you just withheld information," Ben said in a flat voice. He had drawn away from her now, his body again angled away from her. Keeley shook her head in exasperation.

"Seriously? You're going in a mood over that?"

Ben raised an eyebrow at her.

"Did you not think," he said slowly, as if talking to a child, "that considering you were being questioned as to why this woman attacked you, that it would be pertinent to mention something that was obviously a significant part of your conversation with her?"

Keeley stared, feeling annoyance rising in her that she couldn't swallow down.

"Please don't talk to me like that," she said, her voice sounding clipped and cold even to her own ears. "I wasn't trying to 'withhold information,' Ben, I just thought you would prefer it if I told you myself. And," she couldn't resist adding, "if I hadn't been to see Edna, you wouldn't have this information at all, because neither she nor Raquel disclosed it."

Ben shook his head as if he couldn't quite believe his ears. "You think that makes it all right then, that you took it on your own back to go around questioning suspects?"

"Edna wasn't a suspect," Keeley pointed out, "and Raquel approached me. I don't think I've done anything wrong to warrant the way you're being."

"You shouldn't have gone round there." Ben's face was set in stubborn lines that she knew all too well. She took a deep breath, trying to breathe in calm and breathe out her irritation, a technique she often taught at the beginning of class.

"You can't tell me where to go, Ben. But," she conceded, "perhaps I should have mentioned the child when I was being questioned. I suppose I just wanted to tell you myself. It's quite sensitive information."

"Are you sure you were going to tell me at all? That you didn't keep the information back for yourself, so you could go off investigating with me none the wiser?"

Keeley felt her face flush with anger and hurt. Did he really think that of her, that she would keep secrets from him? But then she had, in a way, by being less than open about her decision to help Raquel. Although, she thought mutinously, he had hardly given her a chance, cutting her off every time she had tried to talk to him.

"No, Ben. And I'm upset you would think that," she said. Her voice sounded as if it was coming from far away, and there was an edge to it that she barely recognized as her own.

"Well, I'm upset too," Ben said curtly, staring forward out of the windshield. Keeley felt a wave of sadness wash over her, the day's events coming together in her mind in stark clarity. Her cheek throbbed, and she suddenly felt fragile and in need of comfort.

Something she clearly wasn't going to get from Ben. There was a stubborn set to his jaw. Sighing, she undid her seatbelt and opened the car door. Ben made no move to embrace and she hesitated halfway out of the door, looking back over her shoulder at him.

"Shall I ring you later?" She winced at the note of neediness in her voice.

"If you like." Ben continued to stare through the windshield. Keeley got out of the car and shut the door behind her in a less than gentle manner, walking off into the café without looking back, and feeling hot tears sting her eyes as she heard his car pull off.

She and Ben had never argued—at least, not since they had become a couple—and this was the second time they had in two days.

Keeley went upstairs, glad to find the apartment empty. At least her mother was out enjoying herself. Again.

Still, Darla's strange behavior over the last few days was the least important thing on her mind right now. She sank down onto the sofa, feeling a tidal wave of emotions rush over her, from anger at Ben, fear that their recent butting heads was an indication of something more serious, and sheer shock at the attack from Edna and the sequence of events Gerald's murder had set in place.

Part of her wondered if Ben was right, and she should just keep out of it. But another, larger part of her wanted to get to the bottom of it all, to find out the answers and the truth. Justice was important to her, she knew. Or maybe she was just nosey. She pulled a cushion over her face, shutting her eyes and instantly seeing Ben's face and that hostile expression. The way he had just withdrawn from her, leaving her shut out and unwanted, scared her. As much because of her own reaction as anything else. She obviously hadn't dealt with the rejection and abandonment issues left by her father's death and Brett's betrayal as thoroughly as she had thought, and having Darla here had stirred it all up again too. Perhaps she was using her interest in the case as a foil for her own uncomfortable feelings.

But, an obstinate voice sneaked into her musings, what if Duane and Megan were right? That she did have a knack for it? People did confide in her, they always had, and Raquel at least seemed certain that Keeley could help. Not everyone thought she was as incompetent as Ben currently seemed to. And at least she wasn't under the pressure Ben was to find a convenient scapegoat. His superior's instructions to get the case wrapped up were unjust.

Shaking her head at her own chaotic thought processes, Keeley jumped to her feet. She would have a shower, then spend some time on her mat unwinding and relaxing. Today had left her in more than a little shock, and she knew the importance of being kind to herself when she felt like this. She would phone Ben later, she decided, and apologize while putting her point of view across. Even if she wasn't entirely sure what that was.

She emerged from the shower feeling more at ease, and heard her phone ringing. Seeing Ben's name flash on the screen, she snatched it up, feeling her heart beat faster.

"Hello, babe?" She was about to launch into a rushed apology when Ben's voice stopped her cold.

"I want to go over your statement again. I need to know exactly what was said between you and Edna. There was definitely only the two of you there?" There was a tone to his voice that set butterflies of panic beating frantically in the pit of Keeley's stomach.

"Yes, unless you count the cat. What is it, Ben, what's happened?"

Somehow she knew what he was going to say before he even uttered the words.

"She's dead, Keeley. Edna's been murdered."

Chapter Nine

Keeley sat down, her hand groping behind her for the edge of the bed. The ground felt shaky under her feet. Edna, dead? It had just been a few hours ago that the old woman had been clawing at her face. Ben carried on speaking, his voice sounding as if it was coming from very far away, only just audible through the rushing in her ears. For a moment she heard Megan's voice— *There's an ill wind in Belfrey at the moment*—and she inhaled sharply. She reached for the crystal pendant around her neck that Megan had given her, only to encounter bare skin. It had gone; fallen off perhaps in the tussle with Edna. Edna who was now dead.

Not just dead. Murdered.

Ben was speaking again, his voice louder.

"It looks like the same weapon that Gerald was murdered

with, though as we still don't know exactly what that was, we can't be sure. She was stabbed."

Keeley let her breath out slowly, pursing her mouth into a small "o," trying to relieve the feeling of panic that gripped her before she spoke.

"It must have only just happened. How did you know?"

There was a pause before Ben spoke.

"I went back to ask her about this 'love child' of Gerald's she told you about. Just in case there was any significance. Then I found her. I heard the cat mewling like anything while I was outside, and the door was unlocked so I let myself in. I've been asking all the neighbors if they saw anything, but most people were out. It's quite a secluded area; not really visible from the High Street."

Keeley felt stunned. Who could possibly want to kill an old woman like Edna? Granted, she wasn't the friendliest of souls, but she was an old lady. A sudden thought struck her, bringing with it another rush of fear.

"You don't think this had anything to do with my going round to see her?"

There was another pause. "I don't know," Ben said. "Maybe, maybe not. Who knew you had been to see her? More importantly, who knew what you might have spoken about?"

"Only Megan," Keeley said, reaching again for the pendant that wasn't there. "And Raquel and Duane have been asking me to talk to her. Duane said Raquel knew Gerald had secrets; how much he knows I'm not sure." She thought about Megan's accusations against her cousin and felt her head start to swim. She needed a lie down.

Ben must have picked up on her mood because he spoke in a softer tone. "I'll come round and see you later. Get some rest."

"I will." Keeley lay back on the bed, exhaustion flooding her body. "I'll see you soon."

"See you later." He rang off before Keeley had a chance to articulate the "I love you" that was left lingering on her lips.

She closed her eyes, inhaling a slow breath, but although she felt her body relax there was little that could soothe the chatter in her mind right now. Edna was dead. And there was every chance Keeley's visit to her could have provoked that. She felt remorse wash over her, even as she tried to dampen it with logic. No one other than Megan had known she was going to see the old lady at that time. And there had been no one there to overhear. It could be a coincidence, perhaps, a burglary that got out of hand, or something totally unrelated to Gerald's murder . . . but even as Keeley tried to convince herself of that scenario, she knew she didn't believe it. Life rarely produced complete coincidences, in her opinion. As a yogi, the notion of cause and effect formed a large part of her worldview. And if her visit to Edna had helped result in her murder, then she knew the chain of events wasn't going to stop there. If, a voice nagged at the corners of her mind, Edna had been killed because she knew something about Gerald and Gerald's death, then anyone else who had hinted at knowing secrets about Gerald could be in danger. Such as Raquel and Duane.

Such as Keeley herself.

Her eyes flew open, and as she felt the unease rise up her chest from her stomach she began to breathe slowly again, inhaling and exhaling in a three-part breath technique she taught her more anxious clients. As she felt herself relax, she tried to weigh up the likelihood of that being true. Anyone who had killed an old woman like Edna must be desperate. Whatever it was she had known, it had been enough to kill for. Surely an illegitimate child wasn't as serious as all that?

But no matter how rational she tried to be, that sense of unease continued to nag away at the edges of her mind, the fear gripping and refusing to let go. Eventually she fell into a fitful sleep, broken by images of Edna lunging at her, while a shadowy figure stood in the background raising a sharp weapon.

A noise startled her fully awake and she sat up, sucking in air, to find Darla peering over her with a mixture of concern and irritation.

"Sleeping in the evening, dear?"

"It's practically dusk," Keeley mumbled in her own defense, swinging her legs over the bed and getting up, finding her mother's presence suddenly cloying and wanting to be away from her.

"I shut the café early as it was quiet and you hadn't been back. I thought you were only going to see Megan. You could have let me know what you were doing, Keeley."

Her mother was right. In the aftermath of the attack from Edna, Keeley hadn't really given a thought to the café or Darla.

"I'm sorry. Where have you been?" she asked, wondering if her mother had heard about Edna. It would be all over Belfrey soon. She only hoped the fact of her visit and Edna's arrest hadn't made the gossip mill, but knew that was unlikely. She sighed as she thought of the barrage of questions that would no doubt await her from her customers tomorrow.

"Oh, around," her mother said vaguely, waving her hand in the air. Realizing she seemed to have no idea what had happened, Keeley filled her in, leaving out any mention of the mayor's extramarital shenanigans, watching Darla's eyes go large with shock.

"Well, I always thought she was a disagreeable old bat, but I can't imagine why anyone would want to kill her. I would be less surprised if it had turned out she had been the one to have murdered Gerald."

"That's what I had been wondering," Keeley admitted, thinking over her mother's remark. She wasn't the first person to assume Edna would have been capable of doing someone serious harm. It was quite feasible, then, that whoever killed Edna had done so because of a grudge of their own that had nothing to do with the mayor at all.

But then, that would mean there were currently not one but two killers at large in the local community.

"Did this sort of thing happen when you first moved here?" Keeley asked her mother. Her own memories of a childhood and young adulthood in Belfrey were of a picturesque but rather dull town in which very little happened. That certainly hadn't been the case since she had returned.

Darla looked as though she were considering the question.

"No," she said at last, a faraway look on her face, "I don't ever remember anything like this going on. There was very little crime, really. Your father's shop got broken into once; someone stole all of his best mince. There were always things going on behind closed doors, though; not quite murder but plenty of gossip. Domestic matters, you know."

"And affairs," Keeley said quietly, thinking of Gerald and his mysterious love child, then she realized what she had said as her mother's face flushed.

"I didn't mean that," Keeley said, but her mother was walking off into the bathroom, her face an inscrutable mask.

After their initial phone conversation, in which Keeley had found out more about her mother in twenty-seven minutes than she had in the preceding twenty-seven years, the subject of her mother's infidelity as a young bride, before Keeley's conception, had never been raised again.

Except, that voice nagged at her again, she didn't believe in coincidences. Edna, it seemed, knew quite a few secrets. Perhaps lots of people had reason to kill her?

Keeley grabbed her jacket, overwhelmed by the day's events and all its possible implications.

"I'm going for a walk," she called to her mother as she made her way downstairs. Darla didn't answer, but she hadn't expected her to. Her mother had been acting strangely ever since she had arrived, and her vagueness about her whereabouts also struck Keeley as odd. Still, she had other things on her mind rather than her mother, and she hoped a brisk walk would clear her head. Normally she would take to her yoga mat, but the smallness of her apartment coupled with the late summer heat and the presence of her mother had disturbed her equilibrium.

Once outside the café, she had no wish to walk along the High Street and possibly run into a barrage of questions. News spread fast in Belfrey, and Edna's murder wouldn't stay quiet for long. Of course, no one but Ben, Megan, and Kate was supposed to know she had been there, but who knew who could have been watching? She shuddered at the thought that Edna's killer might have been watching her.

Instead she walked along the path that led behind the café and toward the Water Gardens. Set alongside the Ashbourne

River, the beautiful garden with its Chinese-style pavilions and peacocks were a popular tourist attraction. At this time of day, though, they should be both quiet and peaceful.

But even the serenity of the waterfront couldn't soothe her racing thoughts. Keeley sat on a wooden bench, watching the swans float past her, the water rippling behind them, and wished she could join them in the cool water. Gnats flew around her head, irritating her. They reminded her of her time studying yoga in India. Every day in morning meditation the flies had made a beeline for her fair skin and hair, and it had taken her weeks before she could learn to ignore them. "Accept what is, don't try to change it," the teacher had admonished when Keeley had swatted with fury at the insects buzzing about her head. She felt that same irritation now and stood up, sighing. There would be no peace to be found in the most idyllic of surroundings when her emotions were so disturbed. She could do with a good hour on her mat, but without the presence of her mother. Perhaps Darla would go out again tonight on one of her mysterious jaunts.

She needed to talk to Raquel. The other woman might not have even heard about Edna's murder yet, and would no doubt be wondering about the outcome of Keeley's visit.

Keeley walked back up the path toward the Yoga Café, then continued along it until she reached a small row of stone cottages. One of them, with a painted pink gable and a shiny red sports car outside, stood out like a sore thumb. Raquel's. Keeley walked up the path and knocked sharply on the front door, hoping that Raquel was in and admonishing herself for not checking the diner first.

She needn't have worried. Raquel opened the door on the

first knock, looking flustered and, Keeley thought, more than a bit angry.

"Has something happened?" Keeley asked. Raquel grimaced.

"I thought you were the kids from up the road. They keep knocking my door and then running away before I can answer it. It's their new favorite pastime. That and shouting 'murderer' at me in the street." Although she sounded furious, Raquel looked to be on the verge of tears.

"Duane said you'd been getting some trouble," Keeley said as Raquel held the door open and she stepped inside. The cottage was immaculate, but then it would be. Raquel employed a cleaner.

"It's getting beyond a joke, Keeley," Raquel said, then her eyes lit up. "Have you found out something? Do you know who it is?"

She hadn't heard about Edna, Keeley realized. She took a deep breath.

"You might want to sit down for this," she said. Raquel's eyes went wide as she obeyed, perching on the edge of her white leather couch, her enviously brown legs folded elegantly underneath her.

"Edna's dead," Keeley said, wincing at her own abruptness, the impact of its reality again crashing over her. She needed to sit down herself, and she sat down next to Raquel, who had gone white, her eyes like dark saucers in her face.

"What? How?"

"She was murdered, earlier today." Keeley said quietly. Raquel went from white to gray, then flushed pink.

"Well, it wasn't me," she snapped, "I was in the diner all day." Keeley felt taken aback, not having expected that reaction.

"I didn't actually think it was," Keeley said carefully, reminding herself that Raquel was clearly under a lot of stress at the moment. "I was wondering more if you had any idea who it might be? If we assume it's the same killer . . ." She let the suggestion hang in the air, watching Raquel go white again.

"Who would want to kill Edna? I mean, she was an evil old hag, but surely she couldn't have had long left."

Keeley felt her mouth drop open at the callousness of that remark, and shut it again quickly, taking a deep breath before she continued, reminding herself that she had agreed to help Raquel because she wanted to see justice done, not because the other woman was a nice person.

"Perhaps she knew something she shouldn't? Duane told me that Gerald had a secret daughter; I'm surprised you didn't mention it yesterday."

Raquel shrugged.

"I forgot all about it, it didn't seem that important. I mean, it was years ago, he's never even met her. Surely you're not going to drag that all up? Honestly, Keeley, I thought you were supposed to be good at this sort of thing." Raquel sniffed, as though she couldn't quite believe how disappointing Keeley had turned out to be, and Keeley felt herself stiffen. Why was she even bothering to help this woman? But it wasn't just for Raquel, she reminded herself, it was for Gerald and Edna and the whole of Belfrey, really. As obnoxious as Raquel was, she didn't deserve to get stoned in the street.

"We need to look at all angles here," Keeley said with more patience than she felt. "After all, there isn't a lot to go on. Did Gerald have any more secrets that you know of?"

"I don't think so."

"There has to be someone who has reason to have a grudge against both Gerald and Edna." Keeley sat up straighter as she remembered what Edna had said about John.

"The gardener! Edna said she had an argument with him herself; did you witness that?"

Raquel grimaced. "I heard it. She had a vicious tongue on her, that woman. Come to think of it, half of Belfrey has probably got some motive or other to kill her. I was upstairs with the window open, and John was collecting his tools. I heard him say something to Edna, and then she just started screeching at him. I thought she was going to scratch his eyes out."

Keeley lifted a hand to the scratch on her own face. She could well believe that.

"Did you hear what she said to him?"

"Some of it. She told him he was a cowboy, that he was trying to swindle Gerald out of money, that he hadn't done a proper job. She said she was going to make sure he never worked in Belfrey again."

Keeley thought about that. It sounded like an empty threat, but to a man struggling to support a new family, who had just lost his job—well, who knew what slight was enough to spur a murderer into action? It seemed like a flimsy motive, but she had little else to go on, and who knew, maybe he had stumbled on something of importance concerning Gerald and his housekeeper. It would be worth talking to him.

There was just one problem.

"It can't have been him, though. Tom saw a woman leaving Gerald's house."

Raquel made a derisive sound through her nose.

"Tom said he saw *me*, and you don't believe that," she pointed out.

That was true enough. Keeley nodded. It would give her something to do, rather than twiddling her thumbs waiting for Ben to get in touch. Edna's attack and subsequent death had shocked her, and the best way she knew to deal with that was to keep going and do something useful. Her mother was at the flat, preventing her from doing a yoga session in peace, and she had no cooking to do, so investigating it was.

"I'll go and talk to him. In fact, I might even go now; it's evening time, he's likely to be home. From what I can remember, he doesn't live too far away."

"It's a bus ride away. I'll drive you, if you like, and wait for you round the corner or something."

Keeley looked at her in surprise. "That's kind of you, thank you."

Raquel gave a dismissive wave of her hand. "I've got nothing else to do. And you are helping me, I suppose."

While Raquel got herself ready, Keeley went through the local directory to find John's address. She wondered if she should call first, in case he wasn't at home, but decided against it. What was she going to say? *Oh hi, I just wanted to know if you killed the mayor and his housekeeper, or if you might have any idea who did? Can I come over so we can discuss it?* Better to just take her chances and turn up, and hope she didn't get the door slammed in her face.

Keeley soon wished she had declined Raquel's offer to drive her when the red sports car roared off well over the speed limit, with Raquel casually checking her lipstick in the side mirror.

"Er, do you not think you should slow down?" Keeley asked, watching the cottages whip past at an alarming rate. The car got even louder as they went up the hill.

Raquel looked straight at her.

"Honestly, Keeley, you're still a scaredy cat aren't you? I remember you never wanted to go on the scariest rides at the fair."

"I don't like heights," Keeley said, then closed her eyes as the car veered dangerously near to a tree. "Raquel, please keep your eyes on the road at least?"

Raquel sighed, but she did turn her attention back to the road and slow down until she was only double the speed limit, looking annoyed at Keeley's criticism of her driving.

"How are things with Duane?" Keeley asked, trying to distract herself from the feeling that she was about to die in Raquel's shiny red sports car. She regretted it when Raquel again turned her head fully to face her, which resulted in the car veering off slightly to the left. How on earth had she ever passed her driving test? Perhaps the rather wealthy Mr. Philips had pulled a few strings, or Raquel's driving skills had seriously deteriorated.

"Duane?"

Raquel sounded annoyed, and Keeley wished she hadn't asked. The last thing Raquel's already erratic driving needed was for her to start getting stressed out.

"I just meant, it's nice that you two are friends again; that he's supporting you through this."

Raquel sighed, but thankfully kept her eyes on the road.

"I think Duane would support me even if I had done it," she said with rare insight. "I ought to appreciate him more, I know I hurt him, but he's just not my type."

"Supportive, buff, and handsome isn't your type?" Keeley

asked with a chuckle. Raquel shrugged. "He's just so . . . young. Unsophisticated."

She means not wealthy, or important enough, Keeley thought, knowing that it was true even as she felt mean for thinking it. Duane had never had much of a chance with Raquel, really.

"Ben wasn't my type either," Keeley pointed out. Raquel snorted.

"Oh please, Keeley, you couldn't stop mooning over him at school. None of us could."

"I meant when I came back to Belfrey," Keeley said, feeling herself blush as she remembered her high school crush on Ben. "I thought he was going to be a jerk. And I think he thought I had something to do with Terry Smith's murder."

"Not the last time he was wrong then," Raquel said with more than a touch of bitterness. Keeley bit her lip to stop herself from jumping to Ben's defense. She couldn't tell Raquel that Ben had confided in her about the pressure being put on him by his superior; or that he too was beginning to doubt Raquel's guilt.

"This is difficult for everyone," she said instead, aiming for diplomacy. It would be even more so, now that he had another murder to investigate. Would he question Raquel again? It seemed likely, given that she was the main—only—suspect in Gerald's murder. No wonder Raquel had reacted the way she had to Edna's death. Keeley looked out of the window at the scenery—currently going by too fast—that surrounded Belfrey. It really was a beautiful place, something she hadn't really appreciated growing up. A few years in the hustle and bustle of London and later New York had left her grateful for the rolling countryside she had grown up in, but she had also learned that it wasn't as peaceful as its rolling green hills and chocolate-box cottages made it appear. In the distance, the huge gray cliffs of Matlock swooped up to kiss the sky, which was darkening to the soft purple of twilight. Matlock had a wilder beauty than Belfrey, but really the whole of Amber Valley, nestling in the heart of England, was one of the most visually stunning places Keeley had ever seen. She had just taken it for granted as a child; had walked to school countless mornings without ever raising her head to look at the sights on the horizon. For a moment she felt an intense clutch of gratitude for her hometown, and then anger toward whoever it was who was currently bringing such fear and mayhem. It almost seemed impossible that in the midst of such glorious natural wonder, anyone could be mean and twisted enough to run around committing murders. She wondered if Ben, investigating local crimes on a daily basis, ever felt the same.

"Ben was always pigheaded, even at school," Raquel said, jolting Keeley out of her reverie. Keeley didn't answer, thinking back to her school days when she had been little more than Raquel's shy, chubby sidekick. She had been invisible to popular boys like Ben Taylor—or so she had thought anyway. Ben had confessed to her when they had been reunited that in fact he had had a crush on her too. That wasn't something she was about to tell Raquel, who would no doubt take umbrage at the fact that Ben had taken very little notice of her either.

"We were all different at school," Keeley said, although she often wondered how much of that shy, chubby girl remained inside her. And Raquel? If Keeley was brutally honest, Raquel didn't seem to have changed very much at all.

"Well, you're a lot thinner now," Raquel said, seeming

oblivious to Keeley's answering wince, "but I don't think you changed that much."

"Oh?" said Keeley, bracing herself for a barrage of insults.

"You were always clever, and you never had to work to make people like you; they just did."

It was Keeley's turn to take her eyes off the road and turn to Raquel, staring at her open-mouthed.

"I was always really jealous of you," Raquel said almost matter-of-factly. Keeley blinked in shock. This was turning out to be one of the most bizarre days ever. She went to say something, then let out a little shriek as Raquel swerved the car sharply to one side, causing Keeley to be thrown against the door, her seatbelt cutting into her neck.

"What are you doing?"

"Sorry," said Raquel, getting the car on to a more even keel. "There was a hedgehog."

Raquel was saving hedgehogs? Recent events really had softened her.

"And I've only just had my car cleaned."

Or maybe not.

They spent the rest of the journey in silence, Keeley still mulling over Raquel's words. The idea that Raquel, who she had felt so inferior to as a teenager, had ever been jealous of her back then, before she slimmed down, got a career, and finally bagged the best-looking boy at school, was as unsettling as it was flattering.

"That's it, up there," Raquel pointed to a weatherworn stone cottage nestled in the hill above them. "I'll park just round this corner, you'll have to walk up."

"Okay." Keeley took a few calming breaths, steeling her

nerves. Although she thought it unlikely that the gardener was really the killer, he was the only suspect left, and once again she was walking into an unknown situation alone.

"If I'm not out in thirty minutes, phone Ben," she said. Raquel raised her eyebrows.

"Won't he be angry you're here?"

"Thirty minutes," Keeley said firmly, unbuckling her seatbelt and getting out of the car. Inhaling deeply, she made her way up the steep path toward the house. She paused outside the front door, lifted her hand to knock, then hesitated as she heard a baby crying from inside, then raised voices. *Great.* The last thing she wanted to do was walk into another drama. She looked over her shoulder back down the hill, wondering for a moment if she should just go back and tell Raquel no one had answered. She could come back on her own tomorrow, after a decent night's sleep and time to think about everything that had happened.

Her innate honesty won out, and she knocked, albeit lightly. The voices stopped, then she heard footsteps approaching the door. She smoothed her hair down, trying her best to look calm and even professional.

John opened the door roughly, a thunderous look on his face that softened to confusion and then recognition as he saw Keeley standing there.

"Miss Carpenter? From the café?"

"Yes, that's right. How are you?" she asked cheerfully.

"Er, I'm great, thanks," he said, an obvious question in his voice, but too polite to ask her what she was doing there. Keeley took a deep breath.

"I wanted to talk to you about the time you were working for Mayor Buxby. If it's not a bad time," she added, wincing as the baby let out a high-pitched squeal. John grimaced, and she noticed how exhausted he looked.

"No, it's just Arabella, she screams for hours at the same time every night. The doctors say it's colic, but all the gripe water in the world isn't making any difference. We've just got to wait for her to grow out of it."

"That sounds tough," Keeley said with sympathy. John nodded, then narrowed his eyes at her suspiciously. "What's this about? Has he sent you? I already told that hag of a housekeeper I never stole those tools."

Keeley's eyes widened. He didn't know?

"Erm, not quite. The mayor's dead."

John went white. *Surprise or guilt?* she thought. He leaned forward and looked down the path, as if checking no one had overheard, then stepped back and opened the door for her.

"Come in."

For the second time that day, Keeley stepped into the house of a potential murderer, alone. Still, she reasoned as John closed the door behind her, this time was different. Raquel was waiting for her, and John's wife and baby were here.

"Come through to the kitchen so we don't disturb Mary and the baby," John said. He showed her through to a small but neat kitchen, pulling two chairs out at the old wooden table that sat in the middle of the room, taking up most of the available space. "Now what's this about?" he said as Keeley sat down. She looked at him, hoping her expression didn't betray her suspicion. Could he really not know?

"Mayor Buxby was found dead a few days ago. Murdered in fact." She watched his face closely, but he showed no signs of anything other than genuine surprise. He sat back in his chair, blinking.

"Really? By who?"

"Well, we don't know."

John frowned. "So what does this have to do with me?"

"I'm just trying to get an idea of what was going on with the mayor in the weeks leading up to the murder."

"Right. I suppose your boyfriend's on the case?"

Keeley nodded, feeling guilty as she realized that John must think she was there with Ben's full knowledge—even on his request.

"It's caused quite a stir in Belfrey, as I'm sure you can imagine. I'm surprised you haven't heard about it."

John shrugged. "I've been working away for the last few weeks. I just came home two days ago."

"Oh? Where are you working?" Keeley tried to sound innocent. If John could prove where he was working, that might well give him a solid alibi for the night of Gerald's death.

But not for Edna's. She wondered if she should tell him about Edna's murder, then decided to wait and see if he slipped up. He had been less than complimentary about the old woman at the door, she remembered.

"Down in Birmingham. It was a big job—landscaping for residential homes. I was lucky to get it, after the smear campaign that bastard started. Sorry, I know he's dead, but there was no love lost between me and him."

"What happened?" She wondered how different his version of events was going to be from Raquel's. John sighed and leaned back in his chair again, resting one foot on the opposite knee.

"Where to start? It was a nightmare from start to finish. He moaned about my prices, kept changing his mind about what he wanted doing then trying to get me to lower costs by cutting corners—which I don't do, I like to do things right. Then that housekeeper of his was constantly breathing down my neck, complaining I was making a mess and watching me like she thought I was going to steal something. As for his girlfriend . . ." John broke off, shaking his head.

"Raquel? What about her?"

"Yeah, that was her. Young, dark hair. One of those girls that's all tits and makeup. She was flirting round me something terrible, and I tried to be polite-like, tell her I was flattered but I'm married. Thanks but no thanks, you know? Tried to be nice about it. She was bloody persistent. Next thing I know he's accusing me of harassing her and throwing me off the property. I didn't even get to pick up my tools."

It was what she had expected, Keeley thought, in terms of what had transpired between him and Raquel. On that point at least, she found herself believing him.

"So when did you have the argument with Edna—the housekeeper?"

"A few days later when I went back for my tools. She tried to accuse me of stealing them, said I was taking things from the shed. Bloody load of rubbish. I only ever use my own tools," he said with some pride. "She was threatening to blacken my name, I didn't think much of it, until the next two jobs I had in Belfrey all of a sudden canceled. I don't know how much clout that old bag had, but the mayor certainly would. Really worried, we were. Behind on the mortgage, new baby . . . thank God for this Birmingham gig."

Keeley couldn't help but feel sorry for him, even as she thought that it might well be enough of a motive for revenge.

"That must have been awful. You must have been really angry."

"I was. I would have killed him myself if I had had the chance, trust me."

Keeley felt shocked. It seemed such an insensitive thing to say in the wake of the news. Was he trying to bluff her, to cover the fact it really was him?

"What about Edna?" she asked gently.

"The housekeeper?" John looked confused. "What do you mean?"

"She was found dead earlier today," Keeley said, watching him closely for his reaction. He stared at her.

"She's dead? As well?"

If he was lying then he was very good at it. "Yes, she was murdered too."

John shook his head, looking shocked, then he leaned forward across the table and she wondered what he was about to say.

She never got to find out, as the front door knocked loudly, making them both jump. John got up to answer it, just as his wife called through, "John? It's that detective from downtown."

Ben. Keeley jumped to her feet, feeling her cheeks catch fire. She had to get out of here.

"Oh, here's your other half," John said sarcastically. He must think they were trying to set him up. He went out of the room and Keeley looked around for an escape route, running to the back door and praying it wasn't locked.

It wasn't, and she was running across the small garden and

jumping over the hedge before they could come back, running through the alley and back down the hill, hoping Ben wouldn't spot her. As she ran toward Raquel's car she saw Ben's parked just across the road. Had he seen Raquel? She wrenched open the passenger door and all but threw herself into the car.

"Go, go," she panted. Raquel started the car and took off, staring at Keeley.

"Please keep your eyes on the road," Keeley pleaded, "but don't slow down."

"Okay, okay. What happened up there, did Ben see you? I saw his car pull up and ducked down; I don't think he saw me."

Thank God. Keeley relayed what had happened to an incredulous-looking Raquel.

"You just ran out? Oh my God, Keeley, what will people think? But what did he say? Did he do it?"

"Well, if he did he was hardly going to confess, was he? I didn't get the chance to question him about Edna, but it sounds as though he may have an alibi for Gerald's murder." She wondered how long it would take to get to Birmingham and back; if John had been staying in a hotel on his own while he was away, then in fact his killing Gerald might be plausible—and he could use the trip as a cover.

Keeley repeated her conversation with him to Raquel, though she glossed over his assessment of her. Keeley wondered if his version of events were true and if Raquel felt at all guilty, knowing her lies had resulted in his dismissal.

"He's an out and out liar. He was all over me," she said. Obviously not.

They drove back in silence, until Raquel pulled up outside the Yoga Café and turned to Keeley.

"So now what? Are you still going to help?" Her usual demanding tone was replaced by one of pleading, and Keeley sighed. Ben was going to be furious at her for this. She should have stayed; she had had every right to be there, instead of panicking and bolting like she had. It was too much to hope that John wouldn't tell him.

"Yes. Let me get a decent night's sleep, and I'll reevaluate where we are tomorrow."

"Thank you, Keeley," Raquel said, and she sounded like she meant it. Keeley turned to her in surprise but Raquel was already looking out of the window and getting ready to pull away. Keeley got out, gave her a little wave that went unseen, and let herself into the café, letting out a long, deep breath she hadn't been aware of holding.

Chapter Ten

Keeley was about to go up the stairs to the flat when she heard a car and thought Raquel had forgotten something. But as she looked out of the window she saw Ben outside on the drive getting out of his Mercedes. He looked grim, and her heart began to beat a tattoo of anticipation in her chest. John had told him, of course he had, and she cursed herself for having run off the way she did. She opened the door to let him in and went to go into his arms automatically, then stepped away as she felt him rigid and unyielding against her, a cold feeling of dread coming over her as she saw the inscrutable expression on his handsome face, his usually full mouth pressed into a thin line. He wasn't just angry, she realized, he was furious.

"Is your mother upstairs?" he rapped out his words. "We need to talk privately."

"Yes she is. We can stay downstairs in the café if you like,"

Keeley said, trying not to let her anxiety show in her voice as she reminded herself she had done nothing wrong. She pulled out the nearest chair and sat down, taking a few slow breaths as Ben sat opposite her and put his palms flat on the table, a gesture she recognized. It was as though he was about to question her, like she was under suspicion herself. She felt a flicker of irritation.

"What on earth," he said, emphasizing every word, "did you think you were doing at John Steele's?"

Keeley swallowed, running a few plausible scenarios through her head before settling on the truth.

"I wanted to ask him a few questions about the murder."

"I gathered that. He seemed to think you were there with my knowledge—well, until you bolted anyway."

Keeley squirmed in her chair, embarrassed at her actions.

"I never told him that."

"I bet you let him think it, though." Ben shook his head, looking exasperated. "Keeley, what were you thinking?"

"I was just asking a few questions," she said, hearing the defensiveness in her own voice. "It's not against the law."

"Thanks for reminding me." His tone was dry. "But why were you asking questions? I asked you to keep out of this."

"No, Ben, you told me."

He raised his eyebrows. "That's what this is about? You trying to prove some kind of point? This isn't a game, Keeley; people have been killed."

"I know that," she snapped, feeling her own anger rise. How could he think she didn't understand the importance of it, when a woman she had been talking to just a few hours ago was now dead? "Don't talk to me like I'm a child."

"Then don't act like one," he snapped back. They both sat glaring at each other until Ben spoke again, a note of weariness in his words. "This is about Raquel, isn't it? I passed her car; I know she dropped you off. She asked you to help, and you just couldn't say no." He sounded sarcastic, and Keeley felt herself get hot with indignation.

"Ben, she's really suffering. Kids have been throwing stones at her in the street, for God's sake. And you said yourself she could end up a scapegoat for this. I was trying to help."

"Help who? Not me. Since when do you care so much about Raquel?"

Keeley sighed. It wasn't as though she hadn't been asking herself the same question.

"It's not that it's her, specifically. I just hate any kind of injustice."

"You think I'm being unjust." He crossed his arms, giving her an offended glare.

"No," she said, choosing her words carefully, "but as a police detective, your hands are tied a bit, aren't they? Whereas as an amateur, well, there's a bit more freedom to ask questions and risk looking daft."

The look on Ben's face left Keeley under no illusion that he did, indeed, think she was daft.

"Well, it needs to stop. Now."

"Excuse me?" Keeley widened her eyes, unable to process what she was hearing. Ben had never spoken to her like this.

"I said, it needs to stop."

"I'm not one of your suspects," she said, aware that she was beginning to raise her voice and Darla might hear them, but at the same time feeling too angry to care. "You can't tell me what to do. Just because I asked a few questions."

"You don't know what you're doing," he said dismissively, and Keeley felt her ego bristle at that.

"No? Well considering you were right behind me to question both Edna and John, I was obviously on the right track, wasn't I?"

A muscle twitched in Ben's jaw.

"From now on, Keeley, keep out of this. Or . . ." His words trailed off and he turned his face away from her. Keeley felt a stab of sudden panic.

"Or what?"

He didn't answer her, and it dawned on Keeley that there was something badly wrong, and part of her had no wish to know what that something was. She leaned toward him, trying to keep the worry from showing on her face, but couldn't stop the rising panic as he stood up from the table, folding his arms and looking out of the window as he spoke. Anywhere but at her.

"I can't do this anymore, Keeley."

She frowned. Her brain refused to comprehend what he meant and her words came out in a rush.

"The case? Of course you can, you're a great detective, Ben. It probably just all seems a bit much right now, with the shock of Edna's death. God knows, it's knocked me for six too." Even as she spoke, the knowledge dawned on her that that wasn't what he was trying to say.

"Not the case, Keeley. Us."

Keeley felt the color drain from her face.

"Ben? What do you mean?"

She stood up and reached for his hand, feeling the sting of rejection as he pulled it away from her. He was staring out of the window so she could only see his profile, refusing to meet her eyes. The pulse was jumping in his jaw again, a sure sign that he was emotional and upset, but when he answered her his voice was like ice.

"This, us. Our relationship. I think we need to take a break."

Keeley blinked away hot tears.

"You're breaking up with me," she said, her tone sounding oddly flat. It had been a statement, not a question, but he answered her anyway, the nerve in the side of his voice jumping furiously.

"Yes, I suppose I am."

Keeley held her breath, waiting for him to say something else, her mind scrabbling to make sense of his words. Questions ran through her head, but she said just one word.

"Why?" There was the horrible ring of pleading in it, and she closed her eyes, feeling tears again, this time threatening to spill out onto her cheeks. She tried to practice her deep breathing techniques, but her chest and throat felt tight and constricted.

Ben looked at her then, and for just a second she thought she saw anguish in his eyes, but then he blinked and it was gone, his expression stern and emotionless again.

"It just isn't working, Keeley. I've got so much on with these murders, and you insist on running around getting involved and creating more work. I just don't have time for us right now." His eyes slid away from hers.

"No," Keeley said, angry. Tears burned at her eyes again and this time she let them fall. The muscle in Ben's jaw pulsed, although he gave no other sign of noticing her distress, staring intently out of the window again.

"You can't do this, just like that. I won't let you."

Ben closed his eyes briefly, but not before she saw the hurt in them. She stepped toward him again, trying to force him to look at her, but he flinched away.

"You don't really want this, Ben Taylor, I know you don't."

He took a deep, shaky breath, and for a moment hope flared in her. But then all hint of emotion left both his expression and his voice, as if a mask had come down.

"I'm afraid I do, Keeley."

"Why?" she asked again. She felt anger flare in her when he again failed to answer.

"This is just because I went to Edna's and John's today? Because I asked a few questions before you could get there? That's it, isn't it?" She gave a bitter laugh. "I interfered in your precious investigation, sussed a few things out before the great Detective Constable Ben Taylor, and so now you don't want to see me anymore? This is a joke." She sat back down in her chair, folding her own arms in a defensive gesture, anger momentarily taking precedence over the hurt.

"It's not just a case of interfering," Ben retorted, sounding angry now himself, "you put yourself in danger, and could have jeopardized the whole case. This isn't a TV show, Keeley, for you and Raquel to run around playing Miss Marple."

Keeley felt rather than heard his words, stinging like wasps.

"I know it's not!" Did he really think that about her, that she was some silly girl playing real-life murder mysteries with her friend, as if she didn't understand the full horror of what was happening?

"You should have kept out of it."

"Yes, because you said so," she snapped, then winced at the childishness of her retort. Still, she wanted to hold on to her anger, because she knew once it dissipated there would only be the stark knowledge of her grief, and she didn't want to accept what he was telling her, didn't want to acknowledge what was happening right here and now. She could feel the full realization of the loss she was facing hovering over her, waiting to fall on her with its full, crushing weight.

She softened her voice, letting her arms fall away from her sides in spite of her natural instinct to shield herself from this. She had to try. This was Ben, she loved him. And he loved her, she was sure, in spite of the words coming out of his mouth.

"Ben, please don't do this. We can sort this out."

But her words didn't have the effect she was hoping for. If anything, Ben's posture became even more stiff, his voice so emotionless now it was almost cruel.

"Can we? You don't listen to anything I say, Keeley. And I just don't have the time to worry about you on top of all this. There's a lot riding on this case. The people of Belfrey are scared, and they're looking at me to solve it. I can't do that with you running around causing havoc."

Keeley felt angry again.

"Causing havoc? That's a bit extreme. So let me get this straight—" Her voice began to rise again, loud in the small café, and it sounded almost as though it was coming from someone else, she sounded so hostile and wholly unlike herself. "—you don't want to be with me anymore because I'm jeopardizing your chances of solving these murders? Because you can't pass up a chance to be a hero? Or because you're annoyed I found out something you didn't?"

Ben's jaw pulsed again, though she thought this time it was with temper. She knew how proud Ben could be, how much his career meant to him. Only, she thought with a feeling of desolation, she had never truly realized that it meant more to him than their relationship did. Than she did.

"It's not like that."

"I think it is. I think you're just worried about your precious promotion." She stood up, pushing her chair away and marching toward the door, holding it open. Ben turned out slowly, surprise flickering in his gaze.

"I want you to leave," she said, as firmly as she could, though she heard her voice quavering at the end. "Now, please."

Ben stared at her for a moment, and again she saw the brief look of anguish, and he opened his mouth as if he was going to speak. Her heart jumped, hopeful in her chest, waiting for him to say that he had changed his mind, that he didn't mean it, but then he closed his mouth and the look was gone. He walked over to her and went through the door without looking at her, then paused in the entrance and turned to her. She felt her free hand trembling and shoved it into the back pocket of her jeans, not wanting him to see her distress.

"Look after yourself then. I'll be in touch. About Edna," he clarified, dashing the last flare of hope.

"Fine," Keeley said, although she was anything but, and shut the door on him. Then she walked into the kitchen without looking back, shut the door behind her, and leaned her back against it, inhaling deeply, her eyes staring at the ceiling without looking at anything. She waited for the tears, for the sadness, but felt only a dull ache and a horrible, creeping numbness. As she left the kitchen, locked up, and headed up the stairs, her limbs felt heavy and fatigued. Her thoughts were slow, as though a fog had invaded her brain and she couldn't quite process what had just happened.

Darla was lying on the bed with a face mask and eye pads on, and without talking to her Keeley lay on the sofa and pulled her blanket over her, overwhelmed with a sudden need to sleep. It came quickly, descending on her so that her eyelids closed of their own accord.

She woke with a start in the middle of the night, to hear the sound of an owl hooting and her mother's soft snoring. There were tears on her cheeks, and she lifted her hand to her face to wipe them. As she did so the memory of Ben's words came to her, bringing with them a pain in her chest that was as sudden as it was shocking. She buried herself back under the blanket, horrified to hear a mewling sound escape her lips. Feeling the sobs come she pushed her face into the cushion so she didn't wake her mother, her shoulders and then her whole body shaking. She stayed that way until her eyes were sore and her body drained, and then she fell into a fitful sleep, punctuated by bad dreams. Dreams in which Gerald appeared, his torso twisted and bloody, pleading with Keeley to help him, and Raquel pleading too, her hands outstretched. Edna, attacking her, striking at her with nails that turned into cat claws. And worst of all was the appearance of Ben. She dreamed that she had something desperately important to tell him, but no matter how loud she screamed, he could neither see nor hear her.

BHUJANGHASANA—COBRA POSE

A gentle back bend that tones the abdomen. Used as an individual posture or as part of the flowing sequence of postures known as Sun Salutations or *Surya Namaskar.* The pose takes the shape of a cobra with its hood raised, hence the name.

Method

- Lie on your stomach, toes flat on the ground and forehead touching the floor. Keep your legs closed, with your knees and heels lightly touching. Do not tense. Place your hands under your shoulders, palms touching the floor, keeping your elbows tight to your torso. Take three slow deep breaths here.

- Using your hands for balance, on an inhale lift your head, shoulders, chest, and abdomen, keeping your navel on the floor. Curl your spine vertebra by vertebra. You should now be looking slightly up with your head tilting back, with a gentle arch to your back. Keep your shoulder blades relaxed and down. If this stretch puts a strain on your back, lower down a little to decrease the arch and/or bend your elbows.

- Take five deep breaths before exhaling and lowering down.

Benefits

Benefits to this pose include strengthening of the back and shoulders, the releasing of tension in the shoulders, and improvement in flexibility in the middle area of the back and spine. The expansion of the chest can aid respiratory disorders such as asthma, but do consult your physician before attempting. This pose is also good for circulation and digestion, tones the abdominal muscles, relieves fatigue, and can provide some relief from menstrual cramps.

Contraindications

Pregnancy, hernias, weak wrists, and Carpal Tunnel Syndrome. Consult your physician before attempting if you have any issues with your spine.

Chapter Eleven

Keeley woke with the sun streaming through the window onto her face, a pleasant feeling of warmth that had her smiling until she woke fully and remembered the events of the night before. Then they came back to her with full clarity, bringing a sharp stab of pain that felt almost tangible. She got up and made her way to the bathroom without greeting her mother, who was sitting at the kitchenette counter flicking through a magazine, her hair in rollers.

"Are you okay, dear? You look awfully pasty."

Keeley mumbled an inaudible response and shut the door behind her, leaning on the sink and surveying herself in the mirror. She looked worse than pasty; she was as white as a ghost, apart from the red puffiness around her eyes where she had cried herself back to sleep last night. She felt as though she were moving through fog, an awful numbness dulling the pain to an ache.

It was a feeling she hadn't experienced for a long time, this sense of utter desolation and loss. Not even the sting of Brett's betrayal had affected her like this. In fact, it reminded her of the first few days after the death of her father.

At that thought, she straightened up and shook her head at her own reflection, telling herself not to be so ridiculous. It was just a breakup, it was nothing she couldn't get through. It was certainly nothing compared to the loss of her father. She splashed cold water on her face and went through a few rounds of energizing breathing, which at least made her feel less like the living dead even if it did little to dull the ache in her chest.

It was an ache that stayed with her all morning, leaving her feeling she was just going through the motions as she rolled out her mat for her morning yoga practice, then showered and dressed and prepared to open the Yoga Café. It barely abated as she got on with cooking and serving through the breakfast rush, which for once she was glad of, the busyness keeping her from ruminating over Ben's words. The talk was, as she had expected, all about the murder of poor Edna, who apparently garnered more concern from the locals in death than Keeley imagined she would have in life. Only Jack seemed uninterested in the topic, puffing on his pipe and petting Bambi with a faraway look on his face. Keeley listened to the speculation without commenting, glad that her own visit to the old woman's house didn't appear to be common knowledge. Otherwise, the topic held strangely little interest for her, other than the lurch she felt in her stomach every time Ben's name was mentioned.

Megan came in just before lunchtime when the rush had abated, took one look at Keeley's face, and steered her into the kitchen.

"What is it?" she said, her eyes wide with concern. "Is it what happened with Edna?"

Keeley shook her head, then wrapped her arms around herself, feeling vulnerable and exposed when tears sprang to her eyes, a rush of emotion breaking through the fog.

"No, not really; it's Ben. It's, we're, over." To her horror, she burst into tears again, and Megan pulled her into her arms, resting her chin on Keeley's head and making the kind of soothing noises one would make to a baby. It was oddly comforting.

"I can't believe it," Megan said when Keeley finally composed herself and stepped away, wiping at her eyes. "It just doesn't seem right. Ben's besotted with you."

"Not anymore," Keeley sniffled, then reached for a paper towel and blew her nose. Then she recounted yesterday evening's events and their final conversation. By the time she had finished, Megan looked thoughtful.

"It sounds as though he's just overwhelmed by things, not to mention worried about you getting tangled up in something potentially dangerous." She gave a heavy sigh. "I wish I hadn't encouraged you to go and see Edna and John now; look at the trouble it's caused."

"It's not your fault; I chose to go. Besides, I don't think Ben's being fair. He was so *cold*." She remembered the look of hurt that had crossed his face, but wondered if she had only imagined it and been seeing what she had wanted to see, a way of easing the blow of his dismissal of their relationship. Of her.

"I think you just need to give him time. I can't see this being a permanent thing, Keeley. You two are meant to be; your astrological houses are perfectly entwined."

Keeley fought the urge not to roll her eyes. Megan's brand

of New Age spirituality just wasn't what she needed right now, but she knew her friend meant well.

"I don't think so. He sounded very determined." She knew that when Ben made a decision, he generally refused to budge on it, even if he later regretted it. He was both stubborn and proud, traits she had found endearing before he had turned them on her.

"So talk to him."

Keeley shook her head. She had pride of her own, and no matter how desolate she felt, she wasn't about to plead with him not to leave her. She had all but done that yesterday evening, and he had still walked out on her. That was a wound that she knew would stay open for a long while yet.

"You're both so stubborn," Megan tutted, echoing Keeley's own thoughts. "But I think you're right about him being unfair. He's totally overreacting, which is why I believe he'll come back."

Keeley shrugged, feeling both emotionally and physically drained. Then she heard the door chime and customers walk in. "I'd better go back out front."

"I'll give you a hand," Megan said, and Keeley smiled at her gratefully.

Norma and Maggie stood behind the counter, and Keeley felt her stomach sink. The last thing she needed was this pair dissecting Edna's death.

"Have you heard? Isn't it dreadful!" Norma shrieked, the sheer excitement on her face belying her words.

"Dreadful," Keeley echoed, ignoring Megan, who was making faces behind the pair's back as she began to wipe the tables down and gather up stray crockery. "What can I get you?"

"Oh, just two teas, please. We've just been in the diner for brunch."

"Thought you were staying away from the place," Megan chimed in, her voice amiable enough, but the look of cynicism on her face all too apparent. Keeley shot her a warning look.

"Well, you know, we thought we would go in to offer our support," Maggie spoke up, pulling up a chair and picking up a menu. As much as she needed customers, Keeley hoped they weren't going to order food. Her levels of tolerance and good-will to all were not riding high today. An image of Ben flashed into her mind and she closed her eyes as if she could ward it off.

"But she was very rude. And didn't seem bothered about poor Edna at all," Maggie was continuing.

Norma nodded. "Yes. She always was beastly to her, hounded the woman out of her job. I wouldn't be surprised if she had committed both murders."

"I didn't realize you two were even friends of Edna's," Megan said, again in that deceptively amiable voice. Norma and Maggie's concern for people tended to go only as far as there was an angle of gossip available. Thinking of the two women's propensity for gossip, Keeley found herself asking, "Did you know her and Gerald well?" After all, there was no Ben to tell her off for getting involved now.

Pleased to be asked, Norma sat up straight, all but puffing her chest out as she said in a voice full of her own importance, "Well, I was a very good friend of the mayor's. Had a lot of time for me, he did. Of course, we go back a long way."

"Do you think it's possible that these murders might be connected to something or someone from their past? Assuming," Keeley corrected quickly, not wanting the women to be picking up and expanding on any of her theories for the whole of Belfrey to hear, "that their deaths are even connected."

"Oh but they must be!" Maggie jumped in with obvious relish.

Norma looked thoughtful. "The mayor was a good man, of course, an absolute pillar of society. But, well, I'm not sure I should say this . . ." She paused, obviously waiting for the encouragement to continue. Ignoring Megan's exaggerated eye-rolling, Keeley leaned over the counter encouragingly. "Go on," she prompted.

"Well, I do hesitate to speak ill of the dead," Norma said piously, then went on with no further prompting needed, "but he was a dreadful philanderer in his youth, and even when he was first married. His wife did her best to turn a blind eye, of course, and I'm sure he thought he was being discreet, but people talk, you know. It's awful really, the way some people gossip," she concluded with no apparent irony. Megan stifled a snort of laughter, turning it into a cough. Keeley suppressed a smile. This was interesting, she thought.

"But it was all a long time ago," Maggie took over the story "I wouldn't have thought it could shine any light on his murder. No, I still believe wholeheartedly that it's all down to Raquel, she should be locked up. Honestly, Keeley, I'm surprised your Ben hasn't charged her yet."

Keeley flinched at "your Ben." He wasn't hers, not anymore. Not that people could ever belong to you, Keeley reprimanded herself, pushing away the sudden loneliness.

"I don't see why Raquel would want to kill Edna," Megan chimed in. Keeley sighed. The mention of Ben had reminded her of their argument. He was angry with her precisely because of her interest in this case, and here she was discussing it yet again. She turned away from the other women and began rearranging the shelves of mugs, trying not to listen as the conversation carried on behind her.

"Well, who knows. Perhaps Edna had found some evidence that she killed Gerald?"

"You know," Norma chimed in, "Keeley might have a point. Perhaps one of Gerald's discarded lovers has carried a grudge all these years? And I bet Edna would have known all his secrets."

"Maybe he even had a secret love child or two," Megan said, her voice all innocence. Keeley spun on her heel and glared at her, but Megan gave her a bland smile back.

Norma and Maggie looked excited at the prospect. "He could have a whole brood of them, who knows?"

"Well, evidently Edna did."

"Or Diana," Maggie said. Keeley frowned.

"Diana Glover? Why would she know anything about Gerald?"

"Well, she worked for him alongside Edna a good few years ago, doing the cooking and things when his wife was still alive and he was carrying on his shenanigans. In fact there were even rumors they were involved, and she suddenly stopped working there. Not long after she met Ted."

Keeley felt surprised. Somehow she had never envisaged Diana with any life other than the Glovers' farm, but of course she must have been young once. And pretty, she thought, remembering she had been admiring Diana's bone structure the other day. Had she had an affair with Gerald? Diana had long dark hair, just like the woman Tom had seen. Keeley caught her own thoughts, shocked at the turn they were taking. If she wasn't careful she would end up like Norma and Maggie. The thought made her smile, a welcome relief from the morning's melancholy, as she imagined herself and Megan in thirty years' time, the next generation of village gossips.

"I'm sure Diana doesn't know anything," Keeley said softly, "and it's pointless us debating it. The police will get to the bottom of it."

"We hope." Norma gave a disbelieving snort, but Keeley had already turned away, back to her mug rearranging. Sensing her friend's withdrawal Megan fell quiet too, and realizing they were no longer being listened to, Norma and Maggie soon finished their drinks and left.

Megan raised her eyebrows at Keeley.

"Well, that was interesting. Seems our beloved Lord Mayor had a bit of a racy past."

"We've all got skeletons in the cupboard," Keeley said diplomatically. Megan grinned and cocked her head to one side, surveying Keeley with an amused twinkle in her eyes. "Really? So what's yours? You don't strike me as the secretive type."

"Can't you read it in my aura?" Keeley teased her friend good-naturedly, glad of the light relief. It felt like a long time since she had really smiled. "I don't know. Maybe that I used to be overweight and have a serious chicken nugget addiction? Hardly what you would expect from a qualified nutritionist and yoga teacher. What's yours?"

Megan shrugged. "I don't suppose I've really got anything either. I listen to really cheesy pop music sometimes, instead of the hippie New Age pan pipe stuff people seem to expect me to be into."

Keeley laughed at that, then said on a more serious note, "Gerald's skeletons were a bit more extreme than that. Still, being guilty of a few affairs in years gone by doesn't seem like a very good motive for murder."

"It's definitely not the gardener? He seems to be the most recent person with a viable grudge."

Keeley shook her head.

"He seems to have an alibi. No doubt Ben will check it out."

"That just leaves us with the affairs. Maybe someone never got over him, and was jealous of his relationship with Raquel. Then they killed Edna because they thought she suspected them."

Keeley mulled over her friend's theory. "But if Edna suspected someone, wouldn't she have said, when she told me she didn't think it was Raquel?"

Megan shrugged. "Maybe she didn't want you to know. She was very protective of him. She obviously didn't want anyone to know he had an illegitimate daughter. I wonder what happened to her, if she knows who her dad is?"

"I would imagine she would despise him if so, if he has never had a relationship with her," Keeley said, keeping her voice neutral although a new possibility had occurred to her. Nevertheless, Megan picked up on the words she had left unsaid.

"You think the daughter killed him?"

"It's possible. I mean, growing up with a father who doesn't acknowledge you, it could result in some really deep-rooted issues." In her work with traumatized and difficult adolescents in New York, Keeley had seen firsthand the results of childhood rejection and abandonment.

"She might not even have known," Megan pointed out. "If the mother was married herself, or met someone when the girl was small, she might not even know Gerald was her dad."

Keeley nodded. "It's all speculation. Ben knows about the daughter now, so I'm sure he'll look into it."

Megan gave a wry smile. "If you hadn't gone to speak to Edna, he wouldn't have known about it at all. You would think he would be a little more grateful."

"I think he just thinks I was interfering," Keeley said with a sigh, her lift in mood rapidly dissipating at the thought of Ben. It still seemed surreal, as painful as it was, the idea that he wouldn't be in her life on an intimate level anymore. She hoped he would change his mind, longed for it even, but it wasn't a thought she was going to readily admit to.

Megan went to reply, but was interrupted by the chiming of the door and the entrance of Suzy and Christian. Suzy's pink hair was now lemon yellow, and she carried a large portfolio under one arm. Christian looked as easily handsome as ever. Keeley reflected again on what an odd couple they seemed to make in terms of temperament. Still, who knew what went on behind closed doors? Plenty of people might not have envisaged her and Ben together either.

"I brought some of my paintings to show you, so we can plan where everything's going to go," Suzy said in the surly tone Keeley was coming to realize was characteristic of her.

"That's fantastic." Keeley attempted to sound enthusiastic, but in all honesty she had forgotten all about the art festival given the events of recent days. Neither was she relishing the prospect of a café full of people from outside Belfrey who would have heard about the murders in the regional papers and no doubt be full of questions. Still, at least it would give her the chance to try out her new recipes, and spending the rest of the week concentrating on cooking would hopefully take her mind off Ben.

"How are you?" Christian asked, giving her a sympathetic smile. Keeley smiled back, trying to ignore the venomous look that Suzy gave her.

"I've been better," Keeley admitted, "it's been a tough few days. Thankfully the festival will give me something to focus on. Are you still displaying your work at the diner now that it's open again?"

Christian nodded, looking pleased, and Suzy cut in quickly, opening her portfolio and spreading some pictures over the counter. They were much the same as the images that Christian had shown her on his phone. Beautiful, but somewhat dark in tone. Not really the sort of thing that she thought reflected the atmosphere of the Yoga Café; she would have preferred to be displaying Christian's work.

Suzy was looking around, her face set in concentration.

"I think I'll have the trio of mixed media pictures on that wall there, some smaller pieces along the back wall—you're going to have to move that table, Keeley, it's going to be in the way—and that will leave the window for my new piece, which is going to be quite large. I've nearly finished it."

"She's been working through the night," Christian said, and although his tone was amiable enough there was just the fleeting glimpse of an expression that suggested he wasn't entirely happy with the lack of attention. Keeley imagined he would often find himself coming second best to Suzy's devotion to her art.

"The decor doesn't really go, does it?" Suzy glanced around at the fresh lemon walls with the white coving. "Have you ever thought about a nice purple? Or gray perhaps. That would provide a fantastic backdrop to my work."

Keeley bit her lip, ignoring Megan's snort of laughter at the girl's presumption.

"Er, no. I can't say I have. I don't think that would really reflect what I'm doing here."

"Well, you could always paint it back afterwards," Suzy said, as though that were a perfectly reasonable request. Keeley decided to pretend she hadn't heard and went back to looking at the paintings. She glanced at Christian, who had the grace to look embarrassed.

"I'm sure Keeley wants to keep the café as it is," he reprimanded his girlfriend gently. "It looks lovely; you've done a really good job with the place," he added to Keeley, who felt herself flush with pleasure at his praise. Suzy glared at her and snatched her portfolio back up.

"I'll come in tomorrow to discuss it properly," she said, and turned on her heel, motioning with a jerk of her head for Christian to follow her. He gave Keeley and Megan a sweet, apologetic smile before following. As the door shut behind them Megan raised her eyebrows at Keeley.

"She's certainly the dominant one, isn't she? I can't work out what he sees in her. It's a shame; he's so handsome."

Megan looked almost dreamy for a moment and Keeley grinned, surprised.

"You like him, don't you?" It was the first time since she had met her that she had heard Megan express an interest in a man. Megan colored prettily.

"I just think he's a nice guy. Though there are parts of his aura I can't read; I think he's been through some trauma. Perhaps that's why he likes Suzy, she's a domineering force, it might make him feel protected."

For some reason, Keeley found herself thinking about Diana again. She didn't think she was very protected by the domineering Ted Glover. She pushed away the thoughts and smiled indulgently at Megan, who then surprised her by saying, "It would be no good even if he did get rid of Ms. Tortured Artist. I think he likes you."

"Me?" Keeley wasn't sure she felt entirely comfortable with that idea. She was with Ben. *Correction, I was with Ben,* she thought dismally.

"Yes, it's in his eyes when he looks at you. I'm surprised he hasn't turned up to one of your classes."

"I doubt Suzy would let him," Keeley shrugged. "Actually, yoga might do Suzy some good. I'd suggest it, but she's so prickly."

"Can you believe she suggested you redecorate the café?" Megan said, laughing. Keeley made herself laugh with her friend, but her heart was no longer in it. Thinking about Ben had brought the reality of the situation back home to her. People were dead, and Ben had left her. She felt suddenly drained.

After Megan had left, Keeley went through the rest of the afternoon on autopilot, glad that the café wasn't too busy, then she closed a little earlier than usual and went over to the supermarket for the ingredients for the impending art festival. She would try out her recipe for the goat's cheese and walnut tart tonight.

Even shopping for ingredients failed to cheer her, and as she walked home with her bags she felt a distinct lack of enthusiasm. She had bought a frozen cheesecake too, on impulse, thinking her mother might enjoy a slice. Or at least, that was what she told herself. It had been a long time since Keeley had used processed sugar as a comfort blanket, but then it had also been a long time since she had experienced a major heartbreak. This, she thought, was worse than Brett. She had always known, deep down, that Brett had been no good for her, that if she truly examined it, her "love" for him was based more on her own need to feel loved and wanted. With Ben, it had been different. It had been real. And she had been so sure that their futures would be entwined, and so sure he had felt the same.

When she got back to the apartment, she found her mother shrugging on a linen jacket and spraying on floral perfume. She looked lovely, she thought, as ever envious of her mother's perfect bone structure and effortlessly slender figure.

"Are you going out?" she asked, oddly disappointed. She realized she would have welcomed her mother's company. She was getting used to having her here, and her mother's erratic and haphazard attempts to be a little more, well, motherly, were strangely touching.

"Yes, I'm off to the Matlock Women's Association," Darla said. "I won't be late." She air-kissed Keeley and was gone on a cloud of scent. At least she was making friends, Keeley thought as she took her shopping over to the kitchenette and got her cooking utensils ready. She also put the cheesecake on a plate and left it to defrost.

As she chopped and sliced fresh leeks, carrots, and parsley, she waited for the relief that the simple, repetitive tasks usually brought her, but it was slow and partial in coming. Keeley loved cooking; it was like an extension of her yoga practice in that it enabled her to focus on the task at hand and the present moment, and the benefits that the end result had on her body and mind. Gradually the rhythm and fresh smells began to soothe her, so that as she rolled out the puff pastry and roasted the leeks with the herbs and some lemon, she felt some of the tension in her body unknotting and the pain, if not abated, was at least less acute.

While the tart baked in the oven, Keeley found herself eyeing up the cheesecake. Although she preferred her puddings fresh and homemade, the sugary treat looked tempting. One slice, she reasoned, could hardly hurt.

She sat on the sofa with her cheesecake and picked up the local magazine her mother had left on the cushion. She flicked through the features, not really taking in the information, and ate the cake without truly tasting it. It was gone before she knew she had eaten it, so she went and cut herself another slice, larger this time, determined to enjoy this one.

As she sat back down and picked the magazine back up, she noticed an article about the Matlock Women's Association and their recent bake sale. Remembering that was where Darla had announced she was going, she read it with a vague interest. Then frowned at the part that detailed when meetings were held, on Sunday afternoons and Tuesday mornings. Not Wednesday evenings. Perhaps the writer had gotten it wrong, or Darla had, although that struck her as most unlike her mother.

Or she was lying. As soon as Keeley thought it she felt disloyal, but even so the thought took hold and nagged at her. Darla was acting quite strangely, being far too nice one minute then back to her usual self the next, and going off with "old friends" Keeley had never met. Maybe she was up to something, although quite what she could be up to she had no idea.

The thought that her mother had deliberately lied about her plans for the evening made her feel uncomfortable and agitated, and she found herself going back to the cheesecake and this time not even bothering to cut a slice but bringing the rest back to the sofa with her. As she ate, she thought about her mother, and Ben, and Brett, and her father, and ate faster as if to smother the tears and feelings of loss that welled up inside her.

Then she looked down at her plate and saw she had finished the entire thing. Feeling sick, bloated, and disgusted with herself, and remembering her mother's comments about her thighs, Keeley set the plate down on the floor and then curled up on the sofa under the blanket, trying to fight back the tears that gathered at the corner of her eyes. She didn't want to cry herself to sleep for a second night.

She must have drifted off into sleep, however, as when she opened her eyes again it was getting dark. Hearing something, she sat up to see Darla coming in, her face flushed.

"Have you only just got in?" Keeley felt a sick, heavy feeling and, remembering the cheesecake, she looked down and pushed the plate under the sofa with her foot, feeling ashamed and not wanting her mother to see it and know she had gone back to the habits of childhood. *Using sugar as an alternative to love,* Keeley thought with bitterness and more than a touch of self-pity.

"Yes," her mother said with no word of explanation. The women's association meeting must have gone on for quite a while, and the flush on her mother's cheeks indicated she had been drinking wine. Perhaps they had had a wine tasting session? She remembered the magazine.

"So, did you go to the WA meeting?" she asked, keeping her tone light. Nevertheless her mother gave her an annoyed look.

"Yes, dear, like I told you. Why are you interrogating me? It's your boyfriend who is the policeman, you know."

Wincing at that comment, Keeley took herself to the bathroom to wash her face and clean her teeth. She curled back up on the sofa and went to sleep in her clothes, feeling utterly dejected.

Chapter Twelve

The next morning Keeley stood straight in Tree Pose, standing on one leg, letting her gaze focus on a point on the wall in front of her. She had woken up feeling as sorry for herself as she had the night before, but after getting up and making her way to the bathroom and seeing herself in the mirror, her face puffy and red from crying, she had felt a spark of rebellion. She was not going to allow herself to fall apart over Ben Taylor; she was stronger than that. It was going to hurt, she knew, and hurt badly, but it wouldn't kill her. She still had her business, her friends, her practice, and most importantly her integrity. As much as she loved him, she didn't need him.

Keeley took herself through a series of standing postures designed for strength and balance, and to build resilience. All the things that she needed right now. There was an ever present dull ache of grief, no matter how much she tried to empty her mind of thoughts of Ben, but, she told herself firmly, she was just going to have to get on with it.

Darla remained asleep while Keeley got ready for another early morning session with Diana. Perhaps she had had more wine than Keeley had thought. She thought about her mother's claims that she had only been to the women's association with no small amount of skepticism. Still, it was her business, she supposed.

Diana was chattier than usual, the bruise on her eye faded to nothingness, and as she placed a hand in the small of her back to help her ease into a back bend, Keeley recalled Norma and Maggie's intimation that Diana had known Gerald quite well. She wanted to ask her about it, but couldn't see how to bring it up, though in the end it was Diana who mentioned the subject, shaking her head over the plight of poor Edna.

"I used to work with her, you know, at the Buxbys' before Gerald became mayor. I did a bit of cooking there. She wasn't the easiest person to get along with; a bit of a bully, in fact. Still, she didn't deserve that." Diana shuddered.

"Nobody does," Keeley said quietly.

"I wonder who did it? Does Ben not have any leads?" Diana asked as she relaxed into a lying pose. Then she flushed and brought a hand to her mouth. "I'm sorry, I shouldn't ask that, should I?" She looked mortified.

"Don't be silly, it's perfectly natural to ask," Keeley reassured her, ignoring the twinge of pain at the mention of Ben's name. "But no, I don't think he has." She didn't say they were no longer together; she intended to let people find out in their own time. The only person she had told was Megan, and she was dreading the time when it would become common knowledge. Norma and Maggie would no doubt be around with a barrage of questions, and as for what her mother would say, the longer she could avoid her mother's barbed comments the better.

"I suppose it was that Raquel," Diana offered. Keeley shrugged, suddenly not wanting to get drawn into another conversation about it lest the subject turn back to Ben, but Diana's uncommon chattiness continued. Normally Keeley liked to keep her clients focused on their breath, but it was such a pleasant change to see Diana so communicative that she let her carry on.

"Everyone acted so surprised when he got together with her, but he was always one for the ladies, you know. He even used to flirt with me a lot when I worked there, that was probably why Edna didn't like me."

"Really? Goodness." Since his death it seemed everyone had a tale to tell about the mayor's apparent randiness.

"Oh yes," Diana went on happily, following Keeley's lead and bringing her knees to her chest, "it was the talk of Belfrey for a while. Awful really, that kind of thing can cause so much hurt. Especially when poor George found out . . ." Diana went red and fell silent, a look of horror in her eyes as she realized what she had just said. It took a few moments for the implications of the woman's words to register in Keeley's mind, then when they did she sat up abruptly, her reclining pose forgotten.

"George? You mean my father, don't you?"

Diana sat up too, looking as though she was about to burst into tears. "Keeley, I'm so sorry. I'm such an idiot. Ted always says I should learn when to keep my mouth shut."

Keeley shook her head against the woman's words. "No, Diana, that's an awful thing for him to say. But what did you mean?" When Diana pressed her lips together as if to prevent herself from elaborating further Keeley added, "Please?"

Diana sighed. "There was talk that Gerald and your mother were, you know, involved. It wasn't common knowledge, it all got hushed up. I don't even know the truth of it really." Diana was backtracking.

"It's okay," Keeley reassured her. "I know about what happened when my mum and dad were first married." *I just didn't know it was Gerald my mum had the affair with,* she thought, her mind whirling with half-formed scenarios. Why had Darla not told her when Gerald's death had been announced? After all, Keeley already knew about her mother's past infidelity. Apart from the initial shock at the news, Darla seemed to have taken it perfectly in stride, as though Gerald really was no more than an old acquaintance. Perhaps Diana was wrong, Keeley thought, or rather hoped, but her gut told her the information was accurate.

They finished off the session with Diana back to her more subdued self, unable to meet Keeley's eyes as she paid and made to leave. Keeley felt pity for her, calling her back before she went out the door.

"Diana? Please don't worry about what you said, honestly, it's fine."

Diana gave her a weak smile. "I just hope I haven't upset you, I just didn't think before I spoke. I've had a lot on my plate, you know, running the farm while Ted's away."

"Ted's gone away?" That might explain why Diana had seemed more talkative than usual, given her temporary hiatus from her domineering husband.

"Yes, just on a shooting holiday for a few days. He's back at the weekend." A shadow seemed to cross her eyes at her last words, and she hurried out. Keeley watched her, wishing there was something more she could do for the downtrodden woman. Then her thoughts turned back to this new and unexpected piece of information. Her mother and Gerald? Her every sense rebelled against the thought, but she supposed it wasn't so ludicrous really. They would have been around the same age, and both were very attractive in their youth. She felt a surge of sympathy for her late father. He must have been devastated.

When Keeley had found out about her mother's infidelity, in the wake of her return to Belfrey and the Terry Smith murder, it had shocked and upset her. However, the unusually candid conversation she had had with Darla afterward had left her feeling she knew her mother better, and also enabled her to see just how deeply her parents had loved one another, in spite of Darla's outwardly cold exterior. So any resentment Keeley might have felt toward her for that particular subject had largely dissipated. Even so, she felt shocked at the revelation that her mother's former lover was the recently murdered mayor.

A horrible, creeping suspicion filled her mind. Could her mother possibly know something? That might explain her rather odd behavior and the wine consumption last night. Once again, Keeley wondered if she had really been at the women's association meeting, and she knew that once that thought took hold, it would nag at her until she knew the truth.

Well, there was only one way to find out. Keeley retrieved her phone from where she had left it during her session with Diana, rooted around in the cabinet for the local phone directory, and rang the church hall where the WA group had their meetings.

It was still early, and she half hoped no one would answer, but a croaky voice came at the other end of the line.

"Yes?"

"Good morning," Keeley said brightly, already feeling guilty for the lie she was about to tell, "I wanted to inquire about the women's association meeting on a Wednesday. Is it okay to just come along?"

"It's not a Wednesday, duck," came the voice, old and croaky and of indeterminate gender, "Tuesdays and Sundays after the service, been the same for years."

Keeley felt a curling of dread in her stomach.

"So there was no meeting last night?"

"No, duck," the voice said with a touch of impatience. "Like I said, Tuesdays and Sundays."

Keeley cut the call without speaking, a dreadful thought beginning to take shape in her mind. Why was her mother lying about where she had been? And why had she seemed so blasé about Gerald's death? It was ridiculous to think her mother could have anything to do with what had happened. The two things were most likely unrelated.

And yet.

It made no logical sense; after all, why would Darla want to kill Gerald, a man she had had an affair with twenty-seven years ago? There was no motive. Yet she couldn't deny that her mother's actions were suspicious to say the least: lying about her whereabouts, lying about how well she had known Gerald, when after all Keeley already knew about the affair itself, and her erratic behavior lately. Then there was the fact that the murders had coincided perfectly with the arrival of her mother back in Belfrey. She had to conclude that if Darla was anyone but her own mother, she would see them as a viable suspect.

And so, she realized, would Ben. She wondered if she should tell him, then dismissed the thought straight away. As much as Darla and she hadn't exactly always seen eye to eye, her mother had been making more of an effort recently and she wasn't about to report her to the police just out of a half-formed suspicion. Given that Ben was barely talking to her, she doubted the fact that Darla was her mother would sway him toward sympathy. Ben would, as ever, do his job. The very thing Keeley had once admired about him—his integrity and devotion to his work—now struck her as more of a defect, manifesting in that bull-headed stubbornness and pride that had him walking out on her and the promise of a future together.

No, she wouldn't tell Ben. She would be better off talking to her mother herself.

Keeley was drumming her fingers on the top of the counter, her mind whirling, when she noticed a piece of paper on the floor under the till. She picked it up and turned it over to see a beautiful color sketch of a young girl, with a haunted expression in her eyes. It must have fallen out of Suzy's portfolio the day before. It was very well done, if typical of the artist's subject matter. The girls' eyes seemed to stare at her out of the picture, a look of pleading in them.

The door chimed, startling Keeley, and she turned around to see Christian come in, alone for once.

"Hey," he said with that easy charm of his, and in spite of

her current mood Keeley could hardly help but respond with a warm smile. "I've just been in to see Raquel about showing my work on Saturday, and thought I'd pop in. I'm at a bit of a loose end and Suzy's holed up in the attic."

"Hey yourself. I've just found this, it must have fallen out of Suzy's things yesterday. Could you return it for me?" She passed the sketch to him. Christian took it from her and nodded, staring intently at the picture.

"I haven't seen this one before."

"It's beautiful," Keeley said. Christian nodded.

"Like I said before, she's incredibly talented. Almost makes it worth putting up with her mood swings." He laughed at his own comment, and Keeley laughed with him, glad he had voiced what he knew everyone must be thinking.

"She seems very intense. Are you very passionate about art yourself?"

Christian nodded fervently.

"Oh yes, it's all I've ever wanted to do. I'm interested in all forms of creative expression, though, not just visual art. Performing arts is a big love of mine, and poetry." He looked shy as he said the last, and Keeley felt a shudder of an emotion she couldn't quite name. Ben wouldn't know a thing about poetry if it jumped up and bit him, she found herself thinking, then felt immediately disloyal in spite of the estrangement between them. Once, particularly during what she liked to think of as her "yoga years" in India, someone like Christian would have been her exact type: boyish, laid-back, and a bit arty. Alpha males like Ben she had kept well away from ever since Brett. Now, though, Ben was all she wanted.

The feeling of loss swept over her so suddenly that she had

to turn away to hide the tears that welled up in the corners of her eyes.

"Would you like anything to eat or drink?" she asked, fighting to keep her voice steady. Christian picked up a menu.

"Yes, can I have a peppermint tea, please? And a red pepper, spinach, and potato omelet."

Keeley poured a tea and went into the kitchen to make the omelet, still thinking about Ben. She was just flipping the omelet onto a plate when she thought she heard his voice and jumped. Was she so lovesick she was now conjuring him up in his absence? She carried the plate out, shaking her head at herself, then jumped again when she saw Ben standing by the counter, talking to Christian. She passed Christian his food, her heart thumping in her chest as she looked up at Ben.

"Can I help you?" she said, her voice cool.

Ben glanced at Christian, around the empty café, then back at Keeley. "No," he said curtly, "I just wanted to check you were okay."

"Of course. Why wouldn't I be?" Keeley asked, just as curt. Christian was watching them with interest, and Keeley sat opposite him, giving him a smile.

"So tell me more about your art," she said, effectively freezing Ben out. Ben stared at her for a moment, then turned and walked out. Keeley's face crumpled.

"I take it you two have had a row?" Christian said, handing her his serviette. Keeley wiped her eyes, nodding.

"You could say that."

"Do you want to talk about it? Tell me off if I'm being nosey, but if you need an ear, I'm all yours." He took a bite of his omelet, nodding with satisfaction. "This is really good," he added.

"Thank you," Keeley said, then sighed. "There's not much to say really. These murders, they've upset everyone. He accused me of interfering with the case because I went round to talk to a few people." She stopped, seeing the interest on Christian's face and aware she was saying too much. She didn't want the whole of Belfrey to know she was investigating on Raquel's behalf.

"I heard you solved a murder before," Christian said in between mouthfuls. "You'd think he would be glad of the help."

"I don't know if 'solved' is the right word, I kind of ended up getting involved through circumstances really. I nearly got hurt, so I suppose Ben just feels protective." She found herself defending him.

"Maybe. Or maybe he doesn't want you stealing his thunder."

"That's what Megan said. But that's just ridiculous, Ben isn't like that," she said, even though in her more prideful moments she had come to that conclusion herself.

"Well, I hope you both sort things out," he said diplomatically, giving her a sympathetic smile. Keeley wanted to say she hoped so too, but that hope felt so futile right now that she didn't even want to voice it.

Christian continued to eat his omelet and Keeley got up as two elderly women came in. They ordered two of her summer cream meringues and she busied herself making them, thinking as she did so about the coming Saturday. She really wasn't looking forward to it, in fact she wanted it over and done with as quickly as possible. Usually Keeley would welcome the chance to get involved in the local community, especially something that was likely to drive new visitors to the café and enable her to try out a new recipe, but the thought of spending the entire day with Suzy, surrounded by her stunning but tragic images, didn't

exactly fill her with enthusiasm given the bleakness of her existing mood. More than that, she had a slightly ominous feeling
about the art festival that had been creeping up on her the past
few days, or perhaps she was just being negative, given that events
of the past week had been decidedly less than cheery.

She needed a good, vigorous workout, she thought, looking
at the clock. In fact, if the café stayed this quiet she decided she
would close up early and go and roll her mat out. A few flowing
sequences and yogic push-ups would be just what she needed.

Not to mention the fact that she needed to burn off last
night's cheesecake. Remembering she had left the plate pushed
under the sofa, she hoped Darla hadn't found it when she got
up. She was surprised her mother hadn't yet put in an appearance;
perhaps she was feeling ill from the wine she had drunk. At the
meeting that she hadn't in fact gone to. Again she wondered
why her mother would lie.

The day seemed to drag on, a slow but steady trickle of customers ensuring that she couldn't just leave, and so it was late
afternoon before she went up to the apartment, to find her mother
ironing a dress. Her hair was artfully arranged in a chic updo
and her makeup carefully applied.

"You're off again then?" Keeley said, trying not to sound too
suspicious and then wincing as she heard the tone of her voice
and knew she had failed. Darla pulled a face, pursing her lips.

"I am allowed to have a social life, you know, dear."

"I know, Mum, I'm sorry."

Darla didn't respond but continued to iron her dress. Keeley
watched her, shifting from one foot to the other, wondering if
now was the right time to say anything. To ask her mother where

she had really been last night. Or why she had lied. Or about
Gerald. Although part of Keeley had a burning desire to know
what had happened between her mother and the unfortunate
mayor, another part of her wished she didn't know at all. Keeley
suspected that had as much to do with her own squeamishness
at the thought of Darla and Gerald entangled in some passionate liaison as it did with the fact of his death. The thought of
her mother as some kind of seductress was almost as horrifying
as the thought of her as a murderer.

Darla looked up and frowned at her daughter.

"Is there something wrong?"

Keeley opened her mouth to speak, but then found herself
shaking her head instead.

"No. It's just been a bit of a long day."

Darla raised an eyebrow as she turned her dress over and
began to iron the sleeves with practiced precision.

"You do seem stressed, dear. The café isn't getting too much
for you is it?"

"No!" Keeley protested, feeling suddenly panicked. "Everything's going fine. I love the café."

She fled to the bathroom before her mother could push the
subject further. Somehow her mother had turned the conversation around without Keeley finding out anything.

She emerged from the bathroom and took up her place on
the sofa, waiting for Darla to go out so that she could unfurl
her yoga mat and throw herself into a practice. She didn't want
her mother's eyes on her while she was sweating and contorted.

When Darla left, however, Keeley continued to sit for a few
minutes, ruminating over the day's revelations. Questioning her

mother was unlikely to lead to any concrete answers in any case, she thought, and telling Ben certainly wasn't an option. She could hardly share her new suspicions with Raquel either.

Because now it wasn't just Raquel she was trying to get off the hook. But unlike Raquel, she found she couldn't so easily convince herself of her mother's innocence.

All at once, this case had become very personal indeed.

VRKASANA—TREE POSE

A standing pose that improves both balance and concentration. Like a tree, your standing leg should feel rooted to the earth, your torso strong, and your arms stretching to the heavens.

Method

- Stand with your feet hip-width apart, your spine straight, shoulders back and down, looking straight ahead with your arms relaxed by your side. Focus your gaze on a single point directly in front of you and take three deep breaths. Bring your hands to a prayer position in front of your chest.

- Bend and lift your right leg, then place the sole of your foot against the inside of your left thigh, just above your knee. To make this easier, place your foot against your left shin, or to make it more challenging slide the right foot up toward the groin. Keep your gaze focused ahead and breathe steadily. Find your balance. When you feel comfortable, raise your arms straight above your head. Keep the hands in prayer position if you can, otherwise keep the palms facing each other.

- After three to five deep breaths, replace your foot on the ground and repeat on the other side.

Benefits

Benefits to this pose include strengthening of the thighs, calves, and ankles, and improved flexibility of the groin and inner thighs, chest, and shoulders. Can provide some relief from sciatica.

Contraindications

Migraines or a severe headache, insomnia, and low blood pressure. If you have high blood pressure, do not raise the arms overhead.

Chapter Thirteen

"You can't really think she did it," Megan said, her voice a whisper even though there was no one but the two of them in Crystals and Candles.

Keeley felt guilty even voicing the thought. After her mother had gotten in late last night and went to bed without even speaking to Keeley, smelling of wine, she had begun to wonder if her mother was in fact developing a drinking problem. That might explain the lying about her whereabouts.

Or maybe she was drinking heavily because she felt guilty? Was trying to block out what she had done? Keeley's imagination was running riot.

"No," she nevertheless said to Megan, trying to convince herself as much as her friend, "it can't be. She's probably just got herself a boyfriend." She squirmed in her seat, the idea making her uncomfortable again as soon as she expressed it, and Megan eyed her astutely.

"And how would you feel about that?"

Keeley shrugged. "She's a grown woman, it's up to her."

The truth was she didn't know how she would feel about that. The idea of Darla with anyone but her father was anathema to her, yet as far as she knew her mother hadn't had a partner since her father's death. Ten years was a long time to be alone. No wonder she had gotten so cold and shut off.

"It does look suspicious, though," Megan mused. "What do you think Ben would say?"

"He would consider it grounds to question her, I'm sure," she said.

"Do you think he would expect you to tell him?"

"I'm not going to tell him," Keeley said. She had pondered that question again last night and had no intention of telling Ben about her mother's affair with Gerald. At least not unless she found out something more substantial.

"I was thinking of following her next time she goes out," Keeley admitted. She expected her friend to dissuade her, but instead Megan nodded.

"Sounds like a good idea. After all, if she's already lied once then there's not much point in asking her, is there? She'll only lie again."

"Still, it feels wrong somehow. I mean, she is my mother."

Megan steepled her hands together on the desk in front of her, looking Keeley intently in the eyes.

"If there's even the tiniest chance your mum's up to no good or knows anything about Gerald and Edna, then you're probably doing her a favor by finding out before Ben does."

"You're right." Keeley wondered how Ben was in fact getting on with the case now. For all she knew, there could have been new developments that would put her mind at rest concerning her mother. But there was no way of knowing now; he certainly wasn't going to tell her.

"I wonder if Ben found out anything about Gerald's secret daughter," Megan said, echoing Keeley's thoughts so closely that it made her blink. Sometimes her friend was so attuned to her that she wondered if she wasn't a little psychic after all.

"I lost the amulet you gave me," she said, remembering. "I think it came off when Edna went for me."

Megan looked shocked. "Really? I put a powerful protection on that. I was thinking Edna must have been really very full of darkness to get through that."

"Right," said Keeley, resisting the temptation to roll her eyes. Then she had a thought. "Megan, do you do love spells and things?" She flushed as she heard the words coming out of her mouth and waved her hands in front of her as if she could get rid of them.

Megan bit her lip. "I do, but, I don't really agree with them. It's bending another person's will to suit your own. I could give you something to aid reconciliation, though; some herbs to put in Ben's tea, maybe."

Keeley flushed even harder.

"It was just a general question," she murmured, "I wasn't referring to me and Ben, specifically."

"You don't want the herbs then?" Megan asked, all wide-eyed innocence. Keeley shuffled on her chair. "Well, maybe, if it's only herbs. Although how I would get them into his tea when we're barely talking I don't know."

Megan didn't answer, but got up and went out to the back of the shop. Keeley heard her unscrewing jars, and then she came out with a small bag.

"Put this into your teapot when you're brewing tea. It improves communications and generates feelings of love. You could even use it on your mum."

"Thanks." Keeley slipped the brown paper bag into her hemp satchel, feeling embarrassed.

"I'd better go, I've got a class at the center. Norma and Maggie will be there; I might even ask them a few questions." Keeley was always wary of any information from Norma and Maggie, who were more interested in salacious rumor than fact.

"About your mum?"

"No; I think if they knew anything like that then they would have mentioned it already. But maybe I could get some information on who the mother of Gerald's daughter might be." Keeley still couldn't shake the notion that the mysterious girl might just hold the key to it all.

"Could be a plan; they seemed to think he had had a good few affairs."

They kissed each other on the cheek and Keeley left, deciding to get the bus to the center rather than walk when she saw it winding its way up the street. Buses in Belfrey, although scheduled to run on the hour, were in practice a rare occurrence. She really needed to learn to drive, but so far it was a skill she had found to be beyond her. It was easy for her to stand in a complicated one-legged posture while practicing breathing exercises and giving instructions to a class, but driving seemed to be the skill set of some superior being. The last time she had seriously attempted driving lessons she had reduced not only herself to tears but her instructor too, after a near head-on collision with a truck, due to Keeley driving the wrong way, and in the wrong lane.

On her way to the center, she thought about her half-formed plan. If she could get an idea of the identity of Gerald's ex-lover, the mother of his child, then maybe she could find out where she and said child were now. And then what? She could hardly go bowling up to their house, knock on the door, and say, "Hi, did you kill Gerald Buxby and his housekeeper?" It was a shot in the dark, yet the same intuition that told her Raquel was innocent also told her Gerald's love child was a crucial part of this story.

She hoped she was right. She had to be right; otherwise the only other suspect seemed to be her own mother.

Most of the class were there waiting when she reached the center, and she started with little preamble. There were no newcomers so she went straight into ten minutes of Sun Salutations, walking around and aiding with posture for the second five. Then she began a series of standing balance poses, her eyes on the clock. Her usual serenity and mindfulness of the needs of her class seemed hard to grasp today, and only during the last twenty minutes, when she got everyone down on their mats for some long, deep hip openers, did she begin to feel her usual calm settle over her, and for a while her worries about her mother and Ben and the murders receded into the background. Then the hour came to an end, and as she got up from *Savasana* they all came flooding back.

When Norma and Maggie came over to thank her at the end, Keeley kept them talking until the rest of her clients had left the room. Then she said, glancing toward the door to ensure that no one was listening, "I've been thinking about this philandering of the mayor's." She was rewarded by the eager looks on the women's faces.

"Go on."

"Well, are you sure he had that many affairs? I mean, couldn't it just be gossip?"

Maggie looked offended, shaking her head until her chins wobbled, but Norma answered her eagerly.

"Oh no, there were lots of them. One woman, Jessica Hunter, she was a friend of his wife's originally, but we all knew there was something going on. They were always being seen around Belfrey together, while poor Mrs. Buxby was at home poorly. Travesty it was."

"What happened?"

Norma looked at Maggie, who continued the story for her friend.

"No one knows really. She just left town one day. I heard she got married not long after and had a baby. Of course, it was a long time ago, twenty years or more."

Keeley felt a tingling in her scalp. This was the woman, she was sure of it.

"Why do you want to know?" Maggie peered at her with her shiny black eyes. The smile she gave her was supposed to convey warmth, Keeley knew, but there was something hard and cold about those eyes that made Keeley for a moment wish she hadn't resorted to asking the pair for information.

"For the same reason anyone does, I suppose. We all want to know people's secrets." *Especially when they're not around to hear us,* she thought with an unusual dash of cynicism.

She said her good-byes to Maggie and Norma before they could question her more and hurried off, digesting what the

women had told her. An affair with Gerald, followed by a relo-
cation and a baby? It wasn't a great leap of the imagination to
suppose that the baby was in fact the love child in question. Now
she just had to find Jessica Hunter.

Keeley decided to walk back to the High Street as the
way back was all downhill, and as she passed the library she
did a detour into it. You couldn't beat a local phone directory,
she thought, for a bit of good old-fashioned detecting. Of
course, she had no way of knowing where Jessica had moved
to, but it couldn't be too far away if the news she had had a baby
had filtered back. Keeley picked up the directories for Matlock,
Ripley, Bakewell, and Derby and sat down at a nearby table,
glad that the library was empty except for the librarian, a
plump, mousy-looking woman in a long purple dress who sat
behind the counter with her head buried in an erotica novel, of
all things. That should keep the woman busy enough that she
wouldn't take any interest in anything Keeley was doing.

Her perusal of the phone books proved less than fruitful,
with only one Jessica Hunter appearing. Keeley went outside to
ring her, only to discover that the Jessica in question was ninety-
seven and very nearly deaf. As she went back into the library,
Keeley remembered something Maggie had said and could have
kicked herself for her own stupidity. Jessica Hunter was married.
And, therefore, Hunter would no longer be her name. There
seemed to be no way of finding out any more information without questioning everyone in Belfrey and that, she knew, would
get back to Ben.

Then she had an idea.

"Excuse me," she said to the preoccupied librarian, who

looked up in annoyance at not being able to get on with reading her bodice-ripper, "can I use the computers?"

"There's only one public computer," the librarian said, waving her hand toward an ancient-looking PC in the corner.

"Okay. Well, can I use that one, please?"

The librarian huffed and puffed with annoyance as she put
her book down and wrote login details for Keeley, handing them
over without a word and snatching her book back up. Keeley
resisted the temptation to ask her what the story was about.

Once on the computer, she pulled up the archives for the
local papers, searching for Jessica Hunter. If she had lived in
Belfrey for any length of time then it was likely she had at-
tended a fête or festival of some kind, and may well have got a
mention in the papers. Thanks to Google, there was no need
for Keeley to plough through endless copies of old *Belfrey Times*
editions.

A news story came up straight away, from six years ago, and
it was no mere attendance of a jam stall. Jessica Landry, née
Hunter, was shown weeping, and next to her a picture of a car
crash. A car, stolen by a crowd of teenagers, had crashed and
killed or injured everyone inside it, including the fourteen-year-
old girl in the back.

Jessica's daughter, Lydia. She had been killed instantly.

With her heart pounding, Keeley clicked on the thumbnail
of Lydia's picture. It was a blurry image, with the girl's face
turned away from the camera, but Keeley could see that the resemblance was there. Lydia Landry was Gerald's daughter, and
her death explained why Gerald had suddenly stopped paying
child support.

Keeley walked back to the café feeling sick, and more than a little guilty, as if she had intruded on Jessica Hunter's grief. No matter how long ago it had been, she doubted the loss of a child would ever be less than raw. She was glad she hadn't got through to the woman. She wondered if Ben had found and questioned her yet.

Keeley was just making herself a cup of herbal tea—Darla, once again, was nowhere to be seen—when Ben himself phoned her. Had Norma or Maggie told him about their conversation?

"Hello?" she said, hearing the guilt in her voice.

There was a pause, then he cleared his throat.

"Keeley. How are you?" He sounded heartbreakingly formal, not like a man whom she had been intimate with just a few days before.

"I'm good, thank you. You?"

Another pause, which was loaded with all the things they weren't saying. Then when he spoke again it was in those cold, clipped tones she was beginning to know all too well.

"I just wanted you to know I investigated the information you gave me concerning Gerald Buxby's alleged daughter."

"Oh?" Keeley aimed for nonchalance but felt her cheeks flame and was glad he wasn't there in person to see it.

"Yes. And it was a dead end. John checked out too; he has a cast iron alibi for both murders."

I know, part of her wanted to say, but she bit it back.

"I see," she said instead, wondering why he was taking the time to tell her this, flattered that he would think of her, wondering if he was perhaps looking for a reason to talk to her and if he regretted what he had done. She thought about the herbs in her bag that Megan had given her. Perhaps this was a good time to ask him around for coffee? Then his next words dashed any hope.

"So I want you to leave it there, Keeley. You had no need to go round Edna's, as it turns out it was useless information." The reprimand in his voice set Keeley's teeth on edge.

"Fine," she snapped. There was an uncomfortable silence, broken by Ben clearing his throat again.

"Right. Well I'll see you around. Maybe at the art festival tomorrow." He put the phone down before she could answer. Keeley glared at the phone, a wave of hot anger breaking over her. Who did he think he was, talking to her like that?

"What a jerk!" she said out loud. Then she went into her bag, found the herbs Megan had given her, and threw them angrily into the bin. So much for reconciliation.

Chapter Fourteen

"I wonder what on earth it is?" Megan whispered.

The large canvas stood in the front of the Yoga Café window, covered in a large piece of lilac silk. Suzy was due to do a talk at lunchtime, and would unveil the picture at the end of it. She had carried it in with Christian, seeming very on edge and anxious to ensure nobody saw underneath the fabric. Keeley had to wonder indeed what was being revealed.

"I hope it's not a nude," she whispered back. "She'll give the older residents a heart attack." Although she expected that the majority of her customers today would be visitors to the art festival and that many of her regulars would stay away, Jack had promised to put in an appearance, tempted by the offer of an extra-large slice of her new goat's cheese tart. She was offering it as a special along with her summer cream meringues, and had made an extra pot of her summer stew and added a Halloumi summer salad to the salad bar. Arranging and preparing the dishes last evening and early that morning had reignited some of her passion for her vocation. There was nothing she could do about Ben's attitude toward her, or whatever was going on with Darla, but she could damn well make some good food.

Suzy was currently tucking into some of that good food, a large plate of tofu scrambles and a toasted homemade muffin, making appreciative noises although she looked as sullen as ever. Christian had left to set up his own exhibition at the diner, and Keeley thought that the young artist might be put out at the prospect of her boyfriend spending the day with the diner's glamorous proprietor.

"Right, I'm going to open up," Keeley said, checking the clock. Suzy nodded in between mouthfuls. During the morning, during the run up to the talk, she would be in the corner doing a sketch of the café itself, which Keeley thought was a lovely idea and had been flattered by, even if Suzy had just grimaced when Keeley expressed her delight.

As she opened up the café she looked down at the High Street, coming alive with the morning bustle as the other small-business owners in Belfrey got ready for their own day, the majority of them showcasing a local artist or two, from sculptors to card makers to graffiti artists. Later on, by the afternoon, the High Street itself would be full of stalls, and face painters and henna artists and the like. There was even going to be jugglers and a mobile tattooist from Matlock, Keeley had heard. She smiled to herself. Belfrey was finally coming into the twenty-first century. Growing up here, Keeley had often longed to escape its small-town stuffiness.

The first hour or so was quiet, with only Ethel coming in

for her usual and then rushing off "before the tourists arrive," and Keeley was pleased to see her usual Saturday morning regulars come in for breakfasts and smoothies, though the majority of them also hurried off noticeably quicker than usual. Keeley suspected it may have something to do with Suzy sitting in the corner sketching furiously away, an intent look on her face that was only interrupted by her looking up to scowl when customers asked her what she was working on or about her paintings. She wasn't going to sell any with that attitude, but then Keeley had to wonder if she really intended to sell any at all, given the ridiculously high prices she had put on them.

Megan soon left to open up Crystals and Candles, and Darla made an appearance around midmorning, just as the café began to fill up with art lovers and tourists. Keeley was soon rushed off her feet, and glad when Darla pulled on an apron to help out, albeit with a look of weariness.

"You really need to get more organized," her mother said, though there was no real criticism in her tone, more force of habit.

"Did you have a nice time last night?" Keeley asked before she could help herself as she chopped apples for the blender. Her mother paused, seemed to stiffen and then relax again before she looked Keeley dead in the eye.

"I need to talk to you later, dear," she said in a low tone that sounded ominous to Keeley's ears.

"What about?"

"Not now, dear," Darla said in a firm voice that made Keeley feel about five years old again. "It's very important, and I'm afraid you might be quite shocked." Then she walked into the kitchen, leaving Keeley gaping after her. What could she want to tell her?

The reason behind her odd behavior of late, certainly, but was it going to be the revealing of a new lover or the confession of something much worse?

Lunchtime fast approached, and Suzy stood up to do her talk. The café was heaving now, with a great deal of people unable to sit down and standing around the edges, drinking tea and eating meringues. Keeley had nearly run out of her goat's cheese tart, and she began to cut a large slice for Jack before it ran out.

Right on cue, the door chimed and Jack came in, Bambi following faithfully behind him, woofing quietly and wagging his tail in excitement at the small crowd of customers. Suzy, who had been about to begin speaking, looked over at Jack and glared. Jack stared back, puffing on his pipe, until Suzy looked away, flustered. Keeley suppressed a smile. There wasn't much, she reckoned, that could intimidate the old man.

"Here's your tart," Keeley said, sliding it over the counter toward him, "and there should be enough there for Bambi too." The dog, hearing her mention his name, wagged his tail even harder, knocking into the legs of at least three people behind him.

"What's she going on about then?" Jack asked a few minutes into Suzy's talk.

"She's doing a brief talk on accessing the muse, I believe," Keeley said, "and then she's going to unveil that big painting over there."

"What's with the secrecy? It's just a painting."

"I'm sure it will be very good."

"Well, I can't understand a word she's saying." Jack turned back to his tart, leaning on the counter. Keeley tried to tune in to what Suzy was saying as she went around collecting cups and plates to take in to her mother in the kitchen, who was washing up, in spite of the damage she insisted it would do to her manicure.

"A true artist," Suzy was saying with more than a touch of arrogance in her voice, "should never shy away from the difficult subjects. Grief, anger, even brutality and abuse . . . these are all environments in which great art can grow, like a lotus from the mud."

Keeley grimaced, although around her Suzy's fellow *artistes* were staring at her in admiration. The door chimed, and Keeley looked over the heads to see who it was, wondering quite how she was supposed to fit any more people into the café. A tall, broad-shouldered man came through the door. She couldn't quite see his face, but she knew that physique anywhere.

Ben.

She watched, suddenly frozen to the spot, as Ben made his way through the crowd toward her, his eyes focused on her face. People automatically moved out of the way for Ben, she noticed, without even seeming to register that they were doing so. Megan would no doubt put it down to his "aura."

"Hey," he said. Keeley just nodded, unsure of what to say, feeling her heart starting to pound in her chest and not wanting to say anything that would reveal her reaction to him. He sounded softer, more unsure of himself than he had on the phone the night before, and she felt a flutter of hope.

"Hello," she said, in a formal tone that didn't sound quite like herself somehow. "I didn't think this would be your sort of thing?"

"It isn't," he admitted, "but I thought I would see how you

were getting on. And I wanted to apologize for being short with you on the phone last night. It was a long day."

"Right, I see. Thank you," she said, still in that same tone. Next to her Jack was watching them with undisguised interest. There was an awkward silence. Flustered, Keeley turned her attention back to Suzy in an attempt to regain her composure. The artist was talking louder and faster now, reaching a crescendo, and moving toward the veiled painting, getting ready to reveal it. Keeley watched with genuine interest, eager to see what lay under the shiny fabric.

"As you will see from my latest project, I take inspiration from all that is dark in humanity," Suzy said, lifting up a corner of the silk. "From death. From tragedy . . ." she pulled the silk from the canvas with a dramatic flourish.

"From murder."

Keeley's mouth fell open, and a collective gasp ran around the café. Darla, who was standing behind the counter, made a strangled sound. Bambi, picking up on the atmosphere, growled low in his throat. On the canvas, in a riot of color, was the depiction of a man, sitting twisted in a chair, covered in blood. Not just any man. Gerald Buxby.

Suzy had painted, in lurid and gory detail, the murder of the mayor of Belfrey.

Chapter Fifteen

Someone let out a little scream. Jack whistled low under his breath. Next to her, Keeley felt Ben go stiff. When one of her regular customers retched on her omelet, Keeley pushed her way through the crowd and faced Suzy, who was standing next to her painting, her arms outstretched around it as she presented it to the onlookers, a look of triumph on her face.

"What are you doing?" Keeley said, reaching for the fabric in Suzy's hands. "Cover it back up!"

Suzy put her hands—and the fabric—behind her back, glaring at Keeley.

"It's art," she said loudly. Behind Keeley, a few of the tourists murmured in agreement.

"It's completely inappropriate," Keeley said, angry now. How could Suzy be so insensitive as to unveil such a thing just a week after the mayor's death, in his hometown and in front of people who had both known and liked him? Who had elected him mayor? "And I don't want it in my café."

No wonder Suzy had been so adamant that no one could see what she was working on.

Right now, Suzy looked as if she could cheerfully punch Keeley. "You're ruining my exhibition," she said, a touch of hysteria in her voice.

"You've done that yourself," Keeley said firmly. "Cover it up, or get it out."

"No," said Suzy, a petulant look on her face, the silk still behind her back. Keeley half expected her to stamp her foot.

"Then I'll take it out. I won't have this in here, Suzy." Keeley stepped to the painting and put her arms around one side.

"Ben? Can you give me a hand, please?" She said over her shoulder. Ben started to move toward her, a grim look on his face, and once again the onlookers moved out of the way.

Suzy lunged. She rushed at Keeley, trying to push her away from the painting.

"Get off my work!" she screamed. Her eyes were wide, and her lips curled back from her teeth, giving her such an eerie appearance that it made Keeley lean away from her, still holding on to the painting, just as Suzy grabbed the other end. Keeley stumbled, her knees giving way underneath her as the painting tipped, its full weight leaning on her body.

Then a large, soft body crashed into her and the painting was torn from Keeley's hands. She felt herself fall.

Straight into Ben's arms. She looked up as he caught her, her breath catching in her throat at the proximity of him and the sensation of his arms around her. For a moment she forgot about the painting, and Suzy, and the café, and the small crowd of people watching them. Her whole world dwindled down to her and Ben, and the fact that he was holding her again.

Then he let her go and turned to the chaos in front of them. The world came crashing back in to her consciousness, and the first thing she was aware of was a dreadful snarling sound. The painting had fallen to the floor, and Bambi was on top of it, ripping at it with his teeth, his lips curling. Keeley had never seen the dog react violently to anything. Her customers were milling around, one old lady ineffectively striking at Bambi's back with her umbrella. Suzy was tearing at her hair and wailing.

"My work!" she shrieked. "He's destroying my work!"

"Jack. Call off your dog," Ben said. Keeley thought she detected a hint of amusement in his voice.

Jack made his way over to Bambi, laying his hand on the dog's back. "Bambi. Leave it." He spoke in a voice so quiet it was barely audible, but the dog stopped and raised its head, dropping the canvas, which was now badly ripped. Suzy sank to her knees, sobbing. Bambi looked around, saw Keeley and loped over to her, licking her hand and turning large, expectant eyes to her.

"Reckon he was trying to protect you," Jack said amiably. "it must have looked to his dopey brain that the painting was attacking you."

Keeley ruffled the fur around Bambi's ears. He sat at her feet, panting and wagging his tail. Keeley looked around the café. A few of the regulars were leaving, while those who had come from outside to see Suzy's exhibition had either gathered around the biggest table, talking excitedly, or were thronging around Suzy, trying to comfort her. Darla sat next to the till, observing the scene with her usual personal blend of detachment and contempt.

"We had better tidy this up," Keeley said, hoping people would get the message and start to leave.

"Not yet," Ben said. There was an edge to his voice, and Keeley frowned as he crossed over to Suzy and helped her to her feet. Although she looked at him gratefully, there was no sympathy in Ben's face.

"Interesting subject," he said in a dry tone. Keeley gave a sharp intake of breath as she understood what was coming. "I have to say, it looks very much like the crime scene. I wonder exactly where you did get your inspiration?"

Suzy went pale under her already chalky makeup. An expectant hush settled across the café.

"I don't understand," Suzy said, although Keeley thought she understood very well.

"Could you come down to the station? I'd like to ask you a few questions." It was phrased as a request, but Keeley knew that tone. This was Detective Constable Taylor, not Ben. And he thoroughly expected his requests to be complied with.

Suzy's mouth fell open. "Are you arresting me?"

"No," Ben said, and the *Not yet* seemed to hang, unspoken but still somehow heard, in the now hushed atmosphere of the café. "I just want to ask you a few questions." He held an arm out to Suzy. Suzy stared at it, then took it, leaning on him as if he was the only thing holding her up. Ben led her out of the café. Keeley watched, blinking against the surreality of it all.

She looked around at the café. "I really need to clear this up," she said in a loud voice. "So unless anyone is ordering food or drink, the exhibition is over." The café snapped back to life as people began to get up and leave. The two women who had been crouching next to Suzy began to pick up the remnants of the offending painting.

"We're her friends. We'll look after it," one of them said, glaring at Keeley as though she was personally responsible for its destruction. Which she supposed she partially was, she thought as she glanced over at Bambi, now lying placidly at Jack's feet.

"Thank you," she murmured, and started to clear tables. She waited until the café was clear before sitting at the counter with her mother and Jack.

"Well, well, well," Jack said, then. "Have you got any more of that tart?"

"I'll get you some," Darla said, motioning for Keeley to follow her into the kitchen. Once inside, she turned to her daughter with wide eyes.

"What on earth just happened?"

"You know as much as I do, Mum," said Keeley.

"Well, she's your friend." Keeley went to respond that she would hardly classify Suzy as a friend, but Darla continued. "I don't think those are the sort of people you should be having in the café. And you certainly shouldn't be displaying atrocities like that . . . thing she unveiled."

Keeley felt stung. "That's hardly fair, Mum," she said, wincing as she heard herself revert back to about thirteen years old, "how was I supposed to know she had painted Gerald's death?"

"You should have demanded to know what it was or you wouldn't have unveiled it. Is this your business or not? Take some control, Keeley. That's what I would have done."

"But I'm not you, Mum," Keeley said quietly, then physically flinched at the scathing look her mother gave her.

"I'm well aware of that, dear," she snapped, and went to walk back into the café. Keeley felt a wave of shame and resentment. Still, after all these years, her mother could make her feel worthless with a look. She closed her eyes and took a deep breath, reminding herself she was okay, she was safe, and she was not the image that her mother projected onto her. When she opened her eyes she was surprised to see Darla had paused at the door and half turned to look back at her daughter, an expression on her face that looked like remorse.

"I'm sorry," her mother said. The words sounded new and untested in her mouth. "I didn't mean that, dear. You've done a wonderful job with the café and I'm very proud of you." Then she went quickly into the café before a stunned Keeley could formulate a response. She had thought her mother was acting oddly, but this was beyond bizarre. She blinked back sudden tears, a reaction to hearing her mother express any pride in her daughter, something Keeley had wanted her entire life but had resigned herself to never receiving.

There was definitely something wrong, and she wondered again what it was that her mother wanted to talk to her about. The debacle with Suzy had perhaps opened up a new avenue of suspicion for Gerald's murder, but Keeley hadn't ruled Darla out as a suspect. Perhaps her impending confession had prompted this sudden softness.

Keeley composed herself and joined her mother in the café, where Jack was shrugging on his coat.

"I've got to go walk this old fella," he said, motioning to Bambi, whose ears pricked up at the sound of his favorite word.

The great dog looked so harmless, Keeley could hardly believe that just a few moments ago she had seen him ripping Suzy's painting apart like a wild animal. "Reckon I'll pop back in later."

"That would be great," Keeley said, smiling with genuine affection at the old man. When she had first returned to Belfrey, Keeley had been unsure how to take the old man, whose gruffness could easily come across as rudeness, but she had become very fond of him over the last few months. Even her mother seemed to like him.

Did Jack know about Darla and Gerald? It had been him who had confirmed Edna's tale of infidelity in her family back in April, though he had refused to give her the details, telling her instead to ask her mother. Jack knew a great deal more about most people than he let on, but getting any information from him was like pulling teeth. Even so, Keeley realized he may be the perfect person to find out if her mother had any past motives for a grudge against Gerald or Edna.

Hopefully she would never have to ask him, she thought. Suzy would turn out to be the perpetrator, Ben would arrest her and the whole mess would be over. And maybe, just maybe, she could get Ben to talk about their relationship. She was sure she hadn't imagined the look on his face when she had fallen into his arms earlier. Maybe there was still a chance. Perhaps she shouldn't have been so hasty in throwing Megan's herbal concoction away.

Right on cue, Megan walked through the door, accompanied by David, the sculpting druid, again dressed in some kind of long tunic with loose trousers, but this time in black, and covered in clay.

"What's happened?" Megan said, enveloping Keeley in a hug. "You look as white as ghost."

"I'm surprised you haven't already heard. The whole of Belfrey will be talking about it." This year's art festival would certainly be remembered.

She told Megan and her companion what had happened while Darla made drinks. Megan was suitably shocked, unlike David, who had closed his eyes and sat cross-legged on a chair. Keeley wondered if he ever actually spoke.

"Is he meditating?" Keeley mouthed to Megan, who nodded. "He's absorbing the energies of the café."

"Well, I don't think they'll be very positive today," Keeley said, trying to ignore Darla's loud snort of amusement behind them.

"I knew she was working on something odd, but I never suspected it would be anything like that. She has such a dark energy about her, that girl. I know you don't believe in it, Keeley, but you should really let me perform a cleansing ritual on this place."

"Maybe I will," Keeley murmured, then got up to serve as an elderly couple came in. After she had dished up two plates of salad and Halloumi, Keeley sat back down. The druid had opened his eyes now, although they looked unfocused and otherworldly.

"You think she did it?" Megan said. Keeley shrugged, her palms up.

"Maybe. Who knows? Where's the motive?"

Megan looked excited. "Maybe," she said, leaning over the table and speaking in a tone that Keeley thought was meant to be a whisper, but was in fact so loud half the High Street could probably hear her, "Suzy is the long-lost daughter? She could be around the right age?"

Keeley shook her head. "No." She glanced at the druid, who was now looking at her with interest. "I'll explain later," she said, "but it's definitely not that." There could be a connection, though, she thought. She was beginning to think she had been looking at this case all wrong. There was something she was missing, but she just couldn't pinpoint what that something was.

"Well, let's hope Ben gets it all sorted out," Megan said.

Customers began to trickle back into the café, many of whom had heard about Suzy and her painting and were full of questions. Feeling a headache coming on, Keeley retreated to the kitchen to take care of the cooking and left Darla to man the counter. She was busy making an omelet when she heard stilettos clicking on the floor behind her.

"Have you heard?" Raquel said. "Suzy's been released."

"She wasn't actually arrested," Keeley pointed out. "I think Ben just wanted to ask her a few questions."

Raquel gave a snort of derision. "Well, we all know what that means," she said darkly. "Ben took me in for questioning, and the whole of Belfrey thought I was a murderess. Now it can be Suzy's turn. At least someone finally found out something. You weren't much help," she said dismissively. Keeley bit her lip to keep from retorting, taking a deep breath before saying, "I did what I could, Raquel, but until now there's been nothing to find out." She wasn't about to tell Raquel about Lydia; somehow the fact that the girl was dead seemed too personal and private a matter to confide to someone as unsympathetic to other people's plights as Raquel. And she certainly wasn't going to tell her that she thought her own mother might be in the frame.

"Well, with a bit of luck Suzy will confess. I don't know why no one realized it was her before, it's quite obvious she's crazy."

"We don't even know if she had anything to do with it." Keeley finished dishing up the omelet and took the plate out to the customer who had ordered it, Raquel following her into the café. Jack was coming in, Bambi close behind. He nodded at Keeley.

"Looks like the young artist is off the hook. Just seen her going in to your diner," he added to Raquel.

"That's unfair," she protested. "Ben kept me at the station for hours."

"Like I said, she must be off the hook," Jack said. Raquel glared at him.

"Meaning I'm not? Thanks to you," she snapped at Keeley before stalking out of the café. Keeley shook her head; she had had enough for one day.

After the remaining customers had left, apart from Jack who seemed to have ensconced himself permanently at the counter, Keeley changed the sign on the door to CLOSED and began to clear away. As she did so she watched her mother, wondering what it was she had to tell her, and if she even wanted to hear it. Perhaps not knowing things wasn't so bad, Keeley thought. Darla seemed aware of her daughter's appraisal, avoiding Keeley's eyes as she helped her tidy up. When Keeley went into the kitchen to wash up, Darla followed her and busied herself wiping down and disinfecting the sides.

Keeley had just put the last plate away when Darla laid a hand on her arm, breaking the loaded silence that had been gathering between them.

"I think it's time for that talk, Keeley."

Keeley looked at her, surprised to see that her mother was clearly very nervous. So much so in fact that she was fidgeting and playing with her hair, ruining the perfect lines of her cut. Keeley felt her stomach sink, her suspicions against her mother returning.

"Okay," she said. She leaned back against the sink, taking a long, slow breath. The agitation was coming off her mother in waves.

"I'm not sure how to tell you this." Darla actually wrung her hands together. Unable to keep her calm, Keeley blurted it out.

"Is this about the affair you had with Gerald Buxby?" Darla's face drained of color.

PASCHIMOTTANASANA—SEATED FORWARD BEND

Method

- Sit on the floor with your buttocks supported on a folded blanket and your legs straight in front of you. Press through your heels. Rock slightly onto your left buttock, and pull your right sitting bone away from the heel with your right hand. Repeat on the other side. Turn the top thighs in slightly and press them down into the floor. Press through your palms or finger tips on the floor beside your hips and lift the top of the sternum toward the ceiling as the top thighs descend.

- Draw the inner groins deep into the pelvis. Inhale and, keeping the front torso long, lean forward from the hip joints, not the waist. Lengthen the tail bone away from the back of your pelvis. If possible take the sides of the feet with your hands, thumbs on the soles, elbows fully extended; if this isn't possible, loop a strap around the foot soles, and hold the strap firmly. Be sure your elbows are straight, not bent.

- When you are ready to go further, don't forcefully pull yourself into the forward bend, whether your hands are on the feet or holding the strap. Always lengthen the front torso into the pose, keeping your head raised. If you are holding the feet, bend the elbows out to the sides and lift them away from the floor; if holding the strap, lighten your grip and walk the hands forward, keeping the arms long. The lower belly should touch the thighs first, then the upper belly, then the ribs, and the head last.

- With each inhalation, lift and lengthen the front torso just slightly; with each exhalation release a little more fully into the forward bend. Stay in the pose anywhere from one to three minutes. To come up, first lift the torso away from the thighs and straighten the elbows again if they are bent. Then inhale and lift the torso up by pulling the tail bone down and into the pelvis.

Benefits

Benefits of this pose include relief of stress and low mood (however, it is not recommended for those with moderate to severe depression) and stimulation of the internal organs. Stretches and tones the hamstrings, can improve digestion and soothe anxiety, and provide relief from headaches and menstrual cramps.

Contraindications

Asthma and diarrhea. Consult your physician if you have ever suffered from a back, shoulder, or spinal injury.

Chapter Sixteen

"How did you know?" She made no attempt to deny it.

"Someone told me, but they didn't mean to," Keeley said, wanting to protect the gentle Diana Glover from her mother's wrath. "And it wasn't Norma or Maggie," she added.

Darla frowned. "Well, I wasn't aware it was common knowledge," she said stiffly.

"I don't think it is," Keeley assured her. "But don't change the subject, Mum."

"You're the one changing the subject," Darla snapped, sounding more like her usual self. Keeley frowned, confused.

"Isn't that what you want to talk to me about?"

"Why on earth would it be? It was years ago, Keeley." Darla looked annoyed. Keeley put a hand to her forehead, trying to collect her thoughts.

"Because you didn't tell me," she said quietly. "You told me about the affair, but never about who it was, and you barely seemed to react when you found out about his death."

Darla shrugged. "Well, I was shocked, of course, but I can't say as I had particularly strong feelings about it. Gerald stopped meaning anything to me a long time ago. He never did, really, I was always in love with your father, I was just very young and foolish."

That was exactly like her mother, Keeley thought. Gerald's death didn't have any impact on her life, so Darla was hardly likely to have any strong emotional reaction to it just because she had cared about him once. In hindsight, Keeley wasn't sure why she would have expected anything else.

"I see. I just thought it was odd," she said. Darla tutted.

"Honestly, Keeley, why are you harping on about this? Anyone would think you thought it was me that murdered him."

Keeley, who had thought exactly that, looked down at her feet, hoping that her mother wouldn't pick up on her guilt.

"So what did you want to tell me?" she asked, more to distract her than anything else. When her mother again began to fidget Keeley looked up again, her interest renewed. She heard Jack cough outside in the café and nodded toward the door.

"Shall I ask him to go, so we can have a bit more privacy? I'm shutting up now anyway."

To her surprise Darla shook her head and flushed bright crimson.

"No. Jack's waiting for me."

"Why on earth is Jack waiting for you?"

As her mother flushed even deeper and looked down at her own feet, looking for all the world like a naughty schoolgirl, Keeley felt understanding slowly dawn. This was the reason behind her mother's odd behavior and disappearances. She had a lover all right, but it certainly wasn't anyone that Keeley had been expecting.

"You and Jack? That's where you've been sneaking off to?"

Darla tutted. "I hardly sneak, dear."

Keeley felt a laugh bubbling in her stomach and traveling through her. She tried to disguise it with a cough, but couldn't stop a wide grin from splitting her face. Her mother, and Jack? She just couldn't picture her prim and proper mother with the grizzled old man. He must be at least ten years older than her. And yet, on some level, it made a strange kind of sense. It explained the wine too; Jack was notorious for his home-brewed stuff.

"You and Jack," she said again with something like wonder. After all, Jack was in his early sixties.

"Yes, dear, you don't need to keep repeating yourself." Although Darla had regained her composure, the color was still high on her cheeks.

"Well, I'm very happy for you both," Keeley said, feeling the urge to laugh again and wondering if it wasn't something like shock. "Let's go out, shall we? I want to congratulate Jack too."

She walked into the café, where Jack was still sitting on the counter, tucking into his third meringue. He stopped and looked up, his eyes taking in Keeley and Darla standing behind her. For a moment he too looked nervous, not an emotion she had ever associated with the old man.

"You've told her then." His voice was gruff.

"Yes." Darla sounded unsure, and Keeley was aware of them both looking at her, waiting for a reaction. Keeley walked around the counter, and before she was even fully aware of what she was about to do, threw her arms around Jack. At their feet Bambi gave an excited bark, wagging his great tail. Jack hugged her back awkwardly, then disentangled himself, looking embarrassed. He swiped at his eyes, and Keeley realized there had been tears in them. Had he really been so worried about her reaction? But then, she thought, he had been very close to her father once.

"I'm very happy for you both," Keeley said again, this time really meaning it.

"Well, lass, I'm glad of it," Jack said, picking up his pipe. Darla stood behind the counter, watching them with a strange look on her face. A soft look, Keeley thought, almost loving. She was beginning to feel like she had woken up this morning into some strange warped reality, what with Suzy's crazy painting and now this.

"We're going for a quick drink at the Wheatsheaf, if you'd like to join us, Keeley?" Darla said. Keeley thought about it, then shook her head. She could do with some time on her own to process everything.

"Thank you, but I'm going to get finished tidying up and then go and unwind. It's been a long day."

Her mother kissed her cheek in answer, looking relieved. Keeley watched them go. The hysteria she had felt creeping up on her had subsided, to be replaced with a sense of calm. As odd a couple as they may appear to be on the face of it, somehow she felt instinctively that they were right for each other. That her father would approve, even.

In fact, now that she knew the truth, she felt guilty that she could ever have suspected her mother. Darla had been, in her own way, more open with Keeley in the last few days than she had perhaps ever been in her life, and here she was accusing her of murder. But along with, and stronger than the guilt, was the relief that she had been wrong.

As she finished clearing and locking up, she thought about the rest of the day. Whatever she had been expecting from the art festival, it hadn't been this. Had Ben really thought Suzy had been responsible, just because of a painting? But then, if the details had been that accurate . . . Keeley shuddered as an image of the painting flashed across her mind. Suzy had captured the moment of death in grisly detail, a lurid grimace on Gerald's face, a look of frozen terror in his eyes. Somehow she had captured the depth of his anguish in the painting, the true horror of what had happened to him, stabbed to death in his own living room. There was no doubt Suzy was an incredibly talented artist, and definitely a bit strange, but that didn't make her a murderer.

The case was running out of suspects, Keeley reflected as she locked up the café and pulled down the blinds. It wasn't her mother, she still didn't believe it was Raquel, and Ben had said that Lydia's mother was a dead end. Maybe it was just some psycho, and the fact that the first two victims had known each other well was just a coincidence. But the idea of some crazed serial killer running around Belfrey, as terrifying as that prospect was, felt inherently wrong. These murders felt personal. She had been so sure that they were connected to Gerald's past, and specifically to Lydia, but Ben had seemed certain that wasn't the case, and she was sure he wouldn't dismiss it without reason. Yet it felt like a strong motive; grief over her daughter's death could surely crystallize into rage against the father who had never provided for her.

Keeley rubbed her head as if to clear it of the morbid thoughts and went upstairs to roll out her mat. She could do with a long, restorative practice, she thought, followed by some good hearty food. The goat's cheese tarts were gone, but there was plenty of summer stew and salads left that would feed her well over the next few days. She stood in Mountain Pose, rooting her feet down to the earth, stretching her body tall, and let out a slow, deep exhale, consciously trying to clear her mind. Then she moved into a few deep standing stretches, feeling the tension in her body and mind release and flow through her as she moved into hip stretches and back bends. Almost on impulse she found herself moving through a series of the more difficult arm balances, then lifting her legs up above her head into a handstand.

Keeley found herself thinking about her mother again as she stood on her hands, legs up against the wall in an inverted pose. It had been one of those days when her usual series of postures just wasn't going to cut it. In fact, it seemed quite appropriate to be viewing the world from a different perspective, given the news she had heard today. The notion of her mother with Jack Tibbons had shaken her entire worldview. It seemed opposites really did attract.

At least she knew she wasn't a murderer. Now, she decided, she would leave Ben to get on with catching the killer.

At the thought of Ben she felt her temporary good mood dissipating and brought herself down out of the handstand to rest in Child's Pose, trying to clear her mind of images of him. She knew getting over him was going to be a long and painful process, but she could get a few minutes respite at least.

The doorbell rang just as she had settled into a meditation posture and started her deep breathing, and she bit back a curse as she got up, wiped her forehead with the cardigan laying over the back of the sofa, and went downstairs, wondering who it was likely to be this time in the evening. Megan, maybe.

She knew from the silhouette who it was; knew those strong shoulders and that posture as well as she knew the contours of her own body. She opened the door, her breath catching in her throat.

"Hello, Ben."

"Can I come in? You look busy," he said, his eyes flickering over her, taking in her vest and tight yoga pants. He had always loved her in yoga pants.

"I'd just finished my practice." She held the door open for him, wondering what he wanted. Perhaps he had found the killer; although the look on his face suggested he was anxious rather than triumphant. She hoped nobody else had been hurt, and felt a flutter of panic.

"Can't we go upstairs? This is important," he said when she went to pull out a seat. The flutter of panic increasing, she nodded and opened the door that led to the upstairs apartment. He followed close behind her, so close that she was acutely aware of the nearness of him, of his size and smell. For a moment she missed him so badly it was a physical ache.

She turned to him as they reached her apartment, crossing her arms over her chest defensively and waiting for him to speak.

"Aren't you going to offer me a drink?" he asked, raising an eyebrow.

"Just tell me what's the matter, Ben," she snapped, more aggressively than she had meant to. Ben nodded and visibly swallowed. He looked nervous, she realized, not an adjective she would usually associate with him.

"I've hurt you, haven't I? You've got every right to be mad with me. I acted like a jerk."

Keeley felt her eyes go wide with surprise. Whatever she had been expecting, it wasn't this.

"You did upset me, very badly. But I'm sure you had your reasons," she said stiffly, hugging her arms even tighter around her torso. If Ben had come to apologize for dumping her in a bid to make himself feel better about it, she wasn't intending to make that easy for him. To help him soothe his conscience so he could move on easier, she thought bitterly.

"My reasons were stupid. And maybe a bit selfish," Ben said with sudden passion in his voice. Keeley bit her lip, shocked, but let him carry on.

"I was just so scared of you getting hurt, Keeley, of losing you. When I found you at Edna's with those marks on your face, and then she turned up dead, I just kept thinking it could have been you. And that I couldn't cope if I lost you. You mean the world to me," he finished in a rush.

Keeley's arms dropped down to her sides, and she stared, not knowing what to say, taken aback by this sudden display of emotion.

"That doesn't sound like a stupid reason," she said carefully. Ben took a step toward her, reaching his hands out to her almost pleadingly.

"Can you forgive me?" he asked, his voice imploring. "It was stupid, Keeley, because I was trying to control the situation, to control you, and that was wrong of me. I got this notion in my head that if I was with you then I wouldn't be able to properly protect you, because I'm too close, you see? And selfish because

I suppose my pride was hurt by the idea I couldn't keep you safe. And if I'm honest, by the fact you found things out I hadn't. That was in there too. I'm so pigheaded sometimes."

Keeley nodded, still intent on not giving an inch, not yet, although she could feel the love for him welling up in her chest and she had to blink back tears.

"But these last few days," he went on, "have been torture. I don't want to be without you, Keeley, and I love you the way you are, even if you do infuriate me sometimes. I've regretted what I said ever since I said it, but I was too stubborn to do anything about it. Then when I came in yesterday and you all but ignored me and sat with that painter, and I felt so jealous . . . I just thought, Ben Taylor, are you really going to be stupid enough to let the best thing that ever happened to you go? So here I am, if you'll have me."

Keeley had a moment of reticence, of telling herself she shouldn't give in so easily, that she should make him work a little harder, then she went with her heart and all but threw herself into his arms. Ben hugged her to him, squeezing her as if he would never let her go again.

"I'm sorry," he whispered into her hair. Keeley breathed in the scent of him, overwhelmed by her feelings for him. By the knowledge that he was still, if she wanted him to be, hers.

"I'm sorry too, and you're squashing me," she said, her voice muffled by his chest. He let her go, laughing. His dimples came out when he laughed like that, and he looked almost boyish. DC Taylor was left behind, and he was just Ben. Her Ben.

"I am sorry," she went on more seriously, "I should have been more open with you that I was helping Raquel. It seemed the right thing to do at the time, and I was so worried for Raquel. But I could have spoken to you first."

"No, Keeley, I never gave you the chance. I shouldn't have shut you out. I just didn't want you hurt. And I didn't trust Raquel, and I was worried she was trying to drag you into something for her own ends."

Keeley sighed. "I can understand why you would think like that, but really, you have to just trust sometimes that I can make my own decisions."

"I'll try, Keeley," he promised, "I just get so caught up in wanting to protect you, and fix everything, and solve this bloody case."

Keeley took his hand and led him over to the sofa, where they sat down next to each other, their fingers entwined.

"I don't care about the case right now," Keeley murmured, her eyes on that deliciously full mouth. She leaned over and pressed her lips softly against his, and instantly his arms were around her again and his mouth crushing against hers, and she lost herself in the sensation of him for a few minutes until she pulled back, smiling. He looked into her eyes, his expression serious.

"I'm never letting you go again."

"Good," she quipped, then went on, "Honestly, Ben, I've been so heartbroken at the thought we were over. Don't do this to me again, not unless you're certain you mean it."

"It's never going to happen," he promised, running the pad of his thumb over her mouth. She bit her lip, her eyes automatically going to the bed. He followed her gaze and grinned.

"Let's go and make up properly, shall we?"

She nodded, then gasped as in one movement he pulled her

onto his lap and then stood up, lifting her. Then he carried her over to the bed and proceeded to show her exactly how much he had missed her.

Afterward, she lay with her head on his chest, her hand entwined with his. The world felt right-side up again. She told him about Jack and her mother, laughing when he looked completely bemused.

"Really? I would have never put those two together. Still, if they're happy, I'm happy for them. She might just have met her match there."

"I think so. She seems to really like him. I knew she'd been acting odd lately. I even started wondering if she might be the murderer."

"Your mother?" Ben said incredulously. "Why on earth? I know she can be hard work, Keeley, but why would you think that?"

She told him about Gerald and Ben nodded, understanding dawning.

"Gerald had secrets everywhere. Remember the Terry Smith case, when his finances got him mixed up in that, and now it seems he was having affairs left, right, and center."

"If he was paying out for a secret daughter for fourteen years, maybe that's one reason his finances ended up in a mess," Keeley mused, then saw Ben frowning at her and realized what she had said.

"You know she died when she was fourteen?" Ben asked. Keeley sighed, then nodded. If they were going to get back together, then she wasn't going to start on a lie. She just hoped he wasn't going to be angry again.

"I did do some asking around. I was starting to worry about

Mum and I was desperate for it to be someone—anyone—else. I won't do it again without telling you," she promised, then heard her own words and amended them to, "Well, I'll try not to."

Ben gave her a wry smile. "I don't believe that for a moment, Keeley Carpenter. You've actually got a knack for it, maybe it's a new calling," he teased before saying earnestly, "Let's just tell each other things in the future. I'll be more open about my work, and you don't go rushing off asking questions without at least speaking to me about it first. You never know, you could be quite a good sidekick."

Keeley jabbed him playfully in the ribs. "Less of the 'sidekick.' But yes, that sounds like a compromise we can live with." They kissed again, and then Keeley said, coming up for air, "Does this mean you're going to let me know what's going on now, then?"

Ben pulled her back onto his chest. "Tenacious, aren't you? And I would if there was anything to tell. But I'm just no further along. The problem really is the murder weapon. We haven't found one and don't even really have a clue exactly what it was."

Keeley thought about that. This was the one thing she didn't know much about.

"They were both stabbed, right? With the same weapon?"

"Presumably, yes, but by the look of things not with any normal knife."

"Oh?"

Ben grimaced. "No, we're looking at something very small and very sharp—like a scalpel of some kind."

"A scalpel?" That would imply someone with a medical background surely—or at least access to their tools. She could ask Diana, she said; she had trained as a nurse briefly.

"Yes. Gerald was killed with long cuts to the torso, after what looks like an initial stab to the heart. Almost like someone was trying to perform open heart surgery."

"You're looking for someone with a basic knowledge of human anatomy then?"

"Rudimentary, at least. Think butcher rather than surgeon. Sorry," he said quickly when Keeley shuddered. Watching her father carve up carcasses had helped put her off meat for life.

"How about Edna? Was she killed in the same way?" She felt sad at the thought of someone treating an old woman in that way, and almost relieved when her death proved to be slightly less macabre.

"Same weapon, but she was stabbed in the neck. Right in the jugular. So again, the murderer at least knew where they were aiming."

"Who could do that?" It sounded a very cold, premeditated way to kill people, Keeley thought, not a spur of the moment crime of passion. Whoever the murderer was, they had gone to see both Gerald and his former housekeeper with no intention of leaving either of them alive.

"Well, that's where I'm stuck," Ben said with a bitter laugh. "Anyone with any motive has an alibi. Suzy has a slightly suspect alibi for Gerald, given that it's her boyfriend, but no motive. Even Raquel has an alibi—a real one—for Edna's death. Not that it will prevent her being charged with Gerald's death if CPS decide to do so."

"So she still isn't off the hook." Keeley sighed. It seemed her own investigating had reached the same dead end as Ben's, and she hadn't succeeded in completely clearing Raquel's name either.

"A lead will turn up somewhere," Ben said, trying to sound upbeat. "I've just got to keep digging." He kissed the top of her head. "I need to get back to the station and finish up some paper-work; I came running round here without sorting anything. How about I pick you up for dinner afterwards?"

"That sounds lovely," Keeley smiled. They kissed again, then she swung her legs out of the bed and got up to get dressed. She watched Ben as he pulled his clothes on, a rush of happiness making her feel giddy. God, but she loved him.

She walked him down to the door, and was halfway up the stairs to the apartment when she heard her phone ring. She jogged up the last couple of stairs and picked her phone up from the kitchenette counter, seeing Raquel's name flash up on the screen. She wondered if she was going to ask her to start inves-tigating again.

"Hello?"

"Keeley? I was wondering if you could come over?" Raquel sounded strained. "I'm at the diner."

"Okay," Keeley said slowly. "Any particular reason?"

"It's about Gerald, I think I've found something out. I can't talk over the phone."

"I'll be there in ten minutes." Keeley cut the call, staring at her phone. There had been something off about Raquel's voice. Realizing she could be walking straight into danger, but know-ing she was still going to go, she phoned Ben, cursing when it rang through to the voicemail. She left a message, then stood for a while drumming her fingers on the countertop, wonder-ing what she should do. The phone rang again, making her jump. It was Megan.

"I just found out something," she said excitedly.

"You're not the only one tonight." She told her friend about Raquel's call, then asked, "What is it?"

"I'm in Matlock listening to my friend's band. His mum knows Gerald quite well, I mean knew, and she was just telling me how apparently, a few days before his death, he was getting irate calls from some young woman, an artist, because Gerald had voted to cut funding for the art festival next year, so it won't be going ahead."

"Right," said Keeley, wondering if Megan was being deliberately obtuse or if she was just missing the point, "so what's that got to do with his death?"

"Well, how many angry young female artists do we know? One who seemed to take great relish in painting the manner of Gerald's death."

"Suzy. But she was with Christian. You think he would really cover up for her?"

"Duane did for Raquel," Megan pointed out, "and Suzy and Christian have been together a lot longer."

Keeley recalled what Ben had said about Suzy. Her alibi could be shaky, but she had no motive. Was Gerald's lack of concern for the arts enough of a motive? It sounded flimsy, but there was no denying Suzy was passionate, to say the least.

"She doesn't have long dark hair," she pointed out, referring to Tom's sighting.

"Tom is a space cadet," said Megan with no apparent irony. "He told me he saw unicorns once. Too many magic mushrooms."

"I thought you believed in unicorns?"

"Not when Tom sees them," Megan said firmly. Keeley suppressed a laugh, turning her attention back to matters at hand.

"I'll tell Ben. I'm trying to get hold of him to tell him about Raquel."

"You're on talking terms then?"

Keeley told her of the evening's events and Megan gave a little whoop. Then she agreed to make her way back to Belfrey and meet Keeley at the diner.

"If it is Suzy, she's staying in your house," Keeley pointed out. She rang off, tried Ben again to no avail, and then shrugged on her jacket and started to make her way to the diner. As she walked she thought about what Megan had told her. To Suzy, Gerald's voting against the festival might be motive enough in her mind, but where did Edna fit into that? And what about the murder weapon? Where would Suzy get a surgeon's scalpel from?

Unless, said a voice in her mind, it wasn't a surgeon's scalpel at all. Didn't artists use scalpel-like tools? Suzy worked with glass and also did engravings and sculpture—it was well within the realm of possibility that she used tools that would be sharp enough to kill. And artists were likely to have at least a basic knowledge of human anatomy. Feeling she was on to something, Keeley felt her heart thump in her chest. It still didn't explain where Edna fit in to it all, but perhaps Raquel had discovered something?

She was nearly at the diner now. Stopping, she pulled out her phone and tried Ben again. Still no answer. She left a rushed message, relaying what Megan had told her and her thoughts about the murder weapon, then headed into the diner. The blinds were down, but light peeped through them and the door was open. She knocked and went in.

There was no sign of Raquel. The diner wasn't empty, though. Her heart sank as she saw the young woman leaning against the counter, regarding her with a satisfied smirk.

Suzy.

Chapter Seventeen

Keeley put on a bright smile, though her stomach was twisting with anxiety. Where was Raquel?

"How nice to see you," said Suzy, without bothering to hide the sarcasm in her voice. Keeley wondered if she held a grudge for damaging her painting. If she had truly murdered Gerald just for voting against the art festival, then Keeley might well be next on her hit list. Keeley found herself edging back toward the door.

"Where's Raquel?" Keeley asked, echoing her concerns. Suzy shrugged and looked annoyed.

"I don't know. She phoned me and asked me to meet her here. I expect she's on her way."

That was odd. Taking a few deep breaths to calm her nerves, Keeley took a seat at the table nearest the entrance, reminding herself that she had no real proof Suzy was the killer. She might well be putting two and two together and coming up with five hundred. But why would Raquel want to talk to both of them? She wondered if she had judged the situation all wrong and Raquel was going to confess. Or perhaps she had gotten her manicured nails into Christian and wanted to tell Suzy, with Keeley there to ensure the artist didn't try to scratch her eyes out.

Or take a scalpel to them. Keeley shuddered. Suzy narrowed her eyes at her.

"What's the matter with you? You look like you've seen a ghost."

"I'm just cold," said Keeley, although she knew it was still warm outside in spite of the coming twilight. Wondering when Raquel was intending to put in an appearance, she reached into her bag for her phone. Raquel's number went straight to voice-mail. Keeley was sure that when she had spoken to her, Raquel had indicated she was already at the diner.

"Where's Christian?" she asked. Suzy just looked at her, and Keeley felt a frisson of fear. Had she done something to him too? Perhaps caught him in a clinch with Raquel? Although she couldn't quite imagine the mild-mannered Christian doing such a thing.

"He's gone to see a band in Matlock. Why do you ask?"

"With Megan?" Keeley said, answering Suzy's question with one of her own. Megan hadn't mentioned Christian was there, and when Suzy's eyes went wide with surprise she realized she may have caught the girl out. She looked toward the door, judging the distance and the time it would take her to get out if the girl went for her. She decided she would give it five minutes to see if Raquel showed, and then she was off.

"I'm not sure," Suzy said slowly, looking as if she was thinking hard. Then she glared at Keeley.

"I'm glad you're here actually. I've been meaning to talk to you about reimbursing me for my painting."

Keeley nodded, deciding it was best to humor her.

"Of course. If you come into the café tomorrow, we'll have a chat about it. I'm really very sorry," she said, hoping she didn't sound as insincere as she felt.

"No you're not." Suzy wasn't fooled for a moment. "You hated it."

"No, I think you're incredibly talented," she said with more honesty, "but I suppose the, er, subject matter was a bit shocking."

"Death is one of the most profound inspirations for an artist," Suzy said, rather arrogantly. Keeley looked at her phone again, wishing Raquel would turn up or better yet, Ben. How long would it be before he saw her calls and checked his voicemail?

"I'm sure it is. It was just a bit upsetting for the residents."

"Oh really?" Suzy scoffed. "I haven't heard any genuine grief for the mayor, just a lot of gossip and malicious rumor."

"Edna genuinely grieved him," Keeley said without thinking, and then immediately wished she hadn't mentioned the other murder victim.

"Well, he deserved to die anyway," Suzy said, her face twisting with a cold rage that transformed her pretty, if sullen, features into a visage that left Keeley in no doubt that Suzy was more than capable of murder. She felt herself go cold all over. This was it; the girl was going to confess. Where the hell was Ben?

"What makes you say that?" Keeley asked, being very careful to keep her voice neutral, trying to remember everything she had ever read or seen on *CSI* about talking to murderous maniacs. Suzy's eyes glittered angrily.

"He was going to cut funding to the arts festival. This would have been the last year. Can you believe it? The arts are vital, especially to small communities such as this!" Suzy's voice rose higher as she spoke.

"I agree, they are very important."

Suzy glared at her. "You're patronizing me." She shifted forward in her chair, and Keeley jumped to her feet, her heart thumping in her chest. Suzy sat back, looking surprised again, the anger gone.

"I'm going to go, it doesn't look as though Raquel is coming, and Ben's on his way. Here," she added, hoping Suzy believed her. Every muscle in her body was tense and coiled as she prepared herself to make a run for it. When Suzy just shrugged Keeley blinked, confused.

"Suit yourself. I'll wait for a while. She had better not be with Christian." The girl looked angry again. Keeley felt utterly bemused. Had she got it all wrong, and it wasn't Suzy at all? But the girl had all but admitted she had wanted Gerald to die.

"Right. I'm sure she's not. I'll see you soon." Keeley turned to go out of the door, and bumped straight into a manly chest. She felt a surge of relief for a second until she saw it wasn't Ben, but Christian, who looked from her to Suzy with a strange look on his face. Keeley stepped back to let him in, and he shut the door behind him and stood in front of it, barring the way.

"Excuse me," Keeley said, giving him a friendly smile. Christian ignored her, and didn't move.

"Where were you?" Suzy asked, accusingly. Christian shrugged. "I told you. In Matlock."

"With Megan?" Keeley asked, wondering if Megan had returned with him and where she was. Perhaps she had sent Christian to fetch her? Although that didn't feel right, given that she thought his girlfriend might be the killer.

Christian looked at her properly then. He looked annoyed, and for the first time Keeley thought he wasn't so handsome. In fact, he had a clammy look to his skin, and his eyes were wide, his pupils dilated, almost as if he had been smoking suspicious-looking cigarettes with Tom.

"Sit down," he snapped.

"Excuse me?" Keeley felt affronted at his tone. He turned a look of such menace on her that she found herself doing as he said, a horrible awareness dawning on her. No, it couldn't be, it made no sense.

"Who rattled your cage?" Suzy seemed genuinely bewildered at Christian's tone. Then she asked with suspicion, "Were you with Raquel?"

Christian barked a laugh. The sound was alien to what Keeley knew of him, but then, she didn't really know him at all. He didn't answer Suzy, just looked from her to Keeley with an eerie smile spreading across his face.

"She thinks you did it," he said in a sing-song voice. "Don't you, Keeley?" He raised an eyebrow at Keeley, who swallowed hard and didn't answer.

"Did what?" Suzy said, then the knowledge dawned. "Killed Gerald? That's ridiculous. Even your boyfriend let me go."

Keeley didn't look at Suzy, she was watching Christian.

"It was you," she said in a flat voice, not knowing how, or why, but knowing as well as she knew her own name that she was right. Christian smirked.

"Took you long enough, didn't it? I was worried you were going to work it out with your relentless digging, but perhaps I shouldn't have been so concerned. I could have just let you frame Suzy; that was my original intention. But then it occurred to me she would probably ask you for help just like Raquel did, and then you'd be off again, investigating. Quite the little amateur detective, aren't you?" There was a nasty sneer to his voice.

Suzy, who had gone even paler than usual, stood up. She was visibly trembling, though Keeley wasn't sure if it was with fear or rage.

"You were going to frame me?"

"Of course," said Christian, as if it were the most natural thing in the world. "Well, not at first, but then when you unveiled that painting, I just thought it was too perfect an opportunity to pass up. And being as I had already used your scalpel to kill him, it was almost uncanny. That amazing artist's intuition of yours." He said the last almost reverentially. Keeley shook her head. He was insane.

Suzy looked as though her eyes were about to pop out of her head at this latest revelation. When she spoke, she all but spat her words.

"You. Used. My. Scalpel?"

Christian nodded, looking pleased with himself.

"Yes. It was perfect. I knew you weren't using it for your latest work so you wouldn't miss it as long as I put it back quickly. So I took it, killed our dear mayor with it, cleaned it up, and replaced it. Hidden in plain sight."

Suzy leapt at him, her hands outstretched into claws in a way that was reminiscent of Edna's attack. Keeley got to her feet, seeing her chance to escape, but concern for Suzy made her hesitate.

She dithered too long. As Suzy flew at him, Christian grabbed a ceramic jug that was on the table Keeley had been sitting at and swung it at Suzy's head. Suzy swayed on her feet for a few seconds, then crumpled to the floor in an unconscious heap. Keeley heard a little shriek come from her own mouth and she started forward toward Suzy, but Christian was in front of her, turning to face her, barring her way not just to Suzy but also, she saw with a shudder, to the door. He smiled at her in a way that made her think of a shark.

"Now it's just us," he said.

Chapter Eighteen

Keeley felt the pit of her stomach go icy cold. She looked down at Suzy lying unmoving on the floor, praying she was going to be all right. Where the hell was Ben? Or Megan? Surely she must be nearly back from Matlock. Or for that matter, Raquel. It had been the diner's proprietor who had phoned both her and Suzy after all.

Or been made to. She looked at Christian and felt sick.

"What have you done to Raquel?"

"What makes you think I've done anything to her?"

"She phoned me and Suzy to get us here, so you must have made her do that."

Christian offered her an indulgent smile.

"Still detecting, are we? Maybe you're right, or maybe you're wrong. How do you know me and Raquel aren't in it together?"

Keeley thought about that, and would have laughed if the

situation hadn't in reality been as far from funny as it was possible to get.

"Because she would be here if that was the case. There's no way that Raquel would miss the grand finale in her own establishment, or let you take all the credit."

Christian looked delighted.

"How insightful. And I thought you were just some dippy yoga teacher, I couldn't understand why everyone seemed to hold you in such esteem. Perhaps I underestimated you. So, Miss Clever-Clogs, why don't you tell me why I killed Gerald."

Because you're batshit crazy, Keeley thought. "I have no idea. Why don't you tell me?" If she could just keep him talking until either Ben or Megan got here, she might just be okay . . . She tried not to look at the crumpled form of Suzy on the floor.

Christian shook his head, his fringe flopping into his eyes. He brushed it back, smirking again in a way that made his face look almost rodent-like. How could she have ever thought he was handsome?

"No, that won't do. I want you to work it out. It can be the last case you solve," he said casually, so that it took a few moments for the full impact of his words to hit her. *He meant to kill her.* Fighting the surge of terror that made her want to scream, she inhaled deeply through her nose, willing herself to keep calm. He wanted to talk, to play games with her, that was good, and there was no sign of a weapon on him, so she had a chance of getting away.

As if in answer to her thought Christian reached into his pocket and slowly pulled out a small, thin object, his eyes not leaving hers. With a sinking feeling in her gut, she knew what it was before she looked.

The scalpel.

He tossed it around in his hand almost nonchalantly, and its blade caught the light and glittered, transfixing Keeley. She felt her breath growing shallow and forced her eyes back to Christian's face.

"Well?" he said, impatiently. For a moment she couldn't recall what it was he had asked her. Gerald. He wanted her to figure out why he had killed Gerald.

"Because of the art festival?" she ventured. Christian gave a snort of derision.

"Although I think he was a complete and utter toad for voting to cut the funding, I wouldn't commit murder over it. Come on now, Keeley, you can do better than that."

Keeley thought, hard, going through everything she had already found out, but nothing made any sense.

"It's something to do with his past, his womanizing," she offered, surprised when Christian nodded and looked suddenly angry. She flinched at his expression, then understood the anger hadn't been for her.

"Very good. That's right. So, what's my link?"

Keeley studied Christian's features carefully, looking for any resemblance to the unfortunate mayor. He could be another secret love child perhaps, one that no one yet knew about.

"He's your father?"

Again, the flash of anger, but he shook his head with vehemence.

"Close, but not quite. You're being too obvious, Keeley."

Keeley frowned. How could it be close? His uncle, maybe? Then a snippet of a conversation she had had with Megan came back to her. "Christian had a sister." Had, not has. And Gerald's daughter had died at the age of fourteen.

"Your sister," she said. Christian went pale at her response, then nodded.

"Gerald was her father?"

Christian's hands balled into fists at his side, the scalpel gripped tight. She tried not to look at it.

"You blame him for her death," she said quietly. A look of pure, heartfelt anguish crossed his face at her words, and she couldn't help a stab of sympathy, though it quickly dissipated. She would have felt a lot more pity for him if he hadn't just bopped Suzy over the head with an urn and then threatened to kill Keeley herself.

"He was to blame," Christian snarled, looking even more rodent-like. "Lydia was a beautiful, good girl, two years older than me. I worshipped her. Dad died when we were kids, and Mum pretty much fell apart for a while. Lydia kept us together. Then when she was thirteen she found out our dad wasn't actually her dad, and that her real father wanted nothing to do with her. He had been sending Mum money every month on the condition that she never sought contact with him. She went off the rails after that, started hanging around with a bad crowd, and she died after getting into a stolen car. Mum remarried, and it was like I wasn't there, and after a few years it was almost like she had forgotten Lydia. I never did."

Keeley couldn't help but feel another flash of empathy.

"I'm sorry for your loss," Keeley said, genuinely. She knew how it felt, to lose a father and be left with a mother who was less than nurturing. Still, it hadn't made her want to go around killing people.

But he had lost a sister as well. Grief could do funny things to people. She clung to that bit of sympathy, however fleeting, trying to convey it in her expression. Perhaps if he thought she understood, he might be less inclined to kill her.

"It must have been awful. I lost my father, and I still miss him every day."

Christian nodded. "I miss mine. And Lydia; I miss her so much. She was so pretty; you've seen her picture."

"I have?" Then Keeley remembered the sketch that had fallen out of Suzy's portfolio. That was why Christian had looked odd when she had given it back. Suzy hadn't been the creator; he had.

"You did that portrait." That was also, she realized, why the girl had looked familiar; she looked like Gerald.

"Yes. So you understand. You understand why I had to kill him. But now it's all gotten out of hand. I'm sorry, Keeley." He made to step toward her, the hand with the scalpel rising. Keeley jumped back.

"Wait," she said, her voice coming out as a terrified squeak, "you haven't told me the rest."

Christian stopped, looking confused. "The rest?"

"Why you waited until now to kill him?" Keeley was talking fast, trying to stall him, and sure he would see through her ploy, but to her relief he lowered his hand and relaxed his posture. She looked over his shoulder at the door. In moving nearer to her he had moved away from the entrance, leaving a gap between it and him. If she could run around the table without him catching her, she might just have a chance, but it was a slim one.

"I only found out a few weeks ago who he was," Christian explained. "I saw his picture in the *Amber Valley Telegraph* and the angle of the photo . . . he looked just like her. I went through my mum's things and found old photos of her at parties. He was in them. They were never together, of course, but the fact they had known each other at the right time, and then the resemblance . . . I asked her and she admitted it. She said it was time to let the past rest." Christian shook his head, angry tears in his eyes. "How could she? Lydia died because of him." He stopped speaking, his eyes unfocused.

"So you planned to kill him?" Keeley tried to keep her tone light and interested, admiring even. To keep him talking, and keep him calm.

"No. But I wanted to. Then Suzy mentioned wanting to come for the art festival and having a friend she could stay with. I didn't definitely plan to kill him, not at first, or I knew I wanted to but I didn't know how. Then I was here when he and Raquel argued outside, and I saw a chance."

Keeley nodded. "I understand. So you went round to his house?"

"It was perfect. I had spoken to Raquel, knew she was home alone and that Gerald would likely be alone as he had gotten rid of Edna. So I took Suzy's scalpel, donned a wig and long coat I still had in my case from my days doing performing arts at college, and paid the mayor a little visit." He finished his recounting, sounding triumphant.

A wig, Keeley thought, *that explained Tom's sighting.*

"So what about Edna? What had she ever done to you?"

"I heard you talking to Megan, just after you had been to see her; I was about to come in the back door. She had told you about Lydia. I didn't know how much the woman knew about our family, or what she might have told the police. I had to get rid of her. I wanted to silence you and Megan too, especially you, with your reputation for snooping."

In spite of the seriousness of the situation, Keeley felt stung at being referred to as a snoop.

"But you didn't."

"Well," Christian shrugged, "I couldn't just kill everyone could I? It would have started to look suspicious." There was no apparent irony in his tone.

"So what about now? Me, Suzy, Raquel? All at once? That looks a little suspicious, don't you think?"

Christian grinned at her. "You would think so, wouldn't you? Except, it's not going to be me that gets the blame. Suzy here," he motioned toward the unconscious body of his girl-friend, "is going to kill you and Raquel both, and then slit her own wrists with the scalpel. Very poetic, don't you think?"

He might just get away with it too, Keeley thought with fresh horror, if he managed to carry out his plan and get away before Ben and Megan arrived. *Dammit, Ben, look at your bloody phone!* She was running out of ways to stall him.

"Raquel's still alive then," she said, replaying his words in her head. "You said, going to kill."

"So I did," Christian shrugged. "She's around. In the base-ment, to be exact. I didn't have time to deal with her before you and Suzy turned up, and of course I needed her to make the call. None of this will take me long, don't worry. Speaking of which . . ." He actually winked at her as he moved toward her purposefully, once again raising the scalpel.

Keeley ran for it. Darting around the other side of the table she made a run for the door, only to feel him grab her arm and spin her to face him, the scalpel raised high overhead. Keeley kicked him, hard, but he only grunted in pain and gripped her tighter. She twisted desperately out of the way of the now descending scalpel, then fell to the side as he suddenly let go of her.

A clearly not unconscious Suzy had jumped on him from behind, her hands going for his eyes, and Christian staggered around, flailing with the scalpel, trying to throw her off. Just as Keeley righted herself Christian threw her into a nearby table. He still had the scalpel in his hand, and he turned on Suzy, his face a mask of rage. Keeley leapt at him, only to be knocked flying by the back of his hand. She crashed into the wall, the pain of the impact taking her breath, and she screamed in part fear, part rage as she saw him go for Suzy's throat with the scalpel.

Just as the door flew open and Ben came through it at speed, rugby tackling Christian from behind and throwing him to the floor. The scalpel flew out of his hand and landed on the floor. Suzy made a grab for it, cradling it to her like a baby. She locked eyes with Keeley, who had sunk to her knees with relief as Ben wrenched Christian's hands behind his back and handcuffed him.

"Thank you," Keeley said.

"Well, I wasn't going to let him kill anyone else with my own tools," said Suzy with a weak grin. They both looked at Ben, who was hauling a now sobbing Christian to his feet. Ben looked at Keeley with an unreadable expression.

"What on earth is going on?"

"It was him," said Keeley, feeling a sudden urge to giggle. It must be shock. Suzy waved the scalpel in the air. "And that's the murder weapon," she added.

Ben just stared.

"Keeley Carpenter," he said with something akin to wonder, "you never fail to amaze me."

NATRAJASANA—LYING TWIST

A gentle but powerful relaxing pose, often used toward the end of practice, or any time you are feeling stiff and/or in need of relaxation.

Method

- Lie on your back with arms horizontally stretched out in line with the shoulders. Bend your knees and bring your feet close to your hips. The soles of the feet should be fully on the ground.
- Swing the knees to the left until the left knee touches the ground (the right knee and thigh are resting on the left knee and thigh). Simultaneously, turn the head to the right and look at your right palm.
- Make sure your shoulder blades are touching the ground. While the body is twisted, there is a tendency for one of the shoulder blades to get lifted off the ground. One must work against this tendency for the stretch to be effective.
- Feel the stretch in the thighs, groin, arms, neck, stomach, and back as you hold the pose. With each exhalation, relax deeper into the pose.
- After a few minutes, you may slowly turn the head back to the center, and straighten the torso and legs. Mirror the pose on the other side.

Benefits

Benefits of this pose include a powerful stretch for the spine and hips, the release of tension in the neck, back, and shoulders, improved digestion, and a sense of deep relaxation. Provides stress relief and lowers blood pressure.

Contraindications

Avoid if you have low blood pressure or have had any spinal or back injuries.

Epilogue

Keeley looked over at her friends, laughing over a plate of summer meringues, and smiled to herself. After the events of the last few weeks, it was good to hear laughter in the Yoga Café. The café was back to its spacious and airy self with Suzy's pictures having been removed, the tortured visages no longer casting a dark shadow over the interior.

Suzy herself had moved back to Bakewell for the time being, although she had told Megan she planned to settle in Belfrey, and Christian was in jail awaiting sentencing, after pleading guilty. Duane had moved into the space left in Megan's loft. They were at the table now, along with Ben and Jack, who was pushing Bambi's hairy head from the table as the large dog eyed the meringues with obvious desire. It would have completed the picture, she thought wryly, if Raquel had been there with Duane, but she was nowhere to be seen, having taken up with an older, wealthy man from Matlock. Her brief incarceration in her own basement at the diner had obviously put her off Belfrey for a while. In a funny kind of way, Keeley almost missed her. Fortunately, Duane seemed to have taken Raquel's latest defection in his stride and had even been out on a date with one of his colleagues at the gym, a pleasant girl with a tan that rivaled even his.

Wiping her hands on her apron, Keeley went to sit down with her friends, sliding onto the chair next to Ben and smiling as he reached for her hand under the table and squeezed it, running the rough pad of his thumb over her palm. She was officially moving in with him this week, and Darla would for the time being stay in the apartment upstairs, though Keeley privately thought that it wouldn't be long before her mother took up permanent residence at Jack's.

Ben had asked her to move in with him a week after Christian's arrest, a shy look on his face as he had done so. Keeley had been taken aback. "You're sure you just don't want to keep an eye on me?" she had asked with suspicion. Ben had laughed at that. "If I thought it would keep you out of trouble, I might try it," he had said, then his voice had turned soft as he added, "I want a future with you. And I want it to start now." Keeley had said yes without even pausing for thought.

She looked up now as the door chimed to see Diana Glover coming in, a basket under her arm. Keeley got up to greet her, smiling warmly. Diana gave her a shy smile back, one that didn't quite touch her eyes, which were sadder and more haunted than ever. Keeley sometimes thought she would give anything to see a bit of genuine joy on the older woman's face.

"Here's the eggs and cheese you asked for. I had a batch of muffins that needed eating, so I've popped them in too."

"Thank you." Keeley went to the till to take out the payment for the eggs and cheese, and as she passed it over to Diana she noticed how fragile and small the older woman's hands were.

"Would you like a cup of tea, on the house?" Keeley offered. "We can try these delicious-looking muffins."

Diana looked as if she was considering the offer, then shook her head. "No, I had better get back, Ted's expecting me." She rushed off without looking at the others. Keeley watched her go with a sigh, wishing there was something she could do to help. Looking up, she saw Jack watching her.

"That Ted Glover needs taking down a peg or two," he said, taking a puff of his pipe. "And I reckon he'll get his comeuppance sooner rather than later."

"I hope so," said Keeley quietly, "for Diana's sake."

"You mark my words," Jack said with a decisive nod of his head. "One of these days, there'll be murders up at that farm."

Recipes from the
Yoga Café

SUMMER FRUIT SMOOTHIE

Serves 1

Ingredients

- 225 grams (8 ounces) fresh blackberries
- 225 grams (8 ounces) fresh raspberries
- 225 grams (8 ounces) fresh blueberries
- 1 just-ripe medium banana, broken into pieces
- 150 milliliters (¼ pint) natural plain yogurt
- 150 milliliters (¼ pint) milk
- 1 tablespoon icing sugar, to taste

Method

Measure all the ingredients into a blender and whisk until smooth. Pour into a tall cool glass, garnish with a slice of lime and/or fresh mint leaves, and enjoy.

SUMMER STEW

Serves 4

Ingredients
- 3 pounds chopped green and yellow summer squash
- 1 onion, chopped
- 4 teaspoons chopped fresh rosemary
- 1 teaspoon basil
- 1 teaspoon oregano
- 1 teaspoon chopped fresh garlic
- 2 pounds chopped sweet potatoes
- 6 cups vegetable stock
- Sea salt and black pepper to taste

Method

1. Sauté onion in olive oil and butter for five minutes. Turn heat to medium, add garlic, rosemary, basil, and oregano, and cook for a further three minutes.
2. Add the vegetable stock and cook for seven minutes.
3. Add the squash and sweet potatoes, turn heat to low and simmer for 30 minutes, or until root vegetables soften to taste.

4. Season and serve hot with fresh bread and grated Parmesan cheese.

SUMMER SALAD WITH HALLOUMI

Serves 4

Ingredients

- 250 grams (7 ounces) Halloumi cheese, thinly sliced
- flesh from 1 kilogram (2 pounds, 4 ounces) chunk of watermelon, sliced
- 200 grams (7 ounces) fine green beans
- small bunch mint, finely shredded
- juice of 1 lemon
- 1 tablespoon olive oil, plus extra to drizzle
- toasted pita breads, to serve

Method

1. Heat grill to high. Lay the cheese on a baking tray in a single layer, then grill for 2 minutes on each side until golden.
2. Toss the watermelon, beans, and mint together with the lemon juice and olive oil, season well, then layer on plates with the slices of Halloumi.
3. Drizzle with a little more oil if you like, and then serve with warm pitas.

GOAT'S CHEESE TART WITH LEMON AND WALNUT

Serves 4

Ingredients

- 1 tablespoon olive oil, plus extra to drizzle
- 25 grams (1 ounce) butter
- 2 medium leeks, sliced
- 2 tablespoons chopped thyme leaves
- zest of 2 lemons and juice of 1 lemon
- 375 grams (13 ounces) ready-rolled puff pastry
- 200 grams (7 ounces) soft spreadable goat's cheese
- 50 grams (1.7 ounces) walnut pieces
- chopped parsley, to serve

Method

1. Preheat oven to 220 degrees C, 425 degrees F. Heat the olive oil in a large frying pan, then add the butter. Once sizzling, add the leeks and cook over medium heat until softened but not colored. Stir in the thyme and half the lemon zest, then increase the heat. Add the lemon juice and cook for about half a minute until the lemon juice reduces, then season well. Remove from the heat and cool slightly.

2. Unroll the pastry and lay on a baking sheet lined with baking parchment. Lightly mark a half-inch border around the edges with the tip of a sharp knife, then prick the base all over with a fork.

3. Spread the lemony leeks on top of the pastry, within the border. Crumble over the cheese, scatter with the walnuts,

then season with pepper. Drizzle with some olive oil, brushing the edges with a little oil as well. Put tart in the oven for 15 to 20 minutes until the pastry puffs up around the edges and is golden brown. Scatter with parsley and the remaining lemon zest. Serve hot, warm, or cool.

RED PEPPER, SPINACH, AND POTATO OMELET

Serves 4

Ingredients

- 1 pound medium waxy potatoes
- ¼ cup olive oil
- 1 clove garlic, minced
- 1 small red bell pepper, seeded and thinly sliced
- 1 small yellow onion, thinly sliced
- Sea salt and black pepper to taste
- 2 tablespoons thinly sliced basil
- 8 eggs, beaten
- 2 cups baby spinach
- 3 tablespoons unsalted butter, cubed

Method

1. Boil 1 inch of water in a 4-quart saucepan fitted with a steamer insert. Steam potatoes, covered, adding more boiling water as needed, until tender, about 1 hour. Let cool, then peel and thinly slice.
2. Preheat oven broiler. Heat oil in an oven-proof 12-inch nonstick skillet over medium-high heat. Cook garlic, pepper,

and onion until soft, 3 to 4 minutes. Add spinach; cook until wilted, about 1 minute. Stir in reserved potatoes and the butter, salt, and pepper. Stir in half the basil and the eggs and reduce heat to medium; cook until golden on the bottom, 8 to 10 minutes. Broil until set and golden on top, about 3 minutes. Garnish with remaining basil.

SUMMER CREAM MERINGUES

Serves 4

Ingredients

- 3 egg whites
- 100 grams (4 ounces) caster sugar
- 250 grams (9 ounces) strawberries
- 100 grams (4 ounces) blueberries
- 150 grams (5 ounces) raspberries
- 500 grams (1 pound, 2 ounces) half-fat crème fraîche
- 85 grams (3½ ounces) icing sugar, sifted
- 2 tablespoons toasted flaked almonds

Method

1. Make the meringues: Preheat the oven to 150 degrees C, 130 degrees C fan, 300 degrees F, gas 2. Beat the egg whites with an electric hand whisk until stiff, then gradually add the sugar, beating all the time, until the meringue is thick and glossy and you can stand a spoon up in it. Use a bit of meringue to stick the baking parchment to the baking sheet, then dollop on the meringue in 5 or 6 nests. Bake in

the oven for 20 minutes, then switch it off and leave them for a further 40 minutes. Take out of the oven, place on a wire rack, and leave until cooled.

2. Prepare the fruit by washing and hulling the strawberries and cutting them into halves or quarters, depending on their size. Reserve a few berries for the topping. Mix together the crème fraîche and icing sugar and place the mixture in a large bowl. Add the fruit, then lightly crush the meringues and stir it all together. Serve in individual glasses or dishes, topped with the remaining berries and the almonds.